ይ99

D0934980

OCT 0 1 1990	DATE DUE		
OCT 1 7 1990		MAR 0 9 2008	
NOV 0 5 1990			
NOV 2 0 1990			
DEC 1 8 1990			
DEC 2 9 1990			
JAN 2 6 1991			
MAR 26 1991			
APR 0 6 1991			
MAR 2 8 1992			

BUFO & SPALLANZANI

ALSO BY RUBEM FONSECA

High Art

BUFO &
SPALLANZANI

RUBEM FONSECA

Translated by Clifford E. Landers

A DUTTON **O**belisk BOOK

DUTTON / NEW YORK

DUTTON
Published by the Penguin Group
Penguin Books USA Inc., 375 Hudson Street,
New York, New York 10014 U.S.A.
Penguin Books Ltd, 27 Wrights Lane,
London W8 5TZ, England
Penguin Books Australia Ltd, Ringwood,
Victoria, Australia
Penguin Books Canada Ltd, 2801 John Street,
Markham, Ontario, Canada L3R 1B4
Penguin Books (N.Z.) Ltd, 182–190 Wairau Road,
Auckland 10, New Zealand

Penguin Books Ltd, Registered Offices:
Harmondsworth, Middlesex, England

First published in the United States in 1990
by Obelisk Books, Dutton,
an imprint of Penguin Books USA Inc.

Originally published in Brazil
under the title *Bufo & Spallanzani*.

First printing, August, 1990
10 9 8 7 6 5 4 3 2 1

LIBRARY OF CONGRESS CATALOGING-IN-PUBLICATION DATA

Fonseca, Rubem.
    [Bufo & Spallanzani. English]
    Bufo & Spallanzani / Rubem Fonseca; translated by Clifford E.
Landers. — 1st American ed.
        p.   cm.
    Translation of: Bufo & Spallanzani.
    ISBN 0-525-24872-2
    I. Title.   II.   Title: Bufo and Spallanzani.
PQ9698.16.046B813   1990
869.3—dc20   89-25641
Printed in the United States of America
Designed by Bernard Schleifer

Publisher's Note: This novel is a work of fiction. Names, characters, places, and
incidents either are the product of the author's imagination or are used fictitiously,
and any resemblance to actual persons, living or dead, events, or locales is entirely
coincidental.

I

FOUTRE
TON
ENCRIER

1

"You made me a satyr (and a glutton), that's why I'd like to cling to your back, like Bufo, and like him I could have my leg burned off and still not rid myself of this obsession. But you, now that you're satiated, want me to talk about Mme. X again. All right, I'm getting there. But first I want to tell you about a dream I've been having lately.

"In this nightmare Tolstoy appears to me dressed all in black, his long white beard unkempt, and says in Russian, 'To write *War and Peace* I had to do this two hundred thousand times.' And he extends his bony hand, as white as candle wax, still partially covered by the sleeve of his coat, and makes the motion of dipping a pen into an inkwell. Before me, on a table, are a bright metal inkwell, a long feather, probably from a goose, and a ream of paper. 'Go ahead,' Tolstoy says, 'now it's your turn.' A terrifying sensation passes through me, the certainty that I'll never be able to reach out my hand hundreds of thousands of times to wet that quill in the inkwell and fill the empty pages with letters and words and sentences and paragraphs. I feel the conviction that I'll die before finishing that superhuman task. Then I wake up anxious and unhappy and can't get back to sleep for the rest of the night. As you know, I can't write anything by hand, the way all writers should write, according to that idiot Nabokov.

"You were asking me how I can be so prolific when I spend so much time with women. Look, I never understood what Flaubert meant by *'Reserve ton priapisme pour le style, foutre ton encrier, calme-toi sur la viande . . . une once de sperme perdue fatigue plus que trois litres de sang.'* I don't fuck my inkwell, but then again I have no social life, I don't answer the telephone, I don't answer letters, I only revise my text once, when I revise at all. Simenon has, or had, as many women as I do, maybe more, and he wrote a huge number of books. Yes, it's true, I don't spend just time—all right, and sperm too—on women, I also spend money because, like you, I'm a generous person. The need for money is in fact a great incentive to the arts.

"Can I confess something? Suddenly I'm very sleepy, and if you don't mind I'm going to take a nap. No, I'm not going to dream of Tolstoy, don't wish that on me. Do you know what the Russian said after dipping his pen all those times in the inkwell? 'The spread of printed material is the most powerful weapon of ignorance.' Very funny.

"Would you like to see Mme. X's picture? We agreed that I'd always tell you everything with total frankness but that I wouldn't name names or show any pictures or let you read the letters. With Mme. X it was no different from what happened with the others: I fell in love with her the instant I saw her, which was all your fault, since it was you who awakened me to love. She wasn't an opulent woman, but there was great splendor in her body; her legs, buttocks, and breasts were perfect. Her hair, that day, was tied in a knot behind her head, showing her face and neck in all their whiteness. She moved elegantly and magnetically through the room where, dumbstruck, I looked at her. It was a vernissage, and the painter was toadying to her like mad. I had just published *Death and Sport: Agony as Essence*, attacking the glorification of competitive sports, that institutionalized preservation of man's destructive impulses, an obscene and warlike ritual, an odious metaphor of the arms race and the violence between nations and individuals. Is there anything more grotesque than those hormonal constructs assembled in sports laboratories, those simian dwarf-women on the uneven bars, those giants of both sexes, built like cattle and with an animal's gaze, tossing weights and hammers through the air? All right, all right, let's get back to Mme. X.

"She sat down to watch a slide show, her back upright against the chair, and crossed her legs, allowing her knees to show. She was wearing a silk dress, and the fine cloth outlined the attractive contour of her hips. I felt like kneeling at her feet (*see M. Mendes*) but thought a conventional approach might be better. The slides were of paintings by Chagall. 'Do you like Chagall?' I asked at the first opportunity. She said she did. 'All those people flying,' I said, and she replied that Chagall was an artist who believed in love above all else. On her left hand, the third finger, was a diamond ring. She must be about thirty and married for five years or so, which is when women start seeing marriage as something oppressive, a sickness, unjust and stultifying. Not to mention the sexual deprivation they suffer, since their husbands have already grown tired of them. A woman like that is easy prey; the romantic dream is over, and what's left is disillusion, boredom, moral turmoil, vulnerability. Then some libertine like me comes along and seduces the poor woman. There you had a person who believed in love. *'Que nul ne meure qu'il n'ait aimé'* (*see St. John Perse*), I said. French may be a dead language, but it's pretty and works very well with bourgeois women. 'Unfortunately, the world isn't as the poets might like,' she said. I invited her to dinner; she hesitated and finally agreed to have lunch with me. It was the first time she had gone to a restaurant with a man other than her husband.

"Her husband was a man of wealth and social standing. Their marriage, as I said, had come to that point where routine led to boredom, boredom to apathy, and apathy to anxiety, then lack of understanding, distaste, and so on. She tried to reverse the process by traveling with her husband to India, China, farther away each time, as if their problems wouldn't follow them. She made her husband buy a ranch nearby (their other one was far off in Mato Grosso), and she bottle-fed the baby goats two or three times till it lost its appeal. She tried to have children, but she was sterile; she dedicated herself to charity and got on the board of an association for the rehabilitation of prostitutes and beggars.

"The first time we had lunch she ate practically nothing. She drank a glass of wine. We talked about books, and she said she didn't like Brazilian literature and admitted candidly that she hadn't read any of my books—which, my dear, destroys the theory that she was dazzled by the writer. I asked who her favorite author was, and she named Moravia. She'd read *La Vita Interiore* and *L'Amante Infelice*—in the original, as she made a point of mentioning. The reference to Moravia gave me the opportunity I'd been waiting for to speak of sex. I told her that I looked at sex, in life as well as in literature, in the same way as Moravia— that is, as something that shouldn't be perverted by metaphor, because there is nothing that resembles it or is analogous to it. I developed this astute reasoning, which led naturally to considerations of a personal nature. I expertly broached the old and well-worn themes of sexual freedom, passion without possession, hedonism, and the right to pleasure. It was 5:00 P.M. and we were still in the restaurant, both talking away, nonstop; I don't think there was a single moment of silence between us. I remember that at one point she asked me what the difference was between sex practiced by two people who loved each other and two people who merely desired each other. I answered, 'Confidence; love between two people means that each can trust the other.' To a married woman contemplating for the first time the possibility of an affair, there is no phrase so provocative and so reassuring.

"Our first meeting, at my apartment, was a hellish thing. I

was wild with desire and she looked at me with wide eyes, astounded and yearning. I had to take off her clothes and place her, nude, on the bed, luxurious, her black hair and white skin shining. Then the most horrible thing happened: my penis went limp and shriveled up. It's the worst thing that can happen to a man. I started sweating in panic, kissing her, caressing her in an agonized way that only served to increase my impotence. She tried to help me but became nervous herself and was frightened because she thought (as she told me later) there was someone hiding under the bed. She got up and went to the bathroom. I stayed in the bed desperately fingering my dick, futilely, for a long time. Then I began to cry. Picture a naked fat man crying in a bed, trying to get it up. Finally I dried my eyes, put on a robe, and went to see what she was doing in the bathroom.

"She was sitting on the lid of the toilet, her legs crossed, disconsolate, half bent over and looking at her nails, giving her pristine torso a small belly; the makeup around her eyes had run, and she stared at me with a pathetic expression. I turned on the water heater, perhaps thinking that a bath would purify us, make us forget that horror, fill my penis with blood again. Suddenly the heater blew up. (*See Fonseca*.) I threw myself over her to protect her, we fell to the floor, and in that inferno of fire and smoke our bodies reconciled themselves in a sublime and delirious coupling. It was only later that night that I realized my body was swollen from burns from the explosion. I think it was that day I decided, having proved the dominance of arousal over pain, to write Bufo & Spallanzani. Even with my body smeared with ointment and shedding skin on the sheets, I began seeing her every day, more potent than Maupassant and Simenon rolled into one.

"Daily, around one in the afternoon, she would arrive at my place straight from the health club where she exercised. Until she got there I would pace anxiously back and forth, touching the erection of my penis, talking to myself. When she showed up I would grasp her body with a mad energy and fuck her standing up, in the hall, without her even taking off her clothes, sticking my cock through the edge of her panties while I lifted her and held her by her ass, crushing her against the wall. Afterward I would carry her to the bed and we'd spend the afternoon fucking. Till then she'd never had an orgasm in her life. In the intermissions I would read poetry to her; she especially liked one of Baudelaire's poems that speaks of eating a woman: *'la très-chère était nue, et, connaissant mon coeur.'* et cetera. I always read poetry to her when we finished fucking, just as I do with you, my love. Now let me sleep."

2

Guedes, a policeman who practiced Ferguson's Principle of Perfection—if there are two or more theories to explain a mystery, the simpler is the correct one*—never supposed that one day he would meet the socialite Delfina Delamare. She, for her part, had never seen a policeman in flesh and blood. Like everyone else, the cop knew who Delfina Delamare was, the Cinderella orphan who had married the millionaire Eugênio Delamare: art collector, Olympic equestrian gold medalist for Brazil, the most sought-after bachelor in the Southern Hemisphere. The papers and magazines devoted a lot of space to the marriage between the poor girl who had never left home, where she took care of an ailing grandmother, and Prince Charming; and from then on the couple had never been out of the news.

There was a time when detectives wore coats, ties, and hats, but that was before Guedes joined the force. All he had was an old suit that he never wore, so old it had been in and out of fashion several times. He usually wore a loose jacket over a sport shirt, which served to hide the Colt Cobra .38 revolver under his arm. The Cobra was Guedes's only luxury and his one infraction of regulations. The Taurus .38 furnished by the De-

*Based on the Principle of Parsimony (see *W. Ockham*): *Non sunt multiplicanda entia praeter necessitatem*, also known as Ockham's Razor.

partment was too heavy to lug around. He had originally thought
of storing the Taurus in a drawer, but one day he was on a bus
when a mugger yanked a gold chain off one passenger while
another, armed, threatened the other passengers. Guedes had
had to intervene by shooting the armed bandit—without seri-
ously wounding him, however. (He took pride in never having
killed anyone.) The Taurus continued under his arm until he
bought the Cobra, fifty years old but in excellent condition, from
Detective Raul in Homicide. It was a light weapon, made of a
special steel and molybdenum alloy; it had its limitations, but
that didn't really matter to Guedes, since he hoped to use the
revolver as little as possible.

Delfina Delamare did not always accompany her husband
when he traveled. In reality she wasn't all that fond of travel.
Ships were always crowded with retired old men and ugly women;
they were places of false elegance where the lengthy voyage
brought out an annoying vulgarity in people. Planes had the
advantage of being faster but generated a claustrophobic and
indiscriminate proximity with fat, dozing men with their shoes
off and leaning on you, even in first class. All in all, traveling
had always been an unpleasant experience. She preferred to
stay in Rio and work with her philanthropic activities.

The meeting between Guedes and Delfina took place under
one of the few circumstances possible. It was in the street, of
course, but in a way neither could have foreseen. Delfina was
in her Mercedes, on Diamantina Street, a dead end at the highest
point of the Jardim Botânico district. When he arrived at the
meeting spot, Guedes already knew that Delfina wasn't asleep,
as those who found her thought because of her peaceful expression and the relaxed position of her body on the car seat. Guedes
had already been informed at the station of the fatal wound
hidden under Delfina's silk blouse.

The site had been roped off by the police. Diamantina Street
has trees on both sides, and at that hour of the morning the sun

pierced the tree crowns and reflected off the metallic yellow hood of the car, making it shine like gold.

Guedes followed attentively the work of the forensic experts from the crime lab. The few fingerprints in the car were carefully collected. Various photos were taken of Delfina, some close-ups of her right hand, which held a nickel-plated .22 revolver. A gold watch was on her left wrist. In her purse, on the car's seat, were a checkbook, various credit cards, makeup items in a small case, a vial of French perfume, a white linen handker-chief, a prescription bearing the letterhead of Dr. Pedro Baran (hematology, oncology), and a notice from the branch post office in Leblon for Delfina Delamare to pick up a piece of registered mail. Guedes put the last two documents in his pocket. In the glove compartment, besides documents relating to the car, was a book, *The Lovers*, by Gustavo Flávio, with the inscription *To Delfina, who knows that poetry is as exact a science as geometry, G.F.* The phrase was undated and had been written with a felt pen in black ink. Guedes stuck the book under his arm. He waited for the forensic men to complete their slow work at the scene; he watched the meat wagon arrive and take the dead woman's body away in a dirty, dented metal box to be autopsied at the coroner's. At the hands of the meat wagon attendants, Delfina received the same treatment as beggars who drop dead in the gutter.

For Guedes, police work consisted of investigating crimes and their perpetrators. Investigating an infraction, according to the penal code, meant investigating the infringement of the law. It was not his job as a policeman to make any value judgment about the illicitness of the fact, but merely to assemble proof of its actual occurrence and of the person or persons responsible, taking all measures necessary to preserve any clues left by the infraction. Delfina Delamare could have been murdered or could have committed suicide. In the second hypothesis, unless in-vestigation showed someone to have encouraged, aided, or abetted the suicide, there was no crime to discover. Suicide wasn't a crime; to Guedes arguments about the right to die—both pro and con—were merely an academic exercise. It was useless to threaten the suicide with any kind of punishment. In earlier times they cut off the right hand of suicides, impaled them, dragged them face down through the streets, denied them an honorable burial; if they were nobles they were declared plebeians, outcasts, their shields were broken, their castles demolished. None of this served as deterrent. Not even the threat of hellfire did much good. Let's leave Dona Delfina in peace, Guedes thought. The forensics man asked why such a rich and pretty woman (and certainly a healthy one, since no one could be that beautiful without being in good health) had taken her own life. "Why not?" Guedes answered. He'd been a policeman for a long time and believed that wanting to live was every bit as strange as wanting to die.

Even though he had no doubt it was suicide, Guedes carried out the same investigations as in a homicide case. Diamantina Street was a short street with few apartment buildings and only two houses. Guedes went to the buildings and houses to find out if anyone had information about the case. The problem in this type of work is knowing how to stifle the talkative and draw out the taciturn. Usually it's those who know the least who do the most talking. But no one had seen or heard anything. The crack of a .22 inside a car with the windows rolled up doesn't make much noise.

The cop ate a sandwich at the corner of Voluntários da Pátria, where the building with Dr. Pedro Baran's office was located. First he had stopped in a bookstore and looked up the word "oncology" in the dictionary.

"Yes," said Baran, after Guedes told him of Delfina's death and his suspicion that she had killed herself, "she was my patient, and I'm not surprised at her suicide."

Baran picked up a folder lying on the desk in front of him.

"She first came to my office referred by the physician who treated her, Dr. Askanasi. She complained of night sweats, nervousness, and loss of weight and appetite. Dona Delfina attributed these symptoms to worry about a trip she was about to take. She hated to travel, according to what she told me, and to her the symptoms were merely a psychosomatic reaction. She was wrong. Patients are always wrong when they diagnose themselves. I took a blood sample and told her to come back in two days. But she left on the trip and didn't come back for three months, a few days ago. I showed her the test results, the ones you're holding: presence of myeloblasts, which allows only one diagnosis. She was suffering from leukemia, a sudden and rapid progressive disease and one as yet incurable. Treatment is palliative in nature, debilitating, and painful. I told her I thought she had only a few months to live but advised her to seek a second opinion."

"How did she take it?"

"Very well. She wanted the truth. In any case, there was no one else to disclose the information to; she was separating from her husband, who still hadn't returned from the trip they took together, and there were no children or relatives. I believe a doctor should tell his patients the truth, however bad it may be."

"She took it very well, you say," Guedes said.

"I know what you're thinking," Baran said. "Finding out the truth may have led her to seek death at her own hands, but for some people that's a form of consolation, a reaction against a cruel fate."

From the doctor's office the cop went to the coroner's office. The autopsy hadn't been performed yet. In the last twenty-four hours an unusually large number of homicide and accident victims had come to the morgue. Delfina Delamare, perhaps for the first time in her life, had to wait her turn.

Guedes looked up the name Gustavo Flávio in the phone book

but didn't find it. The phone I was using wasn't in my name; I wouldn't have answered in any case.

I am narrating incidents that I didn't witness and disclosing feelings that theoretically might be secret but are also so obvious that anyone could imagine them without need of the fiction writer's omniscient vision. The cop's mind was difficult to penetrate, I recognize that. As for Delfina Delamare—well, as for Delfina Delamare. . . .

"I phoned to say I was coming, but no one answered," Guedes said.

"I never answer the phone. When I want to talk to somebody, *I* call *them*."

"Do you know Delfina Delamare?"

We were in my office, the cop and I, a large room with walls completely covered with books. I didn't answer right away. I was trying to see if I could discover what kind of person the policeman in front of me was. My initial impression was that he was one of those men who eat and drink so often standing up in cheap luncheonettes beside workers, bums, prostitutes, and lowlifes that they end up identifying with such rabble. The cop was much shorter and thinner than I and didn't have much hair. His eyes were yellow, the color of the circle around an owl's black pupil.

"Not very well," I said finally. "I was at her house once or twice, at one of those parties with a well-balanced guest list. You know, people from various areas—the arts, business, politics, and elegant women. I represented literature: the fashionable writer serving as decoration. Normally such parties irritate me, but I was writing a book about the avarice of the rich. When a guy has a lot of money he wants even more money—not for what he can buy with it; consumption is a thing of the middle class on down. I'm not taking into account the nouveau riche. The rich suffer from a terrible fear: of suddenly becoming poor. That's why they want money—not to buy things but to salt it away, accumulate. The tendency of every rich person is to become a miser. That's my thesis."

"Couldn't it be the other way around: the tendency of every miser is to become rich?" Guedes asked.

"I thought about that. My character is born rich, very rich, and in his youth he has ideals, dreams, writes sonnets, et cetera, and later turns into a sordid accumulator of money. But you're right; the cause-and-effect relationship may be interchangeable. Getting back to the beginning of our conversation: what interest do the police have in Delfina Delamare?"

"She was found dead this morning, in her car. We think it may have been suicide."

"It's not possible! I could never imagine such a thing happening."

Guedes described his visit to Dr. Baran and the conversation that had taken place.

"I didn't know she was sick," I said. "She didn't look sick."

"There was a book in the glove compartment of the car."

"One of my books? Which one? I don't know if you know, but I've written dozens of books."

"*The Lovers.*"

"Oh, yes, *The Lovers.*"

"With a personal inscription you wrote: *To Delfina, who knows that poetry is as exact a science as geometry.*"

"It's a phrase from Flaubert. Who was wrong, fortunately. He didn't know—it arose later—the Philosophy of Uncertainty (*see Laktos*): there are no exact sciences free of ambiguity, error, or negligence, not even mathematics. The value of poetry lies in its paradox, that which poetry says and that which it leaves unsaid. I should have written, 'To Delfina, who knows that poetry is that which it is not.' In reality an inscription doesn't mean a great deal; we never know what to say when we inscribe a book, especially when we want to display our intelligence or profundity."

"When was the last time you were with Dona Delfina?"

I laughed. "You know something? I've written some novels with policemen as protagonists, but I never had the courage to put that phrase 'When was the last time' in the mouths of any of them. I always thought a policeman would never say something like that out of a B movie or cheap novel."

"When was the last time you were with Dona Delfina?" Guedes repeated calmly.

"I don't recall the date very well. It was one of those dinners for hundreds of people. She was very beautiful and elegant, as always. That's all I can tell you."

"As always? But you only saw Dona Delfina twice—"

"Mr. Detective, a writer's head may work differently from the heads you're used to ransacking. To a writer the written word is reality. I read in the social columns so often that Delfina Delamare was beautiful and elegant as always that I didn't hesitate to incorporate that alien cliché as if it were my own perception. We writers work with verbal stereotypes; reality only exists if there's a word to define it."

"Why did Dona Delfina have your book in her car's glove compartment? Any idea?"

"No. Nor do I think it's important."

"To us everything is important."

The cop's calmness was starting to get to me.

"Are the police always this meticulous? You said you have no doubts that Dona Delfina killed herself. But nevertheless you continue investigating, asking questions, wanting to find out things. Is it just voyeuristic curiosity about the life of a famous woman? I ask the question without any intent to offend; I have my own writer's curiosity. Prince Andrew, son of Queen Elizabeth of England, said in an interview that he'd have liked to be a detective, but he didn't explain why. Is it because the policeman has total freedom to satisfy his curiosity, something even princes can't do? Are you familiar with Plautus's phrase

'*Curiosus nemo est quin sit malevolus*'? No one is curious without being malevolent."

Guedes appeared to reflect on what I had said. "You're right. I'm taking up your time unnecessarily."

"I'm going on a trip in a few days, to a place called Falconcrest Retreat. I want to rest a bit before really getting down to writing my new book, Bufo & Spallanzani."

From my house the cop went to the precinct station. The reports from the postmortem and the forensic investigation still weren't ready; he thought about calling the forensic people and asking them to speed up the test results but decided against it. After all, there was no reason for such haste. The case was already solved.

He caught a bus for home. In the luncheonette he had a steak sandwich and a beer. He started reading *The Lovers* right there, standing up, while he ate. Arriving home, he removed his shoes and the holster with the Cobra, stretched out on the sofa, and continued reading. First he looked up in the dictionary the meaning of the word "bufo."

3

Guedes placed *The Lovers* on the floor, turned off the lamp, and went to sleep. He was used to sleeping with his clothes on; often, when he was on duty at the precinct, he didn't even remove his shoes when it was time to sleep. His sleep, after so many years of not sleeping well at night, was a semiconscious state of alertness, a dulled perception of what was going on around him. He woke up tired even when he slept in his bed. That was the way—fatigued—he awoke that day, a little after five, when it was still dark outside. He showered, shaved, got dressed. He boiled water and made instant coffee. He was never hungry in the morning, and his only breakfast was that cup of coffee.

Barata Ribeiro Street, where he lived, was empty when he left. Within a few hours it would be an inferno of car horns and roaring engines. Some mornings, when he felt like it, he would walk from his house to the 14th Precinct at the corner of Humberto de Campos and Afrânio de Melo Franco, in Leblon, a distance of more than three miles.

He went down Figueiredo de Magalhães to Copacabana Avenue. The stores were still closed; beggars, jobless men, residents of doorways were already getting up and silently preparing to vacate the recesses where they slept before the doormen and janitors began hosing down the sidewalks of Portuguese mosaic stone. Empty of cars and pedestrians, that horrendous street was pretty. Guedes liked empty streets; on Sundays he enjoyed going downtown to walk through the deserted avenues.

When he came to Francisco Sá Street the policeman turned right, toward Ipanema. In General Osório Square he sat down on a bench. A stooped old man was defecating beside a tree. Guedes noticed that from the window of an apartment a woman was watching the old man with an expression of repugnance. Later she'll bring her cocker spaniel to shit in the square, the cop thought, and she doesn't want to mix the two kinds.

From the square Guedes walked down Visconde de Pirajá to the Garden of Allah, another beggars' stronghold. To the right rose the complex of buildings of an old acquaintance, the São Sebastião low-rent housing project. The cop crossed the canal, where a solitary fisherman, using a circular net, was trying to catch some fish on their way into or out of Rodrigo de Freitas Lake. On Ataulfo de Paiva the bakeries and butcher shops were already open, along with the few remaining luncheonettes. Schoolchildren in uniforms were beginning to come out of their houses with colorful packs on their backs.

Finally Guedes arrived at Afrânio de Melo Franco. The last customers had just left the Scala, which stood across from the precinct; the nightclub's neon lights, announcing Brazilian Follies, were still lit.

The cops at the 14th were used to Guedes's early morning habits.

"Can you hold down the fort for me?" said Mantuano, who was on duty. "I'm going out for some coffee."

Guedes quickly read the blotter. Homicides, accidental deaths by auto, a fire, a rape, thefts and robberies. According to the penal code, robbery consists of the removal of another individual's goods by means of serious threat and violence to the person, or subsequent to having rendered him in whatever manner incapable of offering resistance. Old people said that in earlier times thefts were common (second-story men taking advantage of an open window, pickpockets, sneak thieves grabbing the chance to profit from their patsy's distraction) and robberies were rare; a light was enough to scare off the thief. Now the number of robberies was greater than that of thefts, and nothing scared off a robber anymore. One of the most recent robberies that Guedes had investigated was an attack on a mansion in upper Leblon that took place during a dinner with over a hundred people present. Not all victims went to the police, and the statistics were unreliable. (Of course, when some victim of violence died it was reported; a dead person is always a bother, and something has to be done about him.) Thefts weren't reported either, except those committed in stores and offices, where the victims were interested in the insurance. Actually nobody believed the police could do any good; the least that was said about them was that they were deficient, violent, and corrupt. Guedes was an honest cop, I have to admit that, and there were many other honest cops, which is extraordinary in a country where the index of corruption at all levels of administration, public and private, is incalculable.

The society columns carried the story of the "tragic death" of Delfina Delamare. Regular readers would know that tragic death without further explanation meant suicide. The captain of the 14th, Ferreira, after reading the newspapers, sent for Guedes. Ferreira had begun his career as a clerk and had been with the police for over thirty years. He had been in practically all the precincts of the Department and at one time had headed a Specialized Precinct. His dealings with Guedes were formal.

"I'd like to have your report on the suicide of that Delfina

Delamare woman as soon as possible. I received a call directly from the Minister asking for information. Have you been to the scene? Who was the detective on duty?"

"Bruno. But he wasn't there when the call came in from the patrolman." Guedes told Ferreira everything he knew about the suicide.

"She was married to an influential man who has already been to the Minister asking to put a lid on the case. Have the reporters been looking for you?"

"No."

Back in his office, Guedes called the morgue. Delfina's turn had finally come and she'd been autopsied. The body had been released and removed from the morgue.

The medical examiner told him that from external observation (rigidity, cooling of body temperature, livor mortis) as well as internal examination (the contents of the gastrointestinal tract), he had concluded that Delfina's death had taken place around 1:00 A.M.

Guedes immediately called Forensics.

"I'm just finishing the report," the lab man said, "but I can tell you right now it wasn't suicide. I ran all the tests. There were no traces of gunpowder on the hand holding the gun. The woman was murdered, Guedes."

The information left Guedes, normally a cold and controlled man, very upset. He checked his notes. Delfina's car had been locked from the inside and the windows rolled up. The key was in the ignition. No one in the neighborhood had heard anything. He decided he had done a rotten job of investigating. He had committed the worst of all errors: subordinating (and thus circumscribing) the investigation to a preconceived notion. To decide a priori that he was dealing with a suicide had been an act of stupidity. A policeman must always keep an open mind to all hypotheses. If he had explored the possibility of homicide he might have uncovered the killer's movements following the crime; now it was probably too late.

Guedes made a face. What the hell was happening to him, negligence? A negligent policeman is one step from cynicism. The cynic is one step from corruption. Guedes kicked the wastebasket, which rolled along the floor.

"The man wants to talk to you," an investigator said, coming up to the inspector's desk.

"Tell him I left," Guedes said, pulling on his grubby jacket. He didn't want to talk to the captain.

Guedes caught a local bus on General San Martín and went back to Diamantina Street. He made his way up by Faro Street. Two hours later he was in a bar on Jardim Botânico, revising the rough sketch and drinking a beer. If he had been in another automobile, the killer, in order to leave Diamantina, would have had to come down Faro, the only one with access to Jardim Botânico Street. Whether or not he was in Delfina's car but assuming he left on foot, the killer would have two routes: he could go down Faro or Benjamim Batista, via Itaipava Street, to reach Jardim Botânico. Faro ran directly into Jardim Botânico, but if the killer went down Benjamim Batista to get to Jardim Botânico he'd have to cross one of three streets: Abade Ramos, Nina Rodrigues, or Nascimento Bittencourt. Plus the steps leading to Pio XI Square, from which one can reach Jardim Botânico via Oliveira Rocha and Conde de Afonso Celso. All of these streets were quiet, so it was possible that someone might have noticed the presence of a stranger at the lonely hour of night when the crime occurred. Unfortunately, it appeared that all the buildings on those streets had automated security systems. It wasn't going to be easy to find a witness—if one existed.

The rich were buried in St. John the Baptist, thought Guedes, catching another local bus. He got off at the intersection of

Voluntários da Pátria and Real Grandeza and walked to where the cemetery chapels were located. In the hot sun the walk seemed longer than it was. Unable to take off his jacket (a policeman doesn't walk around showing his weapon, even if it is an elegant Cobra), Guedes sweated profusely. As he never used a handkerchief, Guedes removed the sweat from his brow and face with his fingers, the way manual laborers do.

Finally he arrived at the site of the chapels, to the right of the cemetery. All the chapels were occupied, but Delfina Delamare's body was not to be found in any of them.

From a pay phone Guedes called the coroner's office and asked where Delfina's body had been sent. A car from the Charity Hospital had performed the service. From the Charity Hospital they informed him that the "delivery" had been made to Sara Vilela Street, a street at the end of Lopes Quintas Street. The body had been embalmed.

By car, Sara Vilela wasn't far from Diamantina. A fact worth taking into consideration.

Guedes walked back along Real Grandeza to São Clemente Street at a rapid pace that took him half an hour. There he caught a bus and virtually retraced the route he had taken from Diamantina to the cemetery. Lopes Quintas Street was a little beyond Faro. Guedes got off the bus at the corner of Jardim Botânico and Lopes Quintas and went up the street till he arrived at Sara Vilela, a street without apartment buildings, only private mansions.

There were several cars parked at the door of the mansion. Guedes rang the bell. A man opened the gate. His eyes were red, as if he had been doing a lot of crying. He was young and wore the uniform of a pantryman.

"Is Mr. Eugênio Delamare in?"

The pantryman looked Guedes over from head to foot. "Please go around to the service entrance." He pointed to a side entrance to the mansion and shut the door.

Guedes rang the bell again.

The doorman answered the gate, this time accompanied by a large man in a navy blue suit, white shirt, and black tie, who Guedes deduced was a chauffeur.

"Is Mr. Eugênio Delamare in?"

"In regard to what?" the chauffeur asked in a truculent manner.

"A matter only he can handle."

"He can't come down right now."

The chauffeur started to close the gate, but Guedes pushed it with his shoulder and went into the garden of the house.

"Take one more step and I'll put a bullet in your head," said the chauffeur, pointing a .45 pistol at Guedes.

"I'm Inspector Guedes of the 14th Precinct," said the cop, unshakable.

"Show me your ID," the man said.

Moonlighting chauffeur and bodyguard, maybe from the police, thought Guedes, showing him the identification.

"Don't take it the wrong way," the chauffeur said, in a different tone of voice after examining the identification. "The mistress died and we're all pretty nervous."

"I know. That's why I'm here. Call your boss."

The chauffeur made a gesture with his head to the pantryman, who was looking at him nervously with an expression of shameless submission. "Move," said the chauffeur.

Guedes observed the chauffeur, who began pacing back and forth. A large part of his body weight was fat. From sitting on his butt all day long in the car, thought Guedes, and having food brought to him at any hour by the pantryman. But at one time he must have led an athletic life; his movements were quick and his body erect.

The doorman returned accompanied by a man of some forty years, suntanned and elegant. He greeted Guedes and dismissed the others with a curt "You may go." Then he took the cop by the arm and led him through the garden to a bench under an enormous oiticica tree. He motioned the cop to sit down. Guedes, who had already walked a great deal that day and whose shirt was soaked with sweat, sat with relief. At once the shade and cool breeze gave him a feeling of well-being.

"I'm grateful for everything you've done for us," Eugênio Delamare said with a sad smile. "You can imagine my suffering, my awful shock at returning from our trip and discovering that my wife had committed suicide and been thrown into some filthy drawer in the morgue. It's a profoundly unhappy moment I'm going through. We were very close, we have no relatives, it was just the two of us. . . . It's a misfortune I can't share with anybody, one I don't want to share with anybody. . . . We always kept to ourselves and led a very discreet life." Eugênio rubbed his hands over his dry eyes.

"Your wife didn't kill herself. She was murdered."

"What?" Eugênio Delamare rose from the bench in surprise.

"Murdered," Guedes repeated.

"It's impossible!" Eugênio sat down again; the golden color had drained from his face. "They told me she'd killed herself. The Minister of Public Safety spoke with me."

"The Minister probably hadn't seen the reports from the medical examiner and the laboratory," Guedes said.

"Was there violence . . . sexual assault, anything like that?"

"No. She died of a bullet in the heart. The murderer didn't touch her body. Nothing was stolen. The revolver was in her hand. All of that led us to think, wrongly, that it was suicide."

"Have the police arrested anyone? Are there any suspects?" Delamare was already under control.

"There hasn't been time. We just found out today that it wasn't suicide."

Delamare looked Guedes in the eyes. "This is a very violent city." His voice was now a businessman's. "I always told her to be very careful, but she wouldn't listen. She would go out by herself in her automobile. . . . But I never thought she'd be robbed, the way it happened."

"I don't believe she was robbed," Guedes said.

"Of course she was robbed."

"I think you didn't understand what I said. Nothing was stolen."

"It's *you* who don't understand what *I* said. I think she was robbed, understand? I don't want any scandal. And what does it matter if it was a lunatic or a thief who killed her? She's dead, and she won't come back to life if we find out." A different tone of voice: "Please, Inspector . . . what's your name again?"

"Guedes."

"Inspector Guedes, I know how to show my gratitude. What I ask of you is very little, but my appreciation will be great."

Guedes remained silent, which Delamare interpreted as acquiescence in what he had just said.

"I'll explain what I want you to do. Prepare everything—the reports, the files, the papers, the whole business—so there won't be any doubt that my wife was killed by a robber. Don't worry if some superior wants to stir up problems; I'm a friend of the Minister of Public Safety. And of people higher up."

Eugênio Delamare put his hand in his pocket, took out a checkbook, supported it on his knee, and made out a check. He held out the check toward Guedes.

"This is just the first part."

There was a silent, motionless moment, Delamare with the check in his outstretched hand, Guedes looking at him, both of them with calm and inscrutable expressions.

"I could accuse you of offering a bribe," Guedes said, taking the check from Delamare, "but I'm not going to, because you're perhaps upset at the death of your wife and don't know what you're doing."

Guedes threw the check to the ground.

Eugênio Delamare bent down and picked up the check. "Think it over," he said. "Did you see the amount I wrote on the check? You don't make that in ten years in your loathsome job. And it's just the first part, goddammit! Go on, take it!" Delamare tried to push the check into Guedes's hand. The cop took the check and tore it up, throwing the pieces to the ground.

"One other thing," Guedes said. "Your driver, or bodyguard, is using a weapon reserved for the armed forces, which is prohibited by law. I'm going to let that pass too. You'll be getting a summons to come to the precinct to make a statement."

Guedes walked through the garden toward the gate. He heard Delamare say to his back, "Don't be stupid!" The guard opened the gate and the cop left. He was sweating heavily again. He quickly descended Lopes Quintas, caught a bus on Jardim Botânico, and got off at Afrânio de Melo Franco. The day was coming to an end. It was Friday and the gas station at the corner of Ataulfo de Paiva was crowded with cars filling up.

"Where've you been? Ferreira's been looking for you all day," the detective on duty said.

"I was out on a call."

Ferreira had gone, leaving a message for Guedes to call him that night. A few reporters had been to the precinct asking about the "suicide" of Delfina Delamare but had gotten no information.

"Care for some coffee?"

It was Marlene, the black woman with her thermos bottle and

basket of corn muffins. She always showed up at the precinct at this time. Guedes drank a cup of coffee and bought two muffins, which he placed in a large brown envelope, already used. From eating so often in cheap luncheonettes, Guedes had lost any pleasure in food. He seldom used the small kitchen in his apartment, to avoid attracting roaches. He hated roaches, and the old building where he lived, despite periodic disinfecting, was always full of the insects.

It was 9:00 P.M. when he picked up the brown envelope with the corn muffins and caught a bus for home. First he had called Captain Ferreira and then the Director of the Forensics Division, who was a friend of his.

"Guedes, don't make any problems for me, please. The chief called and said that the Minister is very angry. It seems you've been overstepping your bounds; the chief even said he's going to haul you up on charges of unnecessary use of force. I don't want to get transferred to Podunk, do you?" Ferreira had said.

Guedes told of his encounter with Eugênio Delamare.

"You think it was him who killed the woman?"

"He wasn't here the day she was murdered; he got back from Europe the next day. I checked with Customs."

"So don't bug the guy, OK?"

The Director of Forensics was an enemy of the Minister of Public Safety, who wanted to replace him with a relative.

"That corrupt coward ordered the chief to call me and make me change the report to show traces of gunpowder on the woman's hand. That sonofabitch. I told him I'd already sent the report to the precinct, which I haven't. A messenger'll deliver the report to you personally first thing tomorrow. Make a quick addition to the blotter; I'd like to see them get rid of *that*."

The conversation with the Director of Forensics left Guedes worried. When he got home the cop took a shower and ate the muffins, taking care not to leave a single crumb for the roaches. Then he lay down in bed in his undershorts and jacket and picked up *The Lovers*. But after reading only a few pages the cop fell asleep. To him, my book was like a sleeping pill. Guedes was not my ideal reader. My books should be read eagerly, without interruption, especially *The Lovers*.

4

Eugênio Delamare had said he wouldn't be upset if the crime had been committed by a lunatic or a thief; after all, his wife was already dead. The proposal he had made, of arranging things so his wife's death could be officially attributed to a robbery, might be immoral and illegal but didn't necessarily mean he was involved in her death. Any bourgeois whose wife had been found dead in her car would have preferred the robbery version over the suicide, even if he wasn't a famous millionaire. Once the murder had occurred, it was advisable that robbery be the motive: either that or the random act of an unknown psychopath.

Guedes pondered the matter in this light as he shaved. He didn't look on homicide as an atavistic throwback, some remote human characteristic that resurfaced sporadically for unclear reasons. He saw homicide on an almost daily basis, committed by individuals of every type, rich and poor, strong and weak, educated and uneducated, and believed that man had always been and always would be a violent animal, a killer of his own kind and of other living creatures, for pleasure. Anyone could have killed Delfina, but it was neither a robber nor a psychopath, he was sure of that. Then who did kill her? A young, rich, beautiful woman can be killed because of jealousy, envy, spite,

hate, money. Her killer may be the husband, the lover, a relative, a broker, a male or female friend—or, of course, the
butler. Guedes wasn't joking when he included the butler; he
had, in fact, a limited sense of humor. By butler he meant any
servant, male or female.

That day Captain Ferreira arrived at the 14th early. He asked
to see the blotter and confirmed that an addition had been made
to the first entry on Delfina Delamare's death, showing the results
of the tests done by the medical examiner and Forensics. It had
all the marks of homicide.

Ferreira called Guedes in.

"Some mess that woman's death is," Ferreira said. "Refresh
my memory about your talk with her husband."

Guedes again related his dialogue with Eugênio Delamare.

"I can't understand his acting like that," Ferreira said.

Guedes spent the afternoon in the National Library reading *O
Globo* and the *Jornal do Brasil*.

Later, still wearing his grubby jacket, he knocked on my
door.

I said right off, "Mr. Guedes, I'm very busy writing my
book, Bufo & Spallanzani, I think I already told you that,
and I'm about to travel, there are some things I have to do
first—"

"I'll be quick," the cop said. "It's about Dona Delfina, that
society lady who was found dead in her car."

I opened the door all the way for him to come in.

"She was murdered," Guedes said.

"Murdered? But just yesterday you told me she'd killed herself."

"Our mistake. She was murdered."

"Have they caught the criminal?"

"Not yet."

"Do they know who it was?"

Guedes remained silent. He ran his finger over his brow, from one end to the other, and wiped it on his jacket.

"Just what do you want from me anyway? I already told you I'm very busy."

"I don't believe curiosity is a malignant thing in a policeman. It's our job." He was referring to our conversation of the day before.

"Maybe it's police work that's malignant," I said.

"That's possible," the cop said, "but somebody's got to do it."

"So?"

"Well," he said, wiping his forehead again, "we suspect that Dona Delfina had a lover. Since you travel in those circles you might have heard something."

"A lover? Absurd. Dona Delfina was a lady of impeccable morals."

"You said in one of your books that fidelity is a bourgeois concept and that a woman's honor has nothing to do with her sexual behavior."

"In what book did I say that?"

"*The Lovers.*"

"You've read *The Lovers*?"

"I'm reading it."

"I'm going to tell you something: the point of view, the opinions, beliefs, assumptions, values, tendencies, obsessions, concepts, et cetera, of the characters, even the main ones, even those in the first person, as is the case of *The Lovers*, are not necessarily those of the author. Often the author thinks exactly the opposite as his character."

"Is Gustavo Flávio your real name?"

What did he know about my past? My job at Panamerican Insurance? My commitment to and escape from the Asylum for the Criminally Insane? I took a good look at his thin face, his yellow eyes. How much did he know?

"We writers like to use pseudonyms. Stendhal was named Marie-Henri Beyle; Mark Twain's real name was Samuel Langhorne Clemens; Molière was the cryptonym of Jean-Baptiste Poquelin. George Eliot was neither a George nor an Eliot, or even a man, but a woman by the name of Mary Ann Evans. Do you know what Voltaire's name was? François-Marie Arouet. William Sydney Porter hid behind the false name of O. Henry." (For reasons similar to mine, though I didn't say that to the detective.) "It's a literary secret, ha ha!"

Guedes didn't insist, but my nervousness increased. I stuck my hands in my pockets. The cop ran his hand over his forehead again.

"I'll turn on the air-conditioning," I said.

"No need to."

"I'm feeling warm myself. I have a machine that cools the entire apartment," I said, heading toward the pantry where the closet with the air conditioner was. The cop followed me.

"Who was her best woman friend?"

"Whose best woman friend?"

"Dona Delfina."

"I haven't the slightest idea. I don't even know if she had a best friend."

"Every woman has a best friend. Hers was Denise Albuquerque," the cop said.

"You know more than I do. Damn, there seems to be something wrong with this machine. How is it you know who Dona Delfina's best friend was?"

"The lives of socialites are in all the society columns: that is, everything but the seamy side. At the moment the lady is traveling, but she should be back in a few days. I plan to have a talk with her."

We went back to my library. Guedes stood there looking at the books as if trying to read the titles on the spines.

"Do you have anything else to tell me?"

"Like what, for example?"

"Do you know her husband?"

"No. Anything else? I'm very busy, I already told you I'm busy, I'm no government employee like you, I only make money if I work, my new book, Bufo & Spallanzani, is way behind, and I'm very sorry but I must ask you to be brief and objective."

Guedes put his hand in his pocket and took out a piece of paper.

"Read this," he said.

It was a letter. Handwritten.

Dear Delfina,

After you left I got to thinking about the talk we had here in Paris. I think what you're planning to do is crazy. Nobody separates from her husband under such conditions. All of them, and I don't need to mention names, you know who they are, got a large piece of the pie when they separated, they became millionaires and lots of them were nothing but cheap whores playing around on their husbands with everybody and his brother. They learned from Jacqueline Onassis how to deal with men and you should do the same. Letting go of everything is stupidity, an act of folly, and Eugênio doesn't even deserve such consideration after the way he always treated you. Anyway, he has so much money that however much you take he won't even miss it. Is that man, that writer, worth such a sacrifice? Don't do anything rash. You struck me as very nervous, very tense, you weren't well (forgive my frankness). I'm enclosing this magazine about Sèvres porcelain. I spent a whole morning at the factory, seeing how porcelain is made. Sensational. That's all for now. I'm coming back on the 15th, don't do anything before I get there. Love and kisses,

Denise.

I sat down on the sofa in the office; Guedes continued to stand.

"The envelope, with the magazine and the letter, was sent by registered mail and for some reason wasn't delivered by the post office, which just sent a notice, which was found in Dona Delfina's purse. I went to the post office and picked up the envelope," Guedes explained.

I reread the letter. The cop must have known of my involvement with Delfina when he came to see me the first time. He had stood there watching me lie; besides being smart he was malicious. And I thought my relationship with Delfina was a secret. There are no secrets; someone always tells their best friend, and so on. In the end a shit-heel cop finds out too.

I returned the letter to Guedes, who carefully put it in his jacket pocket.

"Did you already know the contents of the letter the first time you came to see me?"

"No. I picked up the letter today. I had forgotten the notice from the post office in my pocket. I must be getting old. Well?"

"Yes. Dona Delfina and I did have an intimate relationship. I didn't tell you this for obvious reasons, to protect the lady's reputation. Besides which, it wouldn't have helped in figuring out the suicide or homicide, whichever it was."

"When was the last time you were with her?"

"The night before her death. We talked about what the doctor had told her about the seriousness of her disease. That's

why news of the suicide didn't surprise me. She was very de-
pressed."

"Where did that conversation take place?"

"At her house. She had just come back from a trip to Europe."

"How long had the two of you been having an affair?"

"I loved her."

"Yes, how long?"

"Six months, roughly."

"And she wanted to leave her husband and marry you?"

"The subject was discussed."

"Is there any possibility of her having another emotional involvement at the same time as the one with you?"

"No. Impossible."

"Had you ever seen, or did you see that day, a nickel-plated
revolver in Dona Delfina's possession?"

"She didn't have a revolver. Maybe her husband did, I don't
know. I never saw her with a weapon of any kind. She was
scared to death of weapons."

"Know what our problem is?" Guedes asked. He paused.
"Our problem is that Dona Delfina wasn't murdered by a robber.
A robber would have taken the automobile, which is worth a
fortune; he'd have taken the revolver, the gold watch, the rings,
the credit cards. A robber would have acted in a completely
different manner. It wasn't robbery."

I said nothing.

"Two people emerge, given the circumstances, as possible
perpetrators of the crime." Guedes spoke in a neutral tone as
if he were discussing the plot of a novel. "One is the husband.
But the husband wasn't in Brazil the day she was killed."

"He could have had someone else kill her," I said. "He knew
of my involvement with her."

"Ah, did he? Interesting. I had already thought of that, the
possibility that he had ordered it, but in that case the murderer
would have done everything in his power to make the crime look

like a robbery, by taking the dead woman's valuables. And a professional killer doesn't use a .22 and, if he did, wouldn't leave it at the scene. No, it wasn't the husband or anyone doing his bidding."

We passed a long moment in silence.

"Don't you want to know who the other person is?"

"Who?"

"You."

"Me?" I stood up, furious. "That's it, get out!" I shouted. "You have no right to come into my house and slander me."

5

"Forgive me for disturbing your meditation, my love, but I had to talk with someone after that cop left. When I screamed at him and ordered him out of my house he stood there calmly, looking at me, analyzing me, then walked pensively to the door, neither frightened nor triumphant, and advised me to look for a lawyer.

"You knew that Mme. X was Delfina? Then why'd you let me make such a ridiculous mystery of it? No; we agreed that I would relate my sex life with the women I've had or have but that their identity wouldn't be revealed. That way we would satisfy both your libidinous curiosity and my verbal lasciviousness. In fact, I may even be making up these stories as an outlet for our lubricity. Telling the details of my love for Delfina is a way of not forgetting her. I'll never forget her, just as I'll never forget you. But between us things are different; when we met each other you were sixteen. If it weren't for you, Gustavo Flávio wouldn't exist.

"Defoe, Swift, Balzac—I could go on for hours about writers who went wrong by investing their money or by speculating in one form or another, unsuccessfully. I can be included in that group. When I first met Delfina my financial situation was on the verge of collapse. The bank where I had put my money went bankrupt, and its president, a scoundrel who was once consid-

ered for Minister of the Treasury, fled Brazil with $250 million
that he deposited in a secret account in Switzerland. He still
hasn't surfaced to this day and they don't even talk about him
anymore. I was left penniless, but like Balzac I didn't change
my lifestyle. I started asking my publishers, both here and
abroad, for bigger and bigger advances. I didn't tell you that
before so you wouldn't worry about it. My last book, *The Lovers*,
for all its critical acclaim, was a commercial failure compared
to my other novels. It seems the public wasn't ready for a love
story between a blind woman and a deaf-mute. 'Cripples, the
maimed, the handicapped in general just don't make it in a love
story,' my agent told me. 'The last time it worked was *The
Hunchback of Notre Dame*.' My new novel wouldn't get past the
planning stage. Normally, as you know better than anyone else,
I construct the book in my head by noting down details, vi-
gnettes, scenes, situations. But Bufo & Spallanzani was—and
is—stuck. I started writing it when I met Delfina. For the first
time in my life a love affair interfered with my work. Being in
love, even just being interested in a woman, was always a great
stimulant to my work, you know that. But I began to lose interest,
showing Flaubert was right. The worst part is that I had already
received several advances for Bufo & Spallanzani and owed a
large sum to my agent in Barcelona.

"One day Delfina came to me and said she didn't want to go
on meeting me on the sly. I knew she'd say that one day, but
even so I was terrified. 'I'm leaving my husband,' she said. 'I
want to live with you openly. I don't have children, we won't
make anyone suffer, and I don't think Eugênio cares that much.'
We were in bed. Delfina, who was nude, placed both hands
behind her neck, stretched her marvelous body, and began
talking about her plans. Meanwhile I was confirming to myself
once again that women, however dazzling they may be, always
end up becoming a nuisance to those who love them. Not you,
you're a very special woman, unlike any other I ever knew. The

others, because of a kind of bourgeois decency linked to hypocritical conventionality, always end up subordinating passion to etiquette. To Delfina I represented, or had represented, a fantasy that sprang from the tedium of her six-year marriage. Now she wanted to make me real, make a husband out of me. 'We'll take a long trip, the two of us, wherever you want to go,' she said. I replied that I didn't want to leave Brazil, that I needed to write Bufo & Spallanzani, that there was nothing worse for a book than travel. She said that the book hadn't even been started, I could write on the trip, we'd go by boat, she'd sharpen my pencils for me. 'Have you ever seen a pencil in my apartment, even one? Don't you know I write on a computer?' I asked. To tell the truth, she had no way of knowing; since I met her I hadn't written a single line. While we talked that day I became aware of that fact: for the first time in my life I had stopped writing for a long period of time, and all because of a woman. I listened to her plans for the two of us. Delfina wanted to leave Eugênio immediately, before they went to Paris, which they did every two years, and where they would remain for six months.

"She said she couldn't stand six more months with her husband, even in Paris, especially in Paris, she couldn't stand being away from me for so long, she didn't want to live a secret life anymore, et cetera. 'We should think about it a bit more,' I said. 'Think, think, that's all you do,' she said, which strictly speaking wasn't true. 'What a writer does least is think,' I said jokingly. She said I was making her nervous, she wasn't sleeping at night, she'd lost her appetite, and all because of duplicity, lying, having to go to bed with a husband she didn't love— which might not be unusual but was still horrible. 'This is going to kill me in the end,' she said. I'll confess two things. First, I didn't want to marry Delfina Delamare, despite loving her deeply. Second, I didn't even want her to leave her husband. Delfina had become accustomed to being a rich woman, and separating from Eugênio would certainly be an untimely romantic gesture that would leave her without a dime. 'We should think about it a bit more,' I said, for the second or third time. She got out of bed and sat, nude, before the mirror and carefully made up her face, like an actress applying makeup to go onstage. I attempted, once again attracted by the beauty of her body now that she had stopped talking, to get her back in bed, but Delfina pushed me away. 'I'm going to tell Eugênio everything,' she said. I replied that it would be insane to do so, a brutal and senseless act that would hurt her husband needlessly. 'Deceiving him hurts him even more,' she said. Did you ever see anything more exasperating and stupid than a romantic woman? 'Let's think about it a bit more,' I repeated. She told me I sounded like a parrot and left, with a strange expression on her face. She won't carry out that act of folly, I thought. And really, the next day Delfina came back to my apartment at the usual time. She was very pale and seemed to have lost weight from one day to the next, as if that were possible—a lot of weight, I mean. We went to bed, and at the moment of orgasm her face was wet with tears. 'I spoke with Eugênio. I swore to him that I wouldn't see you again. Eugênio forgave me,' she said. 'Eugênio asked me to go away with him. Goodbye.'

"So she was going on the trip with her husband after all. She didn't know she had an incurable disease, none of us knew, neither I nor she nor her husband. I sat down at the computer to write but gave up at once. I'm not one to perspire. I know there's such a thing as inspiration; any old whore like me who's written over twenty books in little more than ten years knows that our work is hard labor, demanding physical strength, vigor. I began to think I had dried up; that's why Hemingway put a twelve-gauge shotgun to his temple. That day, after Delfina left, I went to a restaurant and stuffed myself with food and then phoned a woman I knew and shoved myself between her legs. But I didn't stop thinking about Delfina for a single miserable second.

"The next day I was at home thinking simultaneously of Delfina and Bufo & Spallanzani when the doorbell rang. That was the time Delfina usually arrived, one o'clock. I felt my heart beat happily. I knew she wouldn't commit the folly of breaking off with me and telling her husband everything. I ran to open the door, and there he was. I recognized him immediately from his picture in newspapers and magazines—the handsome suntanned face, the straight nose, the strong jaw. He was a bit shorter than I had imagined, but then I had always seen him, in photos, riding a horse. And his eyes were blue.

" 'Gustavo Flávio?' he asked. I acknowledged as much. He put his hand on my chest and shoved. I'm no featherweight— I weigh over two twenty—but he had a great deal of strength in his arm, besides the moral force of the outraged cuckold, and his push moved me out of the way, almost throwing me to the floor. He came into the room and, pointing his finger at me, said, 'If you see my wife again I'll kill you, but I won't dirty my hands on you, you filthy pig. I'll have them cut off your balls and let you bleed to death.' I said nothing. Before me stood a deceived husband, exercising his right to squawk. But after he left I had the feeling that this was no idle threat of a cuckold blowing off steam. There was a sinister truth to the warning. This was a dangerous man. He had the money and the willingness to hire a gang of professional killers.

"I spent two days worrying, until I read in the gossip columns that the Delamares had left for Paris. The rest you know. Delfina came back by herself and turned up dead, et cetera. For the moment, I'm worried less about her husband than about Guedes the cop, the poor man's Javert.

"The Delfina case is one of the most interesting and probably the most provocative and intriguing murder to take place recently here in Brazil. It has aspects that make it charming and a pleasure to read about, as it's a mysterious crime taking place in a social class where violence rarely occurs, and the supporting cast and additional violent deaths help make it even more enjoyable. But I'm too involved to be able to write about it, mainly because I loved Delfina and because the great love stories we writers experience seldom get written. The love stories that can be told are the mediocre ones."

6

Two days after Guedes left my house I received a summons from the 14th Precinct to make a statement. The day set for my statement was the eve of my departure for Falconcrest Retreat, a hard-to-reach spot in the Bocaina range. To get there I would have to go to a place called Pereiras, at the foot of the mountain. Then, after going a certain distance—in a bus, I think—I would take a tractor to the retreat, since the road was so steep and uneven that no other vehicle could climb it. I spoke with Minolta and she thought it a good idea. She was returning to Iguaba after spending ten days with me in Rio (but, as we had agreed, not at my apartment) and believed that perhaps Bufo & Spallanzani called for heroic measures, an entirely new routine, if it was to begin making its way onto paper—that is, I would separate myself from all those women, abandon the TRS-80, get away to an isolated ranch with a typewriter. The notification from the police, however, might mess up everything.

I called Martins, my lawyer.

"Gustavo," he said, "I can go down there with you, but I specialize in royalty law. I don't know anything about criminal law; if I think things are getting complicated we'll have to call in another attorney."

I told him I didn't want another attorney.

At the appointed time we went to the station, a small, dirty

44

one-story building. Martins handed the summons to a guy in shirt sleeves at a desk inside a wooden enclosure in a spacious room. The guy told us to wait. About fifteen minutes later a door marked Registry opened and a fat guy, wearing glasses and holding a piece of paper, which I saw at once was my summons, came toward us and asked, "Gustavo Flávio?"

"That's me."

"You're excused," he said.

"How can I be excused? I received a summons—"

"Let's go," Martins interrupted, pulling me by the arm. "Didn't the man say you were excused?"

"I want to know if I have to come back, in any case, and why they called me down here—"

"Let's go." Martins cut me off again. He was uncomfortable in this kind of atmosphere. I think it was the first time he'd ever been in a police station.

"You won't have to come back," said the clerk, who was standing beside us, listening to my conversation with the lawyer.

"Why won't I have to come back here?"

"You'd better ask Inspector Guedes. He was the one who ordered you summoned and later said you were excused."

"I'd like to talk to him," I said. Martins, who had been hanging onto my arm till that point, released me with a sigh of resigned irritation.

"I'll see if he can talk to you," the clerk said.

Another fifteen or twenty minutes. While waiting for Guedes I told Martins, "You can leave if you want to."

"I'm not going to leave you here by yourself," he said.

"They said they don't want anything further from me. There's no danger."

"I'd better stay," he said, looking about him with displeasure. "You know something? I wouldn't be a criminal lawyer even to keep from starving to death."

"So I see," I said.

Guedes was in his uniform, the grubby jacket and the grimy open-collared shirt.

"I owe you an explanation," he said. "Can you wait another five minutes? I'm finishing up a job."

"Five minutes really? I'm his attorney, and I—"

"There's no need for you to stay," Guedes said, walking away.

"He must be in the middle of a torture session and went to apply a few electric shocks to some poor devil," Martins said.

"You can leave," I insisted. "You can go."

"Of course not," he said indignantly.

Less than five minutes later, a mulatto with a revolver in his belt appeared and asked, "Which one of you is Gustavo Flávio?"

We were taken to Inspector Guedes's office. Guedes was seated behind a wooden table, heavily marked by spilled coffee, that held some papers and a medium-sized dictionary. He motioned us to the two chairs in front.

"Yesterday," Guedes said when we were seated and the mulatto had left, "a patrolman on his beat caught an individual named Agenor Silva, an escapee from Ilha Grande, holding up a bakery. When he got to the precinct he confessed he had killed a woman in a Mercedes ten days ago on a street in the Jardim Botânico district. I brought him here to our lockup. At first I didn't believe his story. His confession was spontaneous, and that's very unusual."

The lawyer gave me a meaningful look, as if to say, The only confession that counts for the police is one they get by torture.

"He also couldn't explain very satisfactorily why he took the car to Diamantina Street. He said he didn't know that part of the city and thought he could get from there to Tijuca Forest, where he planned to rape the woman after robbing her. When he saw that Diamantina was a dead end he got nervous, and at that instant the woman started to scream. To shut her up, he shot her. Why did he have a .22? It's easier to hide, he answered. Why didn't he steal anything else? He was afraid someone had heard the shot and he just had time to grab the woman's gold cigarette case. He still had the case on him when he was caught and couldn't explain why he hadn't fenced it. Dona Delfina's husband confirmed that the case belonged to her. We're obliged to charge this individual, despite some unclear points that need explaining. Your statement"—the cop looked at me—"is no longer necessary. Thank you for your help."

"Let's go, Gustavo," Martins said.

Guedes showed us to the door. There he held me by the arm.

"I know—" he began, then stopped. He was going to say something but changed his mind. He said, "Good night." But from his look I had the impression that he was going to say, I know your real name; I know your dark past.

II

MY
DARK
PAST

At twenty I was not yet a satyr or the glutton I am today. I was thin, frugal, and a virgin. And I had no thought of becoming a writer. I greatly enjoyed reading, but not writing. I was a modest and mediocre grade-school teacher. Then I met Zilda, who took me to bed and moved into my apartment. It was my first sexual experience, a very insipid thing. I don't know how I came to live with Zilda. The sight of a woman's body didn't attract me, the proximity of the female genitalia frightened me, and when I would go to bed with Zilda I avoided looking at her vagina, the odor of which repelled me, even if she had just taken a bath.

Zilda was an ambitious woman who convinced me to leave my teaching job and go to work for an insurance company where she knew a guy named Gomes. That's how I started working for Panamerican Insurance, where I became involved in an adventure that changed my entire life.

I had been working at Panamerican for a short time when, one summer afternoon, a man of thirty-four came into the company's office on Graça Aranha Avenue and told the agent who attended him that he wanted some life insurance. As it was a very large policy, the largest ever handled by Panamerican at the time, Mr. Estrucho was subjected to a careful medical examination that confirmed his excellent state of health. His offer

was approved. For some months Mr. Estrucho paid his premiums
punctually, until he died. A lawyer representing the interests
of the widow, Dona Clara Estrucho, appeared at Panamerican
and said he wanted the company's doctors to carry out a postmortem on the deceased in order to establish irrefutably that
his death was from natural causes, as he wished to avoid any
delay in payment of the insurance.

The head of the legal department at Panamerican was named
Carlos Ribeiroles, like all lawyers a cautious type of guy. He
met with his main advisers to look into the matter. When he
received the phone call, after the visit from Dona Clara Estrucho's lawyer, Mr. Ribeiroles's first reaction had been not to do
the postmortem. Like all lawyers, Ribeiroles didn't like to do
anything in a hurry; the workings of the law were based first on
Reason, then Morality, and Reason was the same as Good Sense,
just as Morality was the same as Justice. Neither one nor the
other justified such an unusual examination. Death, suspicious
or not, should follow legal guidelines.

"I think we ought to seek legal authorization to do an autopsy
and not a superficial examination such as the one desired by
the insured's representative," said a young lawyer.

Ribeiroles looked at him as if he had uttered a heresy. He
picked up a folder in front of him and read: " 'Maurício Estrucho,
capitalist, grower, thirty-four years of age, son of Curzio Estrucho and Camila Estrucho, married to Clara Estrucho, née Espinhal. The Estrucho and Espinhal families, in addition to
owning large farms in São Paulo, Mato Grosso, and Goiás, where
they grow coffee, soybeans, corn, and sugar, own alcohol dis-
tilleries and other industries as well as commercial interests in
Brazil and abroad, controlled by the Estrucho & Espinhal Holding Company.' This information comes from our Confidential
Investigation Department. Do you really think, counselor"—
lawyers, like doctors, are formal with each other in their hos-

tility—"that we have grounds to suspect fraud, or some even worse crime, in this case?"

"Everybody in Rio knows that Mr. Maurício Estrucho was a playboy," said the young lawyer.

"Playboy? That's not a legal term," Ribeiroles sneered.

"A wastrel, known for his extravagance in spending money," the young man insisted.

"And you think this justifies not only our suspicion but, even beyond that, our reckless rush to judgment? An autopsy can be performed only in case of accident or death resulting from criminal act or suspicion of same. We have the death certificate, signed by Dr. Albuquerque Gomes, one of our most eminent and respected physicians, who states that Mr. Maurício Estrucho died a natural death as the result of a myocardial infarction. That is not to be set aside lightly."

The two lawyers continued arguing for some time. The petition by Dona Clara Estrucho's lawyer asked that the examination be made without desecrating the body, given the couple's religion. This bolstered the position of the head lawyer. "It's not worth the risk of heaping scorn and opprobrium on Panamerican over a million dollars," he said. The other lawyers at the meeting sided with their boss, justifying their support with the ambiguous rhetoric that jurists are wont to use.

It was finally decided that Panamerican would carry out the examination. Ribeiroles was calm about the decision because of a conversation with Dr. Gervásio Pums, head of Panamerican's medical division and inventor of a technique known as OMSBS, Organic Measurement of Semiotic Biological Systems, used to measure the mental and physical health of individuals. OMSBS analyzed the alpha and beta rhythms of brain waves, the body's involuntary functions (such as heartbeat, blood pressure, contractions of the digestive tract), and finally the rigidity and texture of the fibrous musculature and of bones and skin. Basically, the OMSBS used five instruments invented by Dr. Pums to take these measurements. The ETG (electrotranscardiograph), which evaluated heartbeat and rate of blood flow through the heart; the DAEM (dual-action electromiograph), which determined the electrical activity and tension of the muscles; the DG (dermogalvanometer), to calculate skin resistance; the EOG (electrosteograph), to probe resistance and hardness of bones; and finally the EPROG (electroprosencephalograph), capable of measuring electric currents in the R (reptilian) complex of the limbic system and the neocortex. The OMSBS, being capable of recording and analyzing the vital signs of the organism like no other research technique, could by the same token also investigate signs of death.*

While Panamerican was getting ready, Clara Estrucho, a tall, slim woman of thirty, sat in a chair at Chapel No. 5 of St. John the Baptist Cemetery, her lovely face impassive as she sat by her husband's body. There was no one else in the chapel. Both Clara and Maurício were estranged from their respective families, and Clara had let her relatives know that she didn't wish the presence of any of them at the burial. Chapel No. 5 was empty, but from the next chapel, where vigil was being kept over the body of a young woman who had died in a motorcycle accident, came the sound of voices, at times laughter, or cries of lamentation.

At 7:00 P.M. the medical team from Panamerican arrived at the chapel. Accompanying the doctors was Dona Clara's lawyer, Mr. Ribeiroles, and Mr. Zumbano, head of Panamerican's Confidential Investigation Department (CID). The main members of the team were introduced to Dona Clara, who, her hands maintained tightly at her sides, greeted each of them silently with a nod of her head. When Dr. Pums's machinery was plugged into

---

*These instruments are described in greater detail in my story "The Living Dead," published in the book *Daedalus*.

the wall, Dona Clara said, "I don't want you to desecrate my husband's body." Her own lawyer reminded her that it was she who had requested the test and that the use of the instruments would pose no risk to the *de cujus*. Electrodes were placed on the dead man's head, chest, arms, and legs. For half an hour the doctors, at Dr. Pums's instructions, studied the graphs produced by the several instruments. While the testing was going on, a young man, obviously intoxicated, came into the chapel and asked them to perform the same examination on his fiancée, the dead motorcyclist. After some confusion the man was removed from the chapel and the tests proceeded.

It was almost eleven when they finished. To the disappointment of some of the examiners, the deceased really was dead, according to the OMSBS. Mr. Ribeiroles informed Dona Clara's lawyer that he would provide him with a copy of the test results.

Everyone left. Dona Clara remained, alone. A climate of peace and tranquillity reigned in Chapel No. 5. In the next chapel, the noisy wake continued, even noisier after someone had showed up with a few bottles. It was 3:00 A.M. when the fiancé of the girl killed in the accident told the others in a slurred voice, "That stuck-up broad next door is feeding the dead man through a funnel; come take a look." But apparently no one believed him, and Dona Clara was left in peace.

At 7:30 A.M. a priest arrived at Chapel No. 5 for the commendation of the body, which was merely a quick prayer because burial had been set for 7:00 and the priest was late. The body was placed on a cart, which the gravedigger pushed to the burial site. No one accompanied the bier, only Clara Estrucho. To tell the truth, there was one other person following the coffin, a young man wearing a jacket and tie who hid behind the crypts in order not to be seen. That man surreptitiously observed the burial until the gravediggers finished cementing over the bricks enclosing the grave. That man was an investigator for Panamerican. That man's name was Ivan Canabrava. That man was me.

As I said, I was an elementary-school teacher before I went to Panamerican. I also said I gave up teaching because of Zilda's influence, which isn't absolutely true. I was earning next to nothing as a teacher, and I hated children (I still do to this day). While I was a teacher there was nothing I found so repugnant, so irritating, so annoying, repulsive, and abominable as a pupil of tender years. I felt like killing several of them, before I gave up that nefarious profession.

I followed Clara Estrucho as she walked through the tree-lined cemetery, still maintaining her pose. I caught a cab and followed her to where she lived, on Redentor Street, as I already knew. I watched her as she entered the building. The way she walked, as if trying to disguise the beauty of her body, disturbed me. I had not yet awakened to sex, nor even gone through the stage of appreciating outwardly voluptuous women, but unconsciously I was already aware that the best women are those who don't wiggle their hips.

I went back to Panamerican. Gomes, my co-worker in the Confidential Investigation Department, was doing crossword puzzles as always.

"Gomes—" I began. I was going to tell him everything, that I suspected something was wrong with that million-dollar policy. Nobody takes out a policy that size and dies a few months later. I thought it best to keep my mouth shut. It wasn't yet time to lay it out. I merely said I had to go out on a job that afternoon. I had decided to pay Dona Clara Estrucho a visit.

I went back to the apartment on Redentor. The doorman asked where I was going.

"To Dona Clara Estrucho's apartment."

"Nobody's there," the doorman said.

"What do you mean nobody's there?"

It was three in the afternoon. I had seen her enter the apartment a few hours earlier.

"It's empty. They moved out."

"But I saw Dona Clara go in here today."

"They moved out," the doorman repeated.

"But I'm renting the apartment. Dona Clara said she'd wait for me. She gave me the key and said she'd wait till three o'clock."

I looked at my watch and took a ring of keys from my pocket.

"It's past three; I must be late," I said.

"If you have the keys, you can go up and take a look at the apartment. I can't go with you, I can't leave the door."

The apartment was on the fifth floor, 502 rear. I took out my tool kit and opened the door. How to open doors was the only useful thing I ever learned from Gomes.

I went in. The apartment had a living room, a hall, two bedrooms, pantry and kitchen, a small service area, and maid's quarters consisting of a tiny bedroom and bathroom. It was completely empty. Not quite. There was a bookcase in the living room, without books, and a full garbage can in the service area. I emptied the contents of the garbage can on the floor. There was a bottle with a bit of French wine, Saint-Émilion 1961, the remains of some cheese, an empty box of a tranquilizer, Lorax, an empty box of an appetite suppressant, Moderex (she must take Moderex to control hunger, which makes her nervous, so she takes Lorax to calm down), a plastic rye bread wrapper still containing a few slices, a small plant with round flowers, and a dead toad.

I removed the black plastic bag I always carried in my pocket and placed in it everything I'd found in the garbage can.

As I left, the doorman looked suspiciously at the black bag but didn't challenge me.

———

"Hi, Zilda," I said.

Zilda was watching the seven o'clock soaps and didn't answer.

I went to the bathroom to reexamine Dona Clara Estrucho's garbage. The wine had been drunk that day; it hadn't yet acquired that vinegary taste of wine left in the bottle. The plant appeared to have been crushed as if someone had extracted its juice to make a drink. I tried the cheese. It appeared to be goat cheese.

"What's this? You're eating garbage?" It was Zilda, watching me from the bathroom door.

"Not exactly. I'm working on an investigation."

"Things were better when you taught grammar school," she said.

"Did you know," I said, still holding the piece of cheese, "that a client cheated Panamerican out of a million dollars? Or tried to, that is, but they're not going to get away with it."

"You're the one who should cheat them out of a million. The Beetle broke down on me again in the middle of the street. Why don't you buy a goddam decent car?"

When Zilda began cursing I knew I was in for a bad time.

"When I solve this case, the company—"

"The company, the company, always that goddam shitty company. Fuck the company."

"Sweetheart," I said, reaching out my hand.

"Don't touch me. When I'm mad I don't like to be touched. Either get rid of that cheese or finish eating it."

Zilda screamed. She had seen the toad on the edge of the bathtub. "What's that on top of my bathtub?"

"It's a toad." I tried to be natural, as if I were saying, It's a box of matches.

"A toad! My God, a toad! Zilda, the son of a bitch brought home a toad!" She had the habit of addressing herself as if talking to another person.

"It's dead," I said.

"The bastard brought home a toad!" she yelled at the top of her lungs.

"The neighbors," I pleaded.

"Fuck the neighbors!" Zilda said, in a lower voice. "Get that piece of shit out of here."

Zilda made a nauseated face and ran to the living room.

I placed Clara Estrucho's garbage, including the toad, in the black bag and threw everything down the garbage chute. I hid the plant in a drawer in my dresser.

Zilda was still watching the soap opera.

"There, love. I threw everything out."

"Go wash your hands, then clean them with alcohol," she ordered.

I did as Zilda commanded.

"A toad, he brought home a dead toad. Did you ever see anything like it, Zilda?" She continued to grumble as I, in the bedroom, thought about Clara Estrucho's sudden change of residence. That the place was completely empty of furniture and other objects seemed very suspicious. And what about the toad?

What did the toad mean?

As always between soaps—there were several, and she watched one after the other—Zilda came into the bedroom, this time not to tell me that Patricia was a lying, petty woman, or some other piece of information connected to the soap, but to say, "We're going to the theater tonight."

"What are we going to see?"

"*Macbeth*, by Shakespeare. We're late. Change your shirt and wear your dark jacket." You could watch soap operas on television dressed any old way, but the theater was a different story.

There we were, all decked out, but to the irritation and embarrassment of both Zilda and me, most people were in jeans. The play, which I was seeing for the first time, wasn't all that bad. I mean, the part of it I saw, since we left before the end. The play, as everyone knows, has kings and witches, and somewhere along the way the witches gather around a cauldron and one of them throws in a toad while talking about poison and sleep, things that made me shudder.

"The toad!" I shouted at Zilda. "The Estruchos used witchcraft!"

"Shut up," Zilda said.

"The toad is the clue," I said excitedly.

"Shh!" whispered a guy behind me.

"The toad is going to show me the way," I said.

Zilda got up and headed for the exit with the sour expression she had been wearing a lot recently.

"What was it, love?" I asked outside the theater.

"What was it, love? You retard. You raise a scandal like that in the theater and then ask what was it? You know who was behind us? Dr. Paulo Marcílio, the doctor who lives on the sixth floor. Zilda, what are you doing here, living with a crazy man, poor and besides that not even willing to marry you? Zilda, it's time you did something."

When we got home she said, "It's over, you hear me?" She said it in a soft voice. "You're a good person, but you're an idiot. Don't take it personally. No, not an idiot, Zilda, that's too strong. You live on the moon, you're a dreamer. You shouldn't have given up public school teaching; there are some people who need a third-rate job guaranteed by the government, and you're one of them. You'll never get anywhere in life."

I stood there watching as she packed her bags and cursed.

Before she left I asked, "Do you want to stay? I'll move out and you can stay if that's better for you."

But she didn't answer; she left with her bags and got into the taxi that she had called. I followed her to the door of the building and waved, but Zilda didn't respond. She was looking pretty again, which increased my feeling of sadness.

The next day, from Panamerican, I phoned a shop called Brazilian Fauna and asked if they had toads. No, they didn't. They gave me the number of another shop, and after several calls I managed to get the phone number of the Brazilian Society for the Protection of the Amphibian. The man who answered had a cavernous voice. He said he couldn't give information over the phone. "Come by here," he said. His name was Cerezo.

"Like the soccer player?" I asked. The office of the Brazilian Society for the Protection of the Amphibian was in the Marquês do Herval building, at the corner of Rio Branco Avenue and Almirante Barroso. A small room full of old pictures on the wall and a bookcase.

"How does the soccer player spell his name?" the old man asked. His face was wrinkled like the bark of some ancient tree, and he had an immense shock of curly white hair. "No, no, my name is Ceresso, with two *s*'s," he said as he looked at me. Then he asked, "Do you know what an amphibian is?"

"More or less," I said.

"Name one."

"One what?"

"An amphibian."

"Toad," I said.

"Another."

"Alligator."

"Another."

"Turtle."

"Another."

"Lizard."

"Another."

"Seal."

"Another."

"Sea lion."

"Another."

"Hippopotamus."

"Another."

"Snake."

"You don't know the first thing about amphibians," the old man said with disgust in his voice.

"Submarine," I joked.

"Alligators, turtles, lizards, and snakes are reptiles, belonging respectively to the orders of Crocodilia, Chelonia, and Sauria, with the Sauria encompassing the Lacertilia—that is to say, lizards, among others—and the Ophidia, or snakes. All of them breathe through lungs from the moment of birth, unlike amphibians."

"Seal?"

"The seal is a mammal, my good man. The hippopotamus is a mammal. And so are sea lions. Amphibians belong to three orders: the Gymnophiona, known as cæcilia or worms, among other names; the Caudata, known as tritons and salamanders; and the Salientia or Batrachia, known as frogs, toads, and tree toads. Only those in the last category are amphibians, animals that in the first phase of life breathe oxygen dissolved in water by means of gills and as adults breathe atmospheric air through lungs."

I let the old man talk. Old people don't like to be interrupted. Neither do young people, but the young are more patient.

Finally he said, "You told me on the telephone that you wanted to talk to me about toads and their use in witchcraft."

My heart began beating rapidly at the mention of witchcraft. "It's a long story," I said.

"Then start telling it at once so we don't waste any more time."

I told Ceresso, in summary form, about the death of Maurício Estrucho, my suspicions, and finding the dead toad and the crushed plant in the garbage can.

Ceresso listened to my story in silence. Not in total silence;

occasionally he grunted in what seemed sometimes incredulity, sometimes disdain.

"Come over here." Ceresso led me to one of the walls of the room that featured charts covered with figures of frogs and toads. "Which one of these does the individual you found resemble? Here, not there, those are frogs, blast it!" I think he said blast it. Or perhaps he just muttered in anger. I turned my attention to the chart to which he was pointing. "Go on, which one of these did the toad look like?"

"It was the same as these two here," I said after some time, indicating two toads among the many represented on the chart.

"These two here? How can it be the same as these two here if these two are different types? It's the same as saying that Clara Bow looks like Jean Harlow. This one here is a *Bufo marinus*, better known as the agua toad or cururu, which in the Tupi language means 'large toad.' Influenced by Stradelli— though there is some debate about this—other naturalists such as Spix, d'Abbeville, Rohan, and von Ihering came to adopt the denomination cururu as the common name of that species of large batrachian that exists in Brazil. This other one is *Bufo paracnemis*, commonly known as the bull or giant toad. But they're very dissimilar. The paracnemis has glandular warts on the inner surface of the leg, which, when pressure is applied, exude a milky secretion. The paratoids are smaller and less extensive. And he reaches a length of twenty-two centimeters, while the marinus does not exceed eighteen. But they are absolutely identical in their great usefulness to man."

I looked in confusion at first one toad, then the other. They looked the same to me.

"Well?" the old man said.

"Well, what?"

"Was your toad the *Bufo marinus* or the *Bufo paracnemis*?"

"I don't know," I said disconsolately.

"You are simply too ignorant."

"It's no sin not to know something."

"Blast it! The old safe-conduct of Cicero, the final refuge of every cretin—*nec me pudet ut istos fateri nescire quid nesciam.* Be assured that the only true sin of man is ignorance."

The old man was so furious that he shook his head from side to side, as if a swarm of killer bees were caught in his hair.

"Remove yourself from here," the old man said, after hitting the wall with his fist.

"It's this one!" Divine Providence enlightened me and suddenly I knew, beyond a doubt, which toad was mine. "It's this one here," I said, touching the drawing of one of the toads with my finger.

"*Bufo marinus?*"

"*Bufo marinus.*"

"Hm, grrrr." The old man grunted. "That's the only one it could be. It's the one sorcerers like to use."

When Ceresso said that, my heart started racing again and I felt like kneeling on the floor and kissing the feet in his down-at-the-heels elastic boots. Sorcerers! The word resounded like a song accompanied by drums.

"Sorcerers, tell me about sorcerers," I asked.

"Where's my Marcgrave?" The old man rummaged for some time through the books in the bookcase. As he did so, he continued to talk. "In his *Historia Naturalis Brasiliae,* which he wrote in 1648, Marcgrave already made mention of Brazilian sorcerers' use of venom from *Bufo marinus.* But that's naturalist prehistory. Regarding that subject, read Lamarque Douyon, a researcher from Port-au-Prince who studied Haitian zombies; read Wade Davis's articles in *The Journal of Ethnopharmacology* and his book *The Serpent and the Rainbow;* read the book by E. Nobre Soares, *The Bocors,* and the book by Akira Kobayashi, *Datura and Its Trance-inducing Effects.* As you can see, I did some research after your phone call."

"Where can I find those books?"

"All I have is Marcgrave, but I don't know where it is. The Davis book can be located. I believe it'll be difficult to find the Douyon materials. But try the National Library in any case. Who knows?"

"What about the plant?"

"What plant?"

I took the plastic from my pocket with the vegetable remains that I had found in Dona Clara Estrucho's garbage.

"Could it be toad food?" I asked.

"Toads aren't vegetarians," Ceresso said. "Leave it here. I'll see what it is. Write your phone number on this paper."

I left Ceresso's place mildly disappointed and apprehensive. At one point, when I was certain the old man would provide the clue needed to unravel Maurício Estrucho's phony death, I felt like kissing his boots. But he had told me to do some research at the National Library, and that's where I was now, on the steps of the building on Rio Branco Avenue, recalling the days when I would get out of class at Colégio Pedro II, at the corner of Marechal Floriano Street and Camerino, and walk all the way down Rio Branco to the library. It wasn't easy, in those days, to find the books I wanted; they were never where they should be, or they were being bound, or they simply didn't exist.

After an hour of futile research I had to stop because the library was about to close.

"When you come here tomorrow, look me up and I'll help you find the books," said a young woman who worked for the library. She was pale and had fine, straight brown hair.

As I was leaving, reading the paper with the notes I had made at Ceresso's office, I stumbled over a young woman sitting on the steps. If she hadn't grabbed me I'd have tumbled all the way to the street.

"Hey, zombie, watch where you're going," she said.

"Did you say zombie?" I asked excitedly.

"That's what I said, zombie," she said.

"Incredible, I was just thinking about that."

"About what?"

"Zombies."

"You thought about them and turned into one," she said.

She was dressed like an old-style hippie—long skirt, hair standing on end, sandals, cloth purse—and she had a delightful smell of underarm.

"My name is Minolta."

"There's a bigwig in the international bourgeoisie who named his son RCA Victor Gramophone."

"Nice name," she said.

"My name is Ivan Canabrava."

"Canabrava. Beats Gramophone."

"You a student?" I asked.

"Student? I already studied everything I had to study. No, I invent. I'm a poet. What about you? What were you doing here in the library?"

"Doing research on witchcraft."

"I just love witchcraft," Minolta said.

The employees of the library were leaving, and the librarian who had said she'd help me was staring at Minolta and me. I smiled at her but she didn't respond.

"How about a beer while we talk about witchcraft?" Minolta said. "But you'll have to buy; I'm on empty."

At her suggestion we caught a bus in Cinelândia and got off at Glória. "This tavern has great beer," Minolta said.

In the end we didn't talk about witchcraft. Minolta had been evicted that day. She was thinking about sleeping on the library steps; the proximity of so many books gave her a feeling of security. "Books are a good trip."

"Want to sleep at my place till you find something?"

"It depends. I don't know. Are you into developing your feminine side?"

"What?"

"I'm tired of men who're trying to develop their feminine side. Look at me."

I looked at her. Her eyes were red from spending all morning reading at the beach under a strong sun.

"Your feminine side is inexpressive, unformed, without roots. Give up. Develop your masculine side, which may amount to something," Minolta decreed.

"You didn't answer. My place is at your disposal."

"Do you have a typewriter? I only write with a typewriter."

"Yes," I said.

"OK then."

"What about your things?"

"My things are here," she said, touching the left side of her chest with her forefinger, "and here." A cloth bag that looked like Indian handcraft, over her shoulder.

The minute we stepped inside, the phone rang. I was in the bathroom and Minolta answered.

It was Zilda.

"Who was that woman who answered?" Zilda asked.

"That was Minolta."

"Minolta? That's the name of a bicycle," Zilda said.

"She said that's her name," I said.

"What's she doing there?"

"She was evicted and is going to stay here till she finds a place."

"I turn my back and you bring home the first mongrel bitch you meet on the street," Zilda said. I think she'd forgotten that it was she who had left me.

"She's a good kid," I said.

"A good kid! Good for what? You idiot, you think you're pretty smart, but any two-bit con artist can wrap you around her finger. Throw that cow out or you'll never see me again."

"Sweetheart, I can't do that. She has nowhere to go. Besides which, I already invited her to stay here. I can't go back on my word."

"You can."

"No, I can't."

"Then goodbye. Goodbye! But this time I mean it, you cretin, you weakling, you stupid fool."

"Sweetheart, don't talk like that."

"Go to hell. I hope you drop dead," Zilda said, hanging up.

Zilda was very nervous but she wasn't a bad person. She didn't really mean any of that, but she lost her head easily and said things she shouldn't say.

"Who was that?" Minolta asked.

"Zilda. We used to live together and she had a fight with me and left, and now she's mad because you're here. But she'll get over it by tomorrow."

"Do you like her?"

"Yes. She's very pretty. Let me show you her picture."

I showed her Zilda's picture.

"Not too bad," Minolta said.

"She's prettier in person."

"Could be," Minolta said.

Minolta wanted to sleep in the living room, but I insisted she sleep in the bedroom. "I love sleeping on the sofa," I said.

I woke up quite early, with back pains. I took a bath, shaved. I made coffee, warmed the milk, set the breakfast table. I knocked on the bedroom door.

Minolta opened the door. She was completely nude. With her bag over her shoulder.

"Breakfast is on the table," I said.

"Coming," she said.

"Put on some clothes," I said, returning to the living room. We ate breakfast with few words exchanged.

"I'm leaving for work and will be back around seven," I said.

"Make yourself at home. There's instant coffee, milk, and fruit in the fridge. Should be a few other things as well."

"Where's the machine?"

I showed her where the typewriter was and a large pile of paper. I also showed her where the clean towels were.

I arrived after Gomes, at Panamerican.

"Everything OK?" he asked, looking at me as if my head were wrapped in bloodstained gauze.

"Fine," I said.

"No, really."

I adjusted the knot of my tie. "Really."

There weren't any work orders on the desk. I went to the office of Mr. Zumbano's secretary to say hello to Dona Duda. She always kept me abreast of what was going on. When they changed section heads in Legal and Mr. Ribeiroles took over, she gave me the news before the general bulletin circulated around Panamerican. She was very nice and always gave me a chocolate from the box she kept in her desk drawer.

"I wish I could be like you," Dona Duda said.

"Like me?"

"You eat everything—chocolate, candy—and you're always slim and elegant."

I put the chocolate in my pocket.

"Eat your candy," she said, taking one for herself and devouring it on the spot. "Is everything all right with you?" she asked, swallowing another chocolate.

"Fine," I said.

"Did you see the soap yesterday?"

I hated soap operas. I hated television. I hated children. (I already mentioned that.) But I wasn't going to say that to Dona Duda.

From the moment she got home at seven, she watched the

soaps, just like Zilda. Her dream was to watch the daytime soaps too, when she retired. She also enjoyed watching dubbed movies. The voices of the dubbers were always the same and she liked that. She liked hearing familiar voices. When a new voice came up—which was rare—she would complain. She even wrote a letter to the Globo network:

I didn't like the voice they gave Burt Reynolds in Friday's movie. What happened to the old voice? The one who dubbed Burt also dubbed Lee Majors, Humphrey Bogart, Clark Gable, Telly Savalas, Laurence Olivier, and Sheriff Lobo. Let's just see you put him in those roles too.

Duília Teixeira, Executive Secretary.

Once she fought with me because I told her that to achieve that raspy voice Humphrey Bogart had made the mortal sacrifice of contracting cancer of the larynx and that whoever wanted to dub him correctly should, at the very least, suffer the same. . . . That day, eating my chocolate, I asked which soap Dona Duda was referring to: the six o'clock, seven o'clock, eight o'clock, or ten.

"I never see the six o'clock," she said with a sigh. "The eight o'clock."

"I never see the eight o'clock," I said, dodging the issue.

"Do you know who killed the president of the company, Mr. Max?"

"No."

"Gerard Vamprey. But I already knew because I saw it in *Amiga* magazine. Gerard Vamprey, with that saintly face of his: he was the one who killed Mr. Max." And Dona Duda proceeded to relate the entire episode.

In other words, nothing new in Mr. Zumbano's office.

I went back to my office, mine and Gomes's, and noticed that he was still looking at me oddly.

"You can trust me," he said after a time. "I'm your friend."

"I know, I know," I said, thinking that in some way he must have learned of my investigation of the phony death of Maurício Estrucho. But it wasn't that. Just one of Zilda's schemes.

"Zilda called me and said you had a stress attack."

I let out a sigh of relief. "A stress attack? Is that what she said?"

"Not in so many words. She said you were off your tree, nuts, seeing toads on the wall, eating the neighbors' garbage, and that you threw her out of the house to bring in some hooker from the red-light district."

"It's not like that at all," I said indignantly.

"You mean everything's fine between you two?"

"No, it's not. She moved out, all right, but of her own volition."

"You mean there's no girl at your place?" Gomes had learned questioning from the American manual *Interrogation—Probing and Evaluation*.

"Yes, there is. But, Gomes, you don't know what's happening. Zilda had a fight with me—to tell the truth it was over a toad, but I'm not seeing toads on the wall, don't worry—and moved out. The next day, yesterday"—it was incredible, but it had all happened the day before—"I ran into this girl sitting on the steps at the National Library, her name was Minolta—that's right, just like the camera—and she had nowhere to go and I offered her my place for the night and she slept in the bedroom and I slept on the sofa and as of this moment she maybe isn't even there anymore. Satisfied? If anybody's crazy in this whole incident it's Zilda."

Gomes bit his lips and looked at the floor.

"Satisfied?" I repeated.

He continued biting his lips and scratched the tip of his nose. I don't know if he was convinced or not. In any case it was time to get over to the National Library and continue my research.

"If they ask about me, say I'm on an outside assignment."
Gomes nodded, without looking at me.

At the National Library I looked for the librarian who had offered
to help me. Her name was Carminha. She had sad eyes that
pierced my heart. She knew Ceresso, of the Brazilian Society
for the Protection of the Amphibian, an assiduous patron of the
National Library.

"What are you interested in?"

"Experiments with venom from toads."

"Uh," she said, and her eyes appeared even sadder. "I
thought your interest might be music. Stupid of me. Toads. . . .
Let's see. Is there something special you want, some book?"

"I want to see everything there is. But of course I'd like to
read these." I gave her the list of titles the head of the Brazilian
Society for the Protection of the Amphibian had given me.

Carminha got me *The Journal of Ethnopharmacology* with
Wade Davis's article, the Kobayashi book, and the one by Nobre
Soares.

I plunged into the reading of these fascinating books. The
toad, says Davis, "is a veritable chemical factory," containing,
in addition to hallucinogens, powerful unidentified anesthetics
that affect the heart and nervous system. Davis's discoveries
confirmed those of Kobayashi. Toads possess a substance similar
to the tetrodotoxin encountered by Kobayashi in the baiacu, or
puffer.

People under the effect of this substance appear dead from
a physiological standpoint, retaining only certain mental facul-
ties such as memory. The state is known as zombiism. Buried
or outside the tomb, the zombie remains like a dead man for
ten hours, unless he continues to be fed a mixture of toad venom
and certain of the chemicals found in such plants as pyrethrum
parthenium, in the proportion 1 to 50 mg. In these circumstances

the cataleptic state can be prolonged for some time. Researchers are uncertain as to just how long.

I was so excited after reading and noting it all down that I said to Carminha, "Was I or wasn't I right?"

"If you tell me what you're talking about I could answer."

"A guy can appear to be dead and still be alive."

"And he can appear to be alive and still be dead," she said. She must have a problem, I thought. Poor thing, so young and so pale and so thin and so pretty.

"Are you unhappy?" I asked.

"Me?" she said, surprised. "I never thought about it."

"There was a time in my life when I was unhappy all the time," I said.

"I'm not unhappy," she said. "It's just that . . ."

"That . . . ?"

"I'm not happy. There's a difference."

"I know."

"I have my work," she said. "I enjoy my work."

"I know."

"It's closing time," she said.

I ran to Panamerican, but no one was there but the cleaning staff. I decided to call my boss, Mr. Zumbano, at home. A woman answered and told me to hold for a moment.

"Mr. Zumbano," I said, "it's Canabrava."

"Who?"

"Canabrava, from the office."

"Yes, of course. Canabrava."

"I've found out something important in connection with Mr. Maurício Estrucho's policy."

Zumbano remained silent for a moment. "And this can't wait till tomorrow, when you can tell me about it at the office?"

"Tomorrow's Saturday, the office is closed."

"Ah, yes, so it is, of course. Then why not Monday?"

"Mr. Zumbano, this is very important."

"We can't do anything on Saturday or Sunday, can we? Besides which, I'm just about to leave for my place in Petrópolis. Monday, all right? First thing in the morning."

Minolta was in the kitchen in the apartment. She'd changed clothes.

"Keep an eye on the rice. It's whole grain. You like wholegrain rice? I'm writing a poem about the capuchin monkey, the one they brought back from the United States." She stuck her hand into her bag, which she always carried over her shoulder, and took out a picture. "Did you ever see a cuter little fellow?" It was a monkey dangling from a tree limb. "You know the story?"

"Is whole grain rice that dark kind?"

"It's the only one that's good for your health. The other's nothing but starch, not worth a thing. But this monkey was disappearing in Brazil; it lived near here, in Silva Jardim in the state of Rio, but deforestation was wiping it out. Then they took some couples to the United States and there they were bred in captivity. Now they're coming back, and the problem is whether or not they'll know how to live free."

"Living free is hard," I said.

"What do you mean by that?" Minolta looked at me warily.

"I mean it's hard, that's all."

"You like to live with clipped wings because it's easier, is that it?"

"No, I like living free. It's just that it's difficult, that's all."

She continued looking at me for some time. "If it's difficult for you, just think what it's like for a monkey that grew up in a cage. Fed like a prisoner, he never learned to hunt for his own food. There are poisonous things in nature, even if it seems absurd. The environmentalists recommended that the repatriated females and their young be released here in Silva Jardim, where they're going to be let go, along with a native male, raised in the wild. That male—or macho?—would teach the family to survive. What do you think?"

"Good idea," I said. My thoughts were far away. The only animal I was interested in was the toad—besides, of course, certain rational ones such as Dona Clara Estrucho.

"It strikes me as a solution typical of male chauvinist thinking. Why not put the repatriated males and their young with a wild female native? The female knows how to teach too, doesn't she?" Minolta said.

"It must be to avoid separating the female from her young," I said.

"The female is always the prisoner of convention."

"I don't understand much about monkeys. But why not put the entire repatriated family, parents and young, with a native, male *or* female?" I said.

"Monkeys are monogamous, say the environmentalists. Do you understand the problem?"

"Maybe the males will adopt the offspring of others while the females won't. In any case, under this plan an immigrant couple will have to be separated as well as a native couple—from what you say," I said.

"See what a complicated thing monogamy is?" Minolta said. "I think I'll write a poem about monogamy. I couldn't find the raw sugar. Keep an eye on the rice while I run over to Health Paradise on Dias Ferreira."

Minolta made a dinner consisting of whole grain rice, soy loaf, and boiled chayote squash. I don't know where she used the sugar.

"Is it good?" Minolta asked, eating vigorously and deliberately.

It was horrible. "It's good," I said. Why annoy the girl?

Fortunately, when we were living in hiding in Iguaba, Minolta gave up her macrobiotic fad and we discovered the pleasures of table and bed—but that comes later.

The telephone rang. It was Ceresso, of the Brazilian Society for the Protection of the Amphibian.

"That plant material that you brought me."

"Yes?"

"A botanist friend examined it for me. He said that those scalloped leaves, the ovoid flowers set in paniculate spikelets, the achene fruit, indicate beyond a doubt pyrethrum parthenium, a plant from the family of compounds."

"Dr. Ceresso, it's a substance derived from this plant that, mixed with toad venom, can cause—" I stammered.

"I know," he interrupted. "It's in the Nobre Soares book. It can cause a state of profound catalepsy. Good night." He hung up.

Minolta said, "I'm going out. Lend me the key so I won't wake you. I'll be back late." I was so nervous and excited that I barely heard what she said. I was hot, feverish.

I slept in fits and starts. I think I had several nightmares— I didn't remember them when I woke up, but I knew they were nightmares from the sweat on my forehead and the rapid beating of my heart. Fortunately, daybreak came and I got out of bed— or sofa—feeling the same backaches as before.

I pressed my ear against the bedroom door. I had seen Minolta arrive, quite late, but had pretended to be asleep.

I made breakfast, toasted bread and buttered it, sliced papaya French style, and knocked on the door.

"What is it?" I heard. "Come in."

Minolta always woke up with the same face with which she had gone to sleep. Zilda was very pretty, but in the morning her eyes were swollen. Minolta's face was clean and porcelain-like, that of a healthy child.

"Put on some clothes," I said, closing the door. If I slept

nude I caught a cold. I didn't even have to be entirely nude; it was enough not to wear either top or bottom for me to get a terrible cold, even if I covered myself with the sheet.

"Stop dominating me," Minolta said, coming from the room. "I have to get all dressed up on a hot day like this"—she had put on short shorts and a blouse over bare skin—"just because you make the rules."

"I made breakfast," I said.

"Making breakfast doesn't give you the right to dictate to me."

"I don't want to dictate to you."

"Every man wants to dictate to a woman."

"Not me."

"Liar. Why did the woman who you lived with split?"

"Zilda?"

"Zilda. Were there others?"

"No. Zilda's a very nervous woman."

"You mean: Zilda is a sick woman. That's how men destroy women."

"No. Zilda's not a sick woman."

"Look, Zilda doesn't interest me."

"Right. Let's talk about monkeys."

"I don't want to talk about monkeys either." See a face, forget a nightmare. Her night must not have been so hot either.

"So drink your coffee."

"Don't you have any whole wheat bread?"

"Unfortunately, no."

Minolta picked up the toast and took a small bite. Then another. And another. "This toast is good. How'd you make it?"

"In the oven. I use two-day-old bread, sliced so thin it's almost transparent."

"Delicious. But white bread's not good for you, you know. Once or twice in a lifetime, tops."

"Well, I have to go," I said. "Will you be here when I get back?"

"Maybe."

"I'll come back early."

When I arrived at the office I put the notes I had made at the National Library on the desk and began typing a report for Mr. Zumbano, head of Panamerican's Confidential Investigation Department. I spoke of the toad I'd found in Dona Clara Estrucho's house, the pyrethrum parthenium, the research by Davis, Kobayashi, and Nobre Soares. Despite several interruptions—once from Zilda, on the phone, who said, "Isn't that tramp leaving?" (She had called the apartment and Minolta had answered.) "Either you throw that filthy bitch out or you'll never see me again"—I managed to write a clear, concise, and basic report on the Maurício Estrucho case, proving my point of view that Panamerican was the victim of a massive fraud. "The most Machiavellian and cunning in the history of insurance in Brazil," I concluded my report.

Mr. Zumbano refused to see me.

"He's very busy," Dona Duda told me.

"He told me to see him this morning. I called him at home on Friday. It's urgent."

"But he's very busy. Something to do with the board of directors." For the first time Dona Duda didn't give me a piece of candy from the inexhaustible supply in her drawer. Could my insistence be bothering her?

"Then please do me a favor. Give him this report. Please don't let anyone else see it. Give it directly to him."

"Leave it to me."

"It's very important."

"Leave it to me."

"It's very, very important."

"I know."

"Give it only to him."

"I already told you not to worry."

I gave her the report, waited for her to put it in the drawer, and left after giving her a smile, my nicest smile, the one that showed all my teeth. She didn't respond.

"Zilda just called," Gomes said when I got back to the office.

"I gave Mr. Zumbano a report on the Estrucho case."

"She says she's going to the apartment to throw the girl out."

"What?"

"That wasn't exactly what she said. She said, 'I'm going to kick that disgusting con artist, that slut, out of there.' "

I grabbed the phone and dialed home. The telephone rang and rang, until Minolta answered.

"You interrupted my transcendental meditation," she said.

"Bolt the door and don't let anyone in. Especially Zilda."

"No sweat," Minolta said, hanging up.

"Problems, huh?" Gomes said, looking sidelong at me.

"No, no. Everything's fine."

"Comb your hair," Gomes said.

"I have to talk to Mr. Zumbano."

"Another reason for combing your hair."

"I don't have a comb."

"I'll lend you mine." Gomes handed me a black comb with grayish teeth full of dandruff. Gomes's jacket was always covered with dandruff.

"No, thanks very much."

Mr. Zumbano was leaving when I tried to talk with him.

"What's it about? I'm in a hurry," he said when I asked him if I could have a word with him. Dona Duda looked apprehensive.

"The Estrucho case. Did you read my report?"

"I read it. I read it. I just finished reading it."

"I don't think there's any time to lose. I'll bet if we open the tomb we won't find anything inside," I said.

"Things aren't that simple, Canabrava," Zumbano said, maintaining a certain distance from me. "I have to talk with Ribeiroles. It's a delicate matter."

"Mr. Zumbano, that tomb is empty. There's nobody inside. I don't have the slightest doubt."

"It's always dangerous not to have any doubts," Zumbano said. "Besides, what proof do we have? Are you forgetting the examination done by our own doctors? The man is dead."

"He was in a state of deep catalepsy."

"Deep catalepsy?"

"Didn't you read my report?"

"I read it. I read your report. Do you know what it looked like to me? One of those reports that try to prove the existence of flying saucers or extraterrestrials."

"I don't believe in flying saucers."

"It appears otherwise."

"What if the stockholders found out that we did nothing to defend their interests and let the company be swindled out of a million dollars?"

Mr. Zumbano interrupted me. "Are you threatening me?"

It's true. I *was* threatening Mr. Zumbano. When I realized that, I felt ashamed. I didn't mean to threaten Mr. Zumbano. I wanted to convince him, perhaps persuade him to do what I thought best for the interests of the company. But not threaten him.

"No, I'm not threatening you."

"Don't be so sure of yourself. There are no absolute truths."

"I know. But there's such a thing as simple truth, isn't there?"

Zumbano put on a thoughtful expression. "If truth is relative, then lies are relative. . . . What a provocative thing thinking is." He took a small notebook from his pocket. "I jot down ideas that strike me as important, ideas that might enrich my intellectual capital." He wrote it down, repeating aloud, "If truth is relative, then lies are relative."

The aphorism is Nietzsche's; it's in *Thus Spake Zarathustra,* one of the most boring books I had ever read in my short and meager life. I thought of telling Mr. Zumbano this but decided it was best to remain silent.*

"Well?"

"Well what?"

"My report?"

"Patience, Mr. Canabrava. I sent it to Mr. Ribeiroles. I need an opinion from Legal."

With this, he turned his back, an expression of open impatience and irritation on his face. And his arms. As he walked away, he looked like someone shooing off a beggar who had grabbed him by the coat sleeve.

I got home and found Minolta at the table in the living room with canvases, brushes, and tubes of paint.

"I found some cash in a drawer and bought this stuff to paint with. I'll pay you back later. I'm doing a painting, Nightmare on a Sunny Morning, but don't look. I don't like people to see my paintings while I'm working on them. Oh, that broad was here."

"Who?"

"Your ex. That's some kind of strung-out lady. But no matter." Minolta went back to her painting.

The phone rang.

It was Zilda.

"You worm! That shrew from the red-light district almost killed me. I'm covered with bruises from the beating she gave me. I want to warn you, you festering boil, that I'm taking this to the police. That murderous whore belongs in a cage."

"But what happened, Zilda?"

---

*I was mistaken. Nietzsche's phrase is: "He who knows not how to lie, knows not the truth."

"What happened, Zilda? That psychopathic freeloader with a black belt beat the hell out of me. She said she's a karate champion, which makes her attack all the more serious. She's going to rot in prison, or else I'm going to blow her brains out."

"Take it easy, Zilda."

"Either you get her out of there or I'm coming there with the police. I'm going to the hearing. She'll see who she's dealing with. *You'll* see who you're dealing with."

She made a few more threats and slammed the phone in my ear.

Meanwhile Minolta was calmly painting her canvas. "Hassles?"

"She says you beat her up."

"She's the one who wanted to beat me up. I pushed her away."

"Are you a karate champion?"

Minolta laughed. "I said that to scare the woman. She was yelling a lot and I told her to shut up. She said, 'And you're going to make me shut up, you worm?' So I raised my hands like you see in the movies and said I was a karate champion and jumped toward her yelling 'Sayonara,' the only word I know in Japanese. The next thing I knew she was on the floor; I think she must have slipped, because the blow I landed, if you can call it a blow, wasn't very hard. Want me to show you?"

"Show me what?"

"The blow."

I thought a bit. "No, thanks very much. Zilda says she's bringing the police."

"Bull."

"She's a mean woman."

"She's a lot of hot air. I know those fussy types. No way José. I wasn't born yesterday."

"Do people of your—I mean, your friends; I mean—how old are you?" I asked.

"How old do you think I am?"

"Between sixteen and thirty," I said.

"You got it."

"Do people your age all talk like that?"

"Like what?"

"That mixture of old and new slang."

"Sometimes I like to say stuff my grandmother used to say, like about not being born yesterday; sometimes I invent things; sometimes I use a phrase from the Treasury Department. Polysemy is my thing."

"Would you help me carry out some research?"

"It depends," she said.

"Depends on what?"

"First I want to know what it is. I don't buy a pig in a poke."

"I'm going to take a substance to see if I go into a cataleptic state."

I didn't mention the motives that led me to do this, nor did she inquire.

I phoned Ceresso, of the Brazilian Society for the Protection of the Amphibian.

"Dr. Ceresso, it's Ivan Canabrava. Do you remember me?"

He did. I asked if I could request a favor. He was silent, and I thought he had hung up. "Yes," he said at last.

"I wonder if you could get me a toad and some pyrethrum parthenium."

"What do you think I am, a quick-service storehouse of universal flora and fauna? I have more than enough to do, boy." His voice was harsh and irritated, but he didn't hang up.

"Dr. Ceresso, you are the only person in the world who can help me," I begged. "Please."

"I'm very busy," he said, now merely grouchy.

"I know you're very busy; you're an important scientist dedicated to a noble cause, namely the protection of the amphibian," I said.

"What toad is it that you want, *Bufo marinus*?"

I confirmed that it was *Bufo marinus*, the toad I had identified on the wall in his office.

"Look, boy, you're making some very difficult work for me; the family of compounds is quite large. Pyrethrum parthenium can be in wormwood, sagebrush, arnica, horseshoe pelargonium, the marigold . . ."

I noticed that Minolta had taken off her clothes and was wearing nothing but panties. "It's hot as blazes," she said.

". . . the cardoon, escarole, cockleburs, edelweiss, obviously in the pyrethrum plant . . ."

"Put those clothes on," I said, holding my hand over the mouthpiece while Ceresso recited the names of plants from the family of compounds.

"Why? Do you find my body repugnant? Does my naked body drive you mad? Are you shocked by my nudity? Give me one reason why I shouldn't be naked."

"Well . . . you might catch a cold."

"My last cold was ten years ago."

". . . aster, amaranth, dahlia . . ."

Minolta's body certainly was not repugnant. Maybe her bones stood out a bit more than they should, around the ribs and just above her chest, which could be expected considering her macrobiotic diet. Her rear end was small, round, and muscular; her legs were also muscular, with surprisingly large and well developed quadriceps. I felt a flash of heat in my body, followed by a chill.

". . . tenacet, camomile, chicory, and many others," Ceresso said.

Minolta's breasts were also something unexpected; from that cage of bones projected two solid and upright globes, as if stuffed with silicone.

I missed a bit of what Ceresso was saying.

"When can you get it for me?"

"Didn't I say I'd have everything in two days? Are you deaf, boy?"

"There's something wrong with my phone," I said.

I said goodbye to Ceresso with cloying and subservient expressions of gratitude.

Seeing Minolta nude, painting, for some reason I thought of Zilda. What if she showed up suddenly and saw Minolta walking around the house naked? It was impossible to imagine what could happen.

"If the doorbell rings, don't answer," I said. "Let me go to the door."

"I made a bamboo shoot salad for us to eat at dinner," Minolta said.

As soon as she said this, the doorbell rang.

"Let me get it." Alarmed, I went to the door on tiptoe and looked through the peephole. A man and a woman, their faces distorted by the viewer lens, were probing menacingly, their deformed noses close against the door.

"Who is it?" Minolta asked.

I tiptoed back to where she was, my heart racing in fright.

"Some sinister-looking people," I murmured. "They must be police."

"So what?" Minolta said.

"So what?"—still whispering. "It must have to do with Zilda. I don't know what kind of story she concocted. Do you have anything on you?"

"Anything on me? What kind of thing?"

The bell rang again.

"Drugs, pills," I said into her ear.

"Drugs? That's out, man; the ones who do drugs now are bankers, teachers, butchers, middle-class types. Let the police in."

"With you naked like that? At least put on some clothes."

I led her by the arm back to the bedroom.

"Put on that dress," I said, handing her a long, loose dress, which was in fact the only one she owned. Minolta impatiently pulled the dress over her head as she returned to the living room.

The bell rang again.

I took another look at the two sinister figures through the peephole. The woman seemed to be saying something like "Let's break down the door." They were going to break down the door!

"They're going to break down the door," I told Minolta.

"Shit," Minolta said, putting down her brush. "Let me handle this."

Without looking through the peephole, Minolta opened the door.

"Police, huh?" she said, embracing the two new arrivals. "This is Crab and this is Mariazinha. They make costume jewelry to sell at the Hippie Fair."

"We used to. Got run off by the inspectors. Now we sell in front of the post office in Copacabana," Mariazinha said. "But that's cool."

"Didn't I tell you they were coming for dinner?"

"No, you didn't," I said.

"Sure I did."

"Then I forgot."

"Is this the—" Mariazinha began, then stopped.

"The what?" I asked.

"Go ahead and say it," Minolta said.

"The square?" Mariazinha finished.

"Yeah," Minolta said.

"Nice," Mariazinha said.

"Don't pay any attention to these women," Crab said.

"He said you were going to break down the door," Minolta said.

"Us?" the visitors said in unison, surprised.

"Didn't you say 'Let's break down the door'?"

"Me? I said, 'Let's split, nobody's coming to the door.' "

"When you're scared you neither see nor hear straight," Crab said.

"I have a present for you," Mariazinha said. "I made it myself."

She gave me a small gilded chain with a dangle.

"What kind of animal is that?"

"An armadillo," Crab said.

"Put it on," Mariazinha said.

I put it on.

"I made us bamboo shoot salad," Minolta said.

"We brought some cheese curd that we bought in São Cristóvão," Crab said.

Crab wasn't a nickname, as I later discovered. It was his real name. Despite everything, I liked the couple. After dinner we talked until late. At that hour the buses were few and infrequent, and they lived in Santa Teresa, where transportation was difficult. Minolta invited them to stay over. "You take the bedroom. Ivan and I will sleep in the living room." They didn't want to, but we insisted; they were guests.

"You take the sofa, I'll sleep on the floor," Minolta said after the guests had installed themselves in the bedroom.

"You sleep on the sofa, I'll sleep on the floor. After all, it's my house," I said.

We made a kind of mattress out of the blankets. To tell the truth, sleeping on the floor beat sleeping on the sofa, as I verified upon awaking the next morning.*

The next two days went by in painful anticipation. I was

*At the end of this century sex ceased to be fruition and became communication (*see Moravia*) and as such cannot be ignored by writers. In my books if a man and a woman are alone and she takes off her clothes, something happens. A situation of indifference such as occurred between Minolta and me would be impossible. But in truth that's what happened. I have already stated that my satyriasis was slow to develop. Minolta made me what I am. I owe it all to her. (I think I already said that.)

awaiting news from Ceresso, of the Brazilian Society for the Protection of the Amphibian.

Meanwhile I was working as usual at Panamerican. I knew that Zumbano wasn't going to call me in to talk. I needed to confront him with irrefutable evidence.

Mariazinha and Crab moved into my apartment. They'd been staying temporarily with friends in Santa Teresa and there was some kind of trouble and they had to move the day after they slept at my place. They simply took over the bedroom, which wasn't mine after all but Minolta's. The arrangement of the first day continued, Minolta sleeping on the sofa and I on the floor. But none of that bothered me; all I could think of was the experiment I was going to do as soon as the *Bufo marinus* and pyrethrum parthenium arrived. Besides, Mariazinha and Crab were nice people whose presence didn't bother me. The evening they moved in, I spoke to them and Minolta about the experiment I was planning. They were very interested in what I told them. I asked if they'd like to help me; more than that, if they'd observe the test I was going to carry out and afterward sign as witnesses to the report I planned to prepare for Zumbano if the result was positive, as I hoped. They agreed enthusiastically. Mariazinha had one condition. "I just don't want to handle the toad; they're disgusting."

"I'll handle it. The only thing that disgusts me is cockroaches," Minolta said.

"I'll help," Crab said.

I explained that no one would have to touch the toad. I myself would extract the poison from the animal's glands. It was only necessary to exert a slight pressure on the paratoids. The problem was how much poison to use. As Ceresso, of the Brazilian Society for the Protection of the Amphibian, had told me, *Bufo marinus*'s poison was extremely potent and any animal injected with it would undergo terrible muscular convulsions followed by death. Even the toad itself was sensitive to the effects of its poison and would perish like other animals.

"I read somewhere that if you want to prevent your boyfriend from cheating or leaving you, you should keep a toad under the bed," Minolta said.

"I'd rather lose the boyfriend," Mariazinha said.

At Panamerican I avoided speaking with Gomes. I didn't trust him, not only about company matters but also because I was sure he was spying on me for Zilda. She hadn't carried out her threat to bring the police to my place, maybe because she was cooking up something worse.

Finally Ceresso, of the Brazilian Society for the Protection of the Amphibian, called me.

"I have everything you want. Stop by the society."

"Now? At this very moment?" I tried to speak softly so that Gomes, at the next desk, wouldn't hear what I was saying. Even so, he looked at me with ears pricked.

"Now," Ceresso answered.

"I'm on my way," I said.

I put on my coat and was about to leave when Gomes stood in my path.

"I'm your friend," Gomes said.

"I'm in a hurry; there's an urgent matter to take care of."

"You've been acting very strangely these last few days. Is anything wrong? You can trust me."

"I'm late," I said, squeezing past Gomes and leaving the room.

I caught a taxi that took me to the office of the Brazilian Society for the Protection of the Amphibian.

Ceresso was waiting for me.

"Look what a lovely male I managed to get for you," Ceresso said. It was an immense toad, greenish-yellow, its belly dotted with brown spots. Its entire body was covered with papulose glands, some of them with horny points. I noticed that the toad, as I looked at it, grew in size, its belly swelling in a frightening manner.

"This species is very vain," Ceresso said, "and this individual in particular seems prouder than most. Look how haughtily he puffs himself up."

"No kidding, this creature considers itself pretty?" I asked.

"In reality he thinks you're a snake and is swelling up so you can't easily swallow him." There was a derisive smile on Ceresso's lips. (They weren't exactly lips, just a small line between nose and chin.)

Ceresso took a glass container and began to extract the poison from the glands of the toad. "One must squeeze the glands carefully; otherwise the secretion can be expelled for a distance of over a hundred and fifty feet," Ceresso said. He kneaded the toad, which remained motionless, with extreme caution. A repugnant substance, with a strong odor that I had never smelled before, exuded from the animal's skin. With a small glass rod Ceresso gathered the secretion and placed it in the container.

"Done," Ceresso said. "Here it is. But remember, be careful how you use this."

"Dr. Ceresso, I already told you: I want to unmask a criminal, a swindler, a real wise guy. I'm working on the side of Good."

"That's what Brazil has the most of, wise guys, especially in the scientific world," Ceresso said. "Brash mediocrities who gain their prestige by shrewd and sly theft of the creative work of others. Thieves! Lowlifes! Scoundrels!"

I listened patiently to Ceresso as he railed on. He was right; someone had to put an end to the situation.

In possession of the toad venom and the pyrethrum parthenium, I ran home to my friends who were going to help me: Minolta, Mariazinha, and Crab.

"Brother and sisters," I said, "the moment has arrived. A proportion of one to fifty milligrams, according to the classic authors." At the time I didn't remember whether it was the Portuguese, the Japanese, the American, or somebody else who had determined that proportion. I was possessed by an idée fixe, ready to die for it.

The method would be this: I would take the first dose of the potion and lie down on the bed. Then I'd remain in that position for ten hours and they would feed another dose through a funnel into my mouth, just as Clara Estrucho had done with her husband. Then they'd call a doctor. Then they'd close me up, or rather wrap my head in a plastic sack, to arrest my breathing (it was impossible to arrange for a crypt in the cemetery) for more than twenty-four hours. "You could die, man," Minolta said. "But as long as it's in a good cause that's cool." It was a good cause, unmasking a pair of liars.

Before I drank the liquid Mariazinha made me take a ritual bath. She placed coarse salt in a bucket of hot water, put me naked into the shower stall, and before throwing the salty water over me offered the following prayer, which I repeated: "Guardian angel, guides and protectors, cast thy influence over me, making me to possess strength, faith, and resoluteness of thought, so that by this bath I may feel thy vibrations and thy blessing. So be it."

I didn't believe in sorcery, but for some reason the bath made me feel more confident.

I lay down on the floor. I didn't want to keep Crab and Mariazinha from having the use of the bed. For the purposes of the experiment it made no difference whether I lay on the bed or the floor. "Give me the drink," I said.

"Do you have a mother?" Mariazinha asked.

"Don't be a fool," I said.

"As God wills," Crab said.

"Shit," said Mariazinha. "Now you believe in God?"

"It's turned into witchcraft," Crab said. "God's always involved in witchcraft."

"Do you have a mother?" Mariazinha repeated.

"Why?"

"If something bad happens your mother would want to know."

"Mothers want to know everything *but* the bad things," Crab said. "Don't bug him. Let's do it, man."

I drank the potion.

"Are you feeling anything?" Minolta asked.

"Not so far."

I wasn't feeling anything. Maybe it's a delayed effect, I thought. And blacked out.

I woke up slowly. Smell was the first thing to return, an odor I knew but couldn't readily identify. (It was the Indian incense that Mariazinha burned.) Then I began to hear sounds: muffled voices, the rattling of dishes, a car horn in the street. Sight was the last to come, because I had kept my eyes shut as I began to return to the world of sensation.

The three of them—Minolta, Mariazinha, and Crab—were huddled anxiously over me.

"You gave us one hell of a scare," Crab said.

"You told us you'd look like you were dead, so we were prepared, but we were still worried."

"I never saw a dead person any deader than you. It made me feel like burying you," Minolta said.

"Did you call the doctor?" was the first thing I asked her.

"Yes, and here's the death certificate. He examined you and wrote out the certificate."

"Did you do as I told you?"

"To the letter. When he said you'd had a fatal heart attack I went crazy and said that was impossible, told him to reexamine you, that you were healthy as a horse, and that there'd been a case in your family of an uncle who was thought dead till he sat up in his coffin at the wake and scared the hell out of everybody."

"He didn't buy the story about the uncle; I could tell by his face. He must've thought it was something made up by the poor desperate widow," Mariazinha said.

"But he did the reexamination."

"You were screaming so much."

"Afterward he said, 'I'm very sorry, madam, but your husband is dead beyond a doubt.' That's when I felt like giggling and almost broke out laughing."

"Did he suspect anything at the time?" I asked.

"Not a thing. He gave me some pills to take. He must think I flipped out. I flushed them down the toilet. You won't catch me taking pills."

I picked up my own death certificate, which I read with as much excitement as my state of drowsiness permitted. I had the proof I needed to convince Zumbano and Panamerican's board of directors to open the tomb where Maurício Estrucho was supposedly buried and see for themselves that it was empty. Then it was just a matter of finding the gravediggers who were involved in the scheme and unmasking the pair of swindlers.

A funny thing: in the two days that I was under the influence of the drug, my beard hadn't grown. I shave every day, in the morning and at night, and stiff, prickly hairs darken and completely cover my face. Often, Zilda would order me out of bed to shave, claiming I was scratching her. But that day—when I was in the cataleptic state—not a single hair of my beard had grown.

With the death certificate in my pocket I went to Panamerican.

"What happened?" Gomes asked. "I called your house every day and they said you were on a trip."

"In a way that's true," I said.

"I don't understand."

"I need to talk to Zumbano," I said.

"Take it easy. Don't do anything foolish. They'll fire you."

"Let them."

Dona Duda didn't offer me a piece of candy. She received me coldly, saying "Mr. Zumbano is busy" before I could open my mouth.

"But I must talk with him."

"That's impossible. He's very busy, as I told you."

"I'm very sorry, Dona Duda," I said. I put my hand against Mr. Zumbano's door and went in.

Mr. Zumbano was reading the newspaper. He stood up in surprise, folding his paper.

"I told him you were busy but he went in anyway," Dona Duda said behind me.

"Get out," Zumbano said.

"Only after you listen to me," I said.

"Then I'll have you thrown out. Call Security, Dona Duda, and have them remove this madman from my office." He was so furious that his voice trembled.

"I have proof of the Estruchos' swindle," I said. I took the death certificate from my pocket and shook it in Zumbano's face.

Zumbano's attitude suddenly changed. "It's all right, Dona Duda. I'm going to talk to Mr. Canabrava."

"You don't want me to call—"

"No. You may go." In a different tone of voice, to me: "Please, have a seat, Mr. Canabrava, and tell me everything. Maybe you're right."

I told Zumbano everything. My original suspicions, the research I'd done at the National Library ("That's in the report I gave you"), Ceresso's help, and finally the experiment I had done, inducing in myself the cataleptic state that had led the doctor to believe I was dead.

"Here's the death certificate."

"Hmm," he said, reading the report. "Very interesting. Look, Canabrava, don't talk to anybody about this; it might hamper the investigation. Leave the certificate with me. You've done a fine job. Panamerican needs people with your intelligence and dedication. I'm going to recommend you for promotion."

"Thank you very much."

"Go back to your office. Don't forget: silence. We must take care that the swindlers not get word of it. They may have an accomplice here on the inside."

I hadn't thought of that. It wasn't an outlandish possibility. After all, a lot of money was at stake. When I got back to my office Gomes asked me what the subject was that I had discussed with Mr. Zumbano. I evaded the issue by saying it was something personal, inconsequential. Suddenly I began to suspect Gomes. I recalled he'd been very curious lately, watching me and asking strange questions.

"If you don't want to tell me you don't have to," Gomes said. "I know you're hiding something from me, something serious."

I spent the day doing nothing. Gomes was called to Zumbano's · office and went out on a job. At the end of the day I went home. I told Minolta, Mariazinha, and Crab what had happened. Then I called Ceresso, of the Brazilian Society for the Protection of the Amphibian, to tell him his help had been invaluable. I asked him if he wouldn't like to come to my place for dinner the following Saturday.

"I'm a vegetarian," he said.

"So are we. I want you to meet my friends Minolta, Maria-zinha, and Crab."

Ceresso accepted, saying he'd be there.

"There was a man here today asking questions. Where'd he say he was from, Crab?" Mariazinha said.

"The NHB."

"The National Housing Bank?"

"Right. He wanted to know how many people lived in the

house, our profession, if we had children. It's for some kind of research they're doing on something or other."

"A confused guy, screwed up, a real idiot," Minolta said.

The next day I arrived at Panamerican the same time as always, a short time before it opened. We were well into the morning, and Gomes still hadn't showed up, when I was called to Personnel.

There was a check waiting for me there. I had been fired.

"It's not possible. There must be some mistake."

"Orders from the management," the personnel clerk said. "They told me to figure out what they owe you. It's all taken care of."

I didn't sign the papers. I ran to Zumbano's office. A security guard was in Dona Duda's office, reading a newspaper. The secretary made a sign to him when I entered the office.

"I want to talk to Mr. Zumbano. There's been some kind of mistake and I've been fired," I said.

"Mr. Zumbano isn't in," Dona Duda said.

"He isn't in," the guard said, placing himself in front of the door.

Suddenly, a revelation popped into my mind. Zumbano must be part of the gang! What an idiot I'd been not to have seen it from the start. And I'd given him the death certificate! I had to stay calm; it wouldn't help to play into their hands. Surely Dr. Ribeiroles, the head of Legal, wasn't involved in the fraud. I needed to get hold of another certificate.

The doctor who furnished the certificate was named Pedro M. Silva. His office was on Nossa Senhora de Copacabana Avenue, near the Art Palácio movie theater. He'd been chosen from the phone book because his was the closest office to my apartment, which was on Figueiredo de Magalhães, near the corner of Domingos Ferreira (he wouldn't turn down a patient that nearby), and also because he was a cardiologist. The doctor would be in at two. I phoned Minolta and asked her to go to the office and get another copy of the certificate, claiming she'd lost the original. I said I'd meet her at two-thirty in front of the theater.

It was 11:00 A.M. I had time to kill before I met Minolta. I decided to stop in on Ceresso, of the Brazilian Society for the Protection of the Amphibian, in the Marquês do Herval building, at Rio Branco Avenue and Almirante Barroso.

I was greeted by a woman. "You didn't know?"

"Know what?"

"Dr. Ceresso killed himself last night. The poor man."

"Killed himself? Dr. Ceresso? It's not possible. I spoke with him on the phone last night. There must be some mistake." I couldn't believe what the woman had told me.

"He jumped out of the window of his apartment. In the early morning. The poor man wasn't very well; he was quite sick, did you know?"

I went down in the packed elevator, horrified, feeling the urge to scream. The criminals had killed the old man. I had been stupid to tell Zumbano that Ceresso had helped me with the investigation. They might kill me too. I had to do something quickly. Go to the police? Speak with Ribeiroles? Go to Ribeiroles first or to the police? I was confused. The first thing, I decided, was the death certificate. By now Zumbano must have spread it around the company that I was crazy. Dona Duda and Gomes would substantiate anything along those lines. My situation wasn't good in the least. Probably the guy who'd been at the apartment, claiming to be from the NHB, was a member of the gang.

I called home but nobody answered. It was one-fifteen.

How time was crawling by! My meeting with Minolta, to pick up the copy of the certificate, was at two-thirty. On the bus to Copacabana, I noticed I was talking to myself. I was saying, between my teeth, "How can I prove that Ceresso was murdered?" First I'd have to unmask the criminals inside Panamerican itself; then I'd have credibility to demand an investigation of the death of the president of the Brazilian Society for the Protection of the Amphibian.

At two-forty-five Minolta showed up at the door of the Art Palácio. From a distance, when she saw me, she began gesturing in exasperation, making faces.

"Did you get the certificate?" I asked, my heart tightening, feeling that something awful had happened.

"No, the guy said he never wrote a certificate in the name of Ivan Canabrava and had no idea who he was, and when I got nasty and called him a liar he told his nurse to call the asylum. I kept harping on it and the woman phoned the asylum and told them a patient was having a psychotic episode in the office. I split. What else could I do?"

Then I had a brilliant idea. "There's only one thing to do," I said.

"What?"

I told Minolta my plan.

"It's crazy," Minolta said.

"Will you help me?"

"I'll help. Count me in. Where can we buy the stuff?"

"We can check in the phone book."

"We'll also need a large bag."

"Let's get started; we haven't much time."

It was four-fifteen when we arrived at St. John the Baptist Cemetery carrying a large bag with a short-handled pickax, a small sledgehammer, a chisel, and a shovel, also short-handled.

"You know where the guy's buried?" Minolta asked.

"I know where he *isn't* buried; I was at the fake funeral. The tomb's near a large rococo mausoleum. Easy to find."

My plan was the following: I would break into the tomb and call the cemetery caretaker, the gravediggers, the press, the police, whoever, so they could see the empty tomb. It would create a scandal of such proportions that it couldn't be covered up; it would even be on TV and the criminals would finally be punished.

Over the phony resting place a marble gravestone had been placed, on which was written only *Maurício Estrucho* and the dates of his birth and (fictitious) death.

"You use the chisel and sledgehammer. I'll use the pickax."

That damned marble! It was cemented so well it would have to be splintered before it came out. Evidently they intended the tomb never to be opened. I began swinging the pick furiously against the marble. Minolta was making holes in the smooth surface of the stone with the chisel and hammer. Bit by bit the marble was shattered and we finally managed to remove it, exposing the slab of cement that covered the tomb.

"Stop! Stop!" a voice shouted.

A short way off was a gravedigger, looking at us in surprise. I ran to him. I grabbed him by the arm. "Shut up," I said. "Keep quiet or I'll bury this pickax in your head." I had to finish breaking into that tomb.

"Help!" the gravedigger screamed. "Help!" He must be one of the accomplices in the swindle.

When the gravedigger screamed, Minolta stopped working, not knowing what to do.

"Shut up," I said, shaking the gravedigger, who was an old man with gray hair.

"Help," the gravedigger screamed again, in a weak voice. We were in the middle of the cemetery, a long way from the street, and no one appeared to have heard the shouts.

"Please, be quiet," I begged.

"Help, thieves," the gravedigger screamed in a shrill voice.

I swung the pickax with all my strength against the gravedigger's head. He fell to the ground, his face covered with blood.

"Is he dead?" Minolta asked.

I heard a whistle. In the distance, from beside the chapels, shapes were coming toward us.

"Let's go," I said. But Minolta didn't move. "Is he dead?" she asked, still holding the hammer and chisel in her hand. I took her by the arm, pulled her violently, and she seemed to awaken from a trance and began running headlong with me for the main gate. We abandoned our tools in the street—chisel, pick, everything. We finally managed to catch a taxi.

We packed our bags, and as Minolta was saying "Let's go, there's no time to lose," I decided to leave a note for Mariazinha and Crab. The time I wasted doing this was what led to my imprisonment. Just as we were leaving the building, a police car pulled up. Gomes was inside. I've tried to forget what happened next, but it sometimes comes back in the form of nightmares. I was taken first to one precinct station, then to another, and finally for tests at the Asylum for the Criminally Insane. At the Asylum for the Criminally Insane it became clear that they thought, or had been paid to think, that I was crazy. This irritated me so much that I started acting as if I really were crazy. I had an attack of paranoia, convinced that the doctors were all part of the conspiracy. I started calling the doctors sinister mafiosi, assaulted one of them, and tried to escape from the infirmary. I got myself in deeper and deeper. I saw that I was going to spend the rest of my life there, going from doctor to doctor, until I finally really did go mad or kill someone, thereby justifying my imprisonment. The thought filled me with horror. Today I try to get everything that happened out of my head, and I always do special mnemonic exercises, not to remember but to forget it all.

I shall have little to say about the days I spent as a prisoner in that horrendous hellhole they call the Asylum for the Criminally Insane. Regular asylums, where the rules are less rigid, must be full of people in such conditions. An Asylum for the Criminally Insane is far worse. How many innocents like me, for I killed the gravedigger unintentionally, must there be rotting away in there? I felt I really would go mad after spending so many nights, I don't know how many, trembling with fever, hearing voices, and with all hope gone. I was like the poet of *Paradise Lost*: "So farewell Hope, and with Hope farewell fear, / Farewell Remorse: all Good to me is lost; / Evil be thou my Good."

In the morning of the day my despair reached its height, a guard came to tell me that my sister and a priest had gotten permission to see me. I was lying on the narrow, filthy cot in my cubicle. I stood up in surprise.

"Ivan, dear Ivan," my sister said, embracing me. "I brought Father João to hear your confession."

"Leave us alone," the priest, a man with a black beard, told the guard.

When the guard left, Minolta said, "You're coming with us."

"I'll take your place," Crab said, removing his fake beard and priest's cassock.

"They'll kill you in this hellhole. I can't let you do this for me," I said.

Minolta explained that Crab, unlike me, was not an insane violator of gravesites. They had checked with a lawyer, and the charges Crab might face were nothing serious. They finally convinced me.

I made it through all the doors in my priest disguise, consoling a poor young woman who was crying so hard that no one looked at me. It was a relief for the guards to be rid of Minolta's screams. One of them grabbed me by the arm (which nearly scared me to death) and said, "Get that girl out of here, Father."

From the hospital we went straight to the bus station. In the station bathroom I put on the clothes Minolta had brought in a suitcase, removed the beard, and put it and the cassock in the suitcase. We caught a bus and went to a place in the lake region called Iguaba.

We stayed there for ten years. Minolta suggested I become a writer and gave me the idea for my first book. Minolta took the book to the publisher and got it published. My pseudonym, Gustavo Flávio, was chosen as an *hommage* to Flaubert; in those days, like Flaubert, I hated women. Today I would have honored some other writer. Minolta taught me to love. She taught me to enjoy eating. We would make love several times a day, every day. I put on sixty-five pounds. I became famous.

One day Minolta came to me and said, "I think you can return to Rio. Nobody remembers Ivan Canabrava anymore."

"Will you go with me?"

"No. But I love you and want to see you always. I want to stay here among these deserted beaches, writing my poems. Be good to the women." She knew she had awakened me to the pleasure of loving women.

And in the ten years since I returned to Rio, Minolta comes to see me every six months. I tell her about my love affairs. The last one was my romance with Delfina Delamare.

Getting back to the romance with Delfina, which I stopped telling about to recall my dark past: after Eugênio Delamare's threat I spent two days worrying until I read in the newspapers that the Delamares had embarked for Paris.

"The rest you know. Delfina came back early and turned up dead. Her husband worries me less than that poor man's Javert, Inspector Guedes."

This is what I said to Minolta before going to the precinct, where Guedes told me a holdup man had confessed to Delfina's murder.

I returned from the precinct worried, afraid that Guedes would discover my dark past. Minolta put my mind at ease by saying that was impossible. Too much time had passed.

"I'm more worried about your not being able to write Bufo & Spallanzani," she said.

It was around that time that the idea arose of my spending a few days in a place called Falconcrest Retreat, in the Bocaina range. I don't recall exactly when.

"Maybe you should get away from the TRS-80 a bit. You're hooked, and that's no good. An author should be able to write under any conditions," Minolta said.

III

FALCONCREST
RETREAT

I can't truthfully be accused of underestimating Guedes. Like all people, respectable or criminal, I had an evident aversion to the police. As I've already said, I had suffered greatly at the hands of the guardians of law and order, whether cops, judges, prosecutors, doctors, or orderlies, during my internment in the Asylum for the Criminally Insane. Can anyone underestimate tetanus, for example? But I'm getting ahead of myself and losing the sequence, and writers detest confusion and disorder. That's part of our inherent schizoid incoherence. (*See W. Whitman.*) We reject chaos but also repudiate order. The writer must be essentially a subversive, and his language can be neither the bamboozlement of the politician (and the educator) nor the repression of the ruler. Our language should be that of nonconformity, nonfalsity, nonoppression. We do not wish to bring order to chaos, as some theorists suppose. We always doubt everything, including logic. A writer must be a skeptic. He must be against morality and good habits. Propertius may have been too bashful to recount certain things he saw with his own eyes, but he knew that poetry seeks its best material in "bad habits." (*See Veyne.*) Poetry—art itself—transcends criteria of utility and malignancy and even of comprehensibility. Every highly intelligent means of expression is mendacious.

I say this today, but I can't guarantee that a month from now

I'll still believe this or any other declaration, for I have the fine quality of inconsistency. As for what the others say or think— Guedes, Orion, Suzy, Delfina, Minolta herself—I have nothing to do with that. Their opinions are not mine.

Let's get back on track. I was the first to arrive at the square in Pereiras, the small village at the foot of the mountain. I sat on a bench in the garden, which was still shrouded in fog. Despite being, today, a lazy man, I am also nervous and dislike waiting. I could have read, but the books I had brought were still in the suitcase. So I took a notebook from my pocket and tried to overcome my incompetence at writing anything by hand (aggravated in recent years by my being hooked on the TRS-80) and make some notes about Bufo & Spallanzani. At that instant an enormous limousine pulled into the square, and a woman (I always notice women first) and a man got out. The woman, with a bored air, ran a disinterested glance over the square, passing over my head, which must have been deliberate, for I'm rather too large and attractive to be ignored by any woman in an empty square. The man watched the driver take three large soft-leather suitcases from the car, after which he dismissed the employee with a slight nod.

How to define these people? Memorable? Extraordinary? Since I had the notebook in my hand (and how different what you write is from what you think!), I wrote: *Unforgettable and strange—uncommon, marvelous, unusual? Or merely extravagant—insanus, stultus?* They were especially svelte (more than elegant and graceful), with all the sensual charge that svelteness suggests to a monumental fat man like me. The woman was wearing loose pants that still did not hide the thickness (no, not thickness—the rounded solidity) of her long thighs; the points of her round, firm breasts seemed to be trying to pierce the weave of her blouse. Certain words that I associate only with women came to mind: magnificence, opulence. Her face, however, seemed despicable to me, at least at that moment of hatred.

I hate all women as long as they're unattainable. I think all satyrs are like that.

As for the man, in spite of his strong chin and broad shoulders, there was something of the spoiled child in him, a fussy way of opposing one lip over the other, of turning his head, of inserting and removing his hands from his pockets. The pair, I should mention, struck me as vaguely familiar.

I was absorbed in the couple and didn't see where the guy with the small suitcase came from who appeared in the middle of the little square. As no car other than the limousine had arrived, maybe he was already there before me, hiding behind a tree. He was the kind of person who hides from others; he had a frightened air about him, aloof and deceitful. He was wearing faded jeans and a loose, wool-lined nylon jacket. Now and then he rubbed his hands together as if he were cold. When two taxis stopped in the square he appeared to panic and ran to hide behind a tree.

From one of the taxis another couple got out. The woman was young and had a round face dotted with dimples; her platinum-blond hair shone under the sun, which was beginning to rise, very white, behind the distant blue mountains. Her breasts were large and inviting. She moved slowly, like someone walking in mud up to the ankles. The man with her was also on the heavy side, with long hair and a hooked nose; he was carrying a black violin case, which he carefully placed on the two suitcases that they removed from the taxi.

From the second taxi emerged a pale young man with very short blond hair. He was wearing a long, loose blue velvet jacket that made him look even thinner. His mien was sad and insecure, mildly suspicious, though not as much as the one who had hidden behind the trees.

I noted then that, counting myself, there were seven people awaiting transport to Falconcrest Retreat. That made me quite irritated. I was facing this trip to the end of the world, which would doubtlessly be unpleasant and tiresome, so I could be alone and write Bufo & Spallanzani. I felt like leaving. Then I remembered that the man from the retreat had said I could have my meals in the bungalow and that I wouldn't even be aware of the other guests if I wanted to be alone.

Getting back to what matters: two more people arrived, two women, who pretended to ignore the looks cast in their direction. Both were pretty, one quite a bit older than the other, and they were dressed with discreet care. A microbus, painted yellow, soon arrived. From it emerged a very fat and florid man, large, pot-bellied, with abundant, tousled white hair. He said he was Mr. Trindade, from Falconcrest Retreat, and that he was the one we had dealt with on the phone. The driver, named Sebastião, also got out of the bus, a man so black he appeared navy blue. Sebastião gathered everyone's luggage and put it in a compartment on the bus. The neurotic with the black suitcase hesitated a little but finally got in the bus. The man with long hair kept the violin in his hands. The pale young man in the velvet coat sat on the rear seat.

Before the bus pulled out, the frightened-looking guy got out with his black suitcase and went running off through the square, to the surprise of all. This created a small but short-lived disturbance. Soon we were all resettled and we set out.

During the trip we learned it would take two hours to get to where the tractor was, and then two hours more in the wagon behind it. Someone asked if there were snakes at the retreat, and Trindade replied that there were horses, deer, cavies, otters, thousands of birds and stars, and, of course, falcons. The nights were cold. At that instant I heard the elegant woman tell her companion that she should have brought her mink coat.

So she has a mink coat, I thought, that base predator, that ridiculous show-off. I looked at her beautiful but cold profile. At moments when the bus dipped in one of the many holes in the highway, almost everyone bumped their heads on the car's ceiling. She was the only person whose movements didn't become grotesque; she managed to be tossed up and down with the grace of a ballerina—that is, of course, if some choreographer invented a ballet to be danced sitting down. The broad-shouldered man beside her also kept the jolts under control. The platinum blonde clutched her husband and emitted small happy shouts. The young man appeared not to feel the effects of the unpleasant oscillation, perhaps because he was so thin.

As we entered the forest the air became cooler and the sun penetrated through the thick tree crowns in fine rays of light. Then we arrived at a clearing where our tractor squatted, like some gigantic sleeping zooid.

After we got into the tractor wagon, the road became steeper and steeper and there were moments when the passengers seemed to fear it would fall over backward in a kind of somersault. By the conversation that took place in the bus and later in the wagon, I was able to make a survey of the people traveling with me. The two women, Suzy and Eurídice, were cousins, two pretty women, but they didn't attract me as much as the one with the mink coat, whose name, I found out, was Roma. Roma and her husband, Vaslav, were dancers with the Colón in Buenos Aires, although they were Brazilians. (I must confess that if there is one artistic form that holds no interest for me, it's ballet.) The man with the violin was a conductor of some renown, Orion Pacheco, and his wife was the well-known prima donna Juliana Pacheco. The skinny guy in the blue coat was named Carlos and said virtually nothing about himself; he probably committed poetry in secret.

"I'm scared to death of snakes," Juliana said. Seen up close, with her fear of snakes, the singer lacked the splendor that she displayed on stage. The conductor seemed worried about the chasms on each side of the road.

"At the retreat you'll see animals you've probably never seen in your lives: deer, cavies, armadillos, otters—"

"Otters?" Roma asked.

"I think I'll leave here with a fur coat," Suzy said. Suzy owned a boutique in Rio de Janeiro.

"It's also known as water dog," Trindade said.

"Let's call it otter, since it's prettier," Roma said.

"Besides nature, you'll marvel at the stars in the sky. It's such a fantastic spectacle that I've even become something of an amateur astronomer since I've been living here. Self-taught, understand. But I've read lots of books."

"Can we see the Southern Cross?"

"Of course. We're at twenty-four degrees latitude, and at this time of year it's visible in its entirety till four in the morning."

Finally we saw the main structure of the retreat, which Trindade called "the Big House." It stood on a wide, immense plateau surrounded by trees. The tractor stopped at a spacious gate painted blue. From both sides of the gate extended a thick hedge of hibiscuses, allamandas, and euphorbia that disappeared into the trees of the forest. Orion asked how large the property was. Trindade explained it was some six hundred *alqueires*, each of which contained 48,400 square meters. "We have a lot of room," he said. The vehicle stopped beside the Big House. It housed the common facilities—restaurant, kitchen, several large rooms, and living quarters for Trindade, his wife, Rizoleta, who ran the kitchen, and the other employees of the retreat. The guests' bungalows were not visible. A Toyota jeep was parked at the door of the Big House. Sebastião got out and removed the bags from the wagon.

"Sebastião will take each of you to your bungalows in the jeep. It'll only hold two," Trindade said.

Calmly, as if they had the right-of-way, Orion and Juliana Pacheco installed themselves in the vehicle, which departed at once.

The others went to the porch of the Big House, with the exception of Carlos. There were some horses grazing in the distance, and Carlos walked toward them. The horses saw him approaching and raised their heads and sniffed the air, as if capturing his scent.

"They're tame, aren't they?" said Roma, when she saw Carlos stroking the neck of one of the animals.

"No, that dark chestnut is very skittish and wild, so much so I don't let the guests ride him. We once had a serious accident here with that horse. Rizoleta! Come see something."

Rizoleta appeared on the porch.

"Take a look at Belzebum," Trindade said.

At that instant Carlos hugged the horse's neck.

"That's strange. I wouldn't have believed it," said Rizoleta in her strong backlands accent.

"Do you know what Belzebum means?" I asked.

"Yes. I tried to change his name, but the animal's so headstrong I decided to leave it the way it was," Trindade said.

"What does Belzebum mean?" Roma asked.

"It's a corruption of Beelzebub, the Devil," I said.

"The Prince of Darkness," Trindade said.

"He deserves the name—he's black as night."

"There's something about that fellow," Roma said, referring to Carlos, "something different."

"His pallor," Suzy said ironically. "He has the color of a croupier."

Sebastião returned with the jeep.

"Can the two of us go now?" Suzy asked. She was irritated. The two installed themselves in the jeep. I noticed that Suzy gave Eurídice a slight nudge or a pinch; I couldn't see which.

Finally, only Carlos and I were left waiting for a ride. We didn't speak to each other. I, who for so many years had suffered from chronic lack of appetite, was famished and could think of nothing but what they would serve for lunch. Since there were just the two of us, Carlos and I, we went in a single trip to our respective bungalows. The jeep followed a dirt roadway that

went around the Big House and quickly plunged into a narrow
road surrounded by dense forest. There was an infinite variety
of shades of green. At Carlos's insistence the jeep dropped me
at my bungalow first.

The bungalows were located at distances that rendered them
invisible, and inaudible, to one another. They were made of
wood and were quite spacious, consisting of a bedroom, living
room with fireplace, and a bathroom. The wood, both interior
and exterior, was varnished. The roof, made of tiles, was probably not as old as it looked. There was no electricity. This made
me worry a bit about the food. Did they have refrigerators to
store the perishable ingredients?

In a small brochure on the living room table I read:

Welcome to Falconcrest Retreat. For those who wish to
flee the tensions of large cities, the Retreat offers tranquillity, silence, pure air, an atmosphere of peace, and
communion with nature, in the heart of a virgin forest where
the fauna, the flora, and the water and air have not been
spoiled, polluted, or destroyed by man's predatory acts.
Although we know this warning is unnecessary, we wish
to remind our guests that it is forbidden to hunt, damage
the vegetation, or pollute the water of the rivers and
streams. We most earnestly request that no fires be lit
during outings except under the strict supervision of a guide
from the Retreat.

According to the brochure there were thousands of species
of animals and plants in the area, many of which were listed.
Under fauna it spoke of lizards (calangos, iguanas, tejus), birds
(tanagers, manakins, bellbirds, doves, falcons obviously, par-
tridges, guans, hummingbirds, tyrant birds, flycatchers), mam-
mals (deer, marmosets, margays, otters, cavies, armadillos,
tapetis, anteaters, skunks, coatis, giant river otters, ocelots,

monkeys). There wasn't the slightest mention of snakes, spiders, and rats. On the road to the bungalow I had seen huge shining webs that looked like gigantic bridal veils. And now I recalled Trindade's dissimulated tone of voice as he asked, "Have you ever seen a snake near the retreat?" and Sebastião answering, without great conviction, "No, sir." I know a liar's tone of voice. They probably didn't want to scare the women, who (like monkeys) have an uncontrollable fear of snakes.

A confession: I feel a great attraction toward ophidians in general, perhaps because they are so unfeminine. Minolta told me on a certain occasion that I pretended to like snakes to justify my satyriasis, but I never quite understood what she meant. It's true that I like snakes and women. And in my liking for these two animal species I've learned a thing or two about them. For example: Snakes exist in every region of Brazil, especially where nature has not yet been totally defiled. And there, in the paradise of Falconcrest Retreat, there must be at least pit vipers, the poisonous fer-de-lance, and rattlesnakes, whose ignominious scientific name is *Crotalus terrificus*. Terrificus to monkeys and women. Monkeys, as we all know, are afraid of three things—of falling, of the dark, and, above all, of snakes. This fear on the part of monkeys and women could be a primeval carryover of our reptilian brain. We, men and women, are reptiles turned into primates that came to reject their ancient origins. Maybe I'll write about it someday. I've always been intrigued by knowing there is an archaic part of our brain known as the reptilian complex—responsible to some for the more "human" side of our behavior and to others for the more "animal" side. The brochure also included information on how to light the gas lamps, mealtimes, and the scheduled outings.

I showered. The gas heater didn't work too well, so the water never reached the necessary tepidness, but the shower made me even hungrier. I dressed and decided to go to the Big House to see how lunch was coming along. I was worried about that problem of food. Being a glutton, I appreciate a plate of beans as much as ikra caviar. But the food has to be tasty; nothing irritates me more than dishes (whatever they are, delicate or crude) poorly prepared.

A small path led from the bungalow to the dirt road over which I had come in the jeep. There, a sign with a drawing indicated the road to take to get to the Big House. There wasn't a cloud in the sky. I walked in the sun, breathing the pure air, with a pleasant sensation of sensuality and energy.

The Big House appeared empty. There was no one on the large porch or in the dining room, where tables were already set. Dona Rizoleta and another fat woman with a ruddy face were laboring before an enormous wood-burning stove, an iron machine, black and a thing of great beauty. The pans gave off a delicious fragrance of food. Physical desires are highly intertwined. The odor and sight of those steaming pans made me long for a feminine presence. It would be very nice, for example, if Roma were to arrive at that moment.

I went to the porch, which was still empty. I sat in one of the canvas lounge chairs lined up as if on the deck of a ship, disappointed at not finding Roma. I tried to think about Bufo & Spallanzani. After all, I'd come to the retreat to write and, secondarily, to undertake an exercise in asceticism by temporarily renouncing one of the pleasures of the flesh (and of the soul also, why not?), which was sex. But those aromas from the kitchen had broken my willpower. The smooth muscles of my internal organs, my endocrine glands, rippled in an anticipatory refulgence of the delights of the repast.

At that moment Dona Rizoleta appeared on the porch and said that lunch was ready. I ran to the table. The dining room was still empty. No matter. When I'm devouring delicacies I don't think about women, and vice versa. I started with the turnip soup! Then grilled trout and finally roast kid with broccoli!

As I ate, my ever-fuller stomach gave me a contented sensation of serenity, of happiness, of joy. When I ate the broccoli, which I later learned had been picked that morning before sunrise, still covered with dew, I felt like crying. Tender, a flawless green, its delicate flavor went perfectly with the roast kid, enchantingly browned. Later Trindade explained to me that since they had no refrigerator (they could have had a gas-driven one but didn't want it), the produce they consumed was always fresh. The animals—kids, rabbits, chickens—were devoured the same day they were slaughtered; the fish—trout, tilapia, and carp—were caught, in their respective tanks and ponds where they were raised, the day they went to the pan. "You must see how we raise trout," Trindade said. I also had to see the garden where vegetables and greens were grown without insecticides, as well as the purebred cows that provided the milk for the cheese we ate.

When I had finished talking with Trindade, Roma arrived with her husband. She had changed clothes and was elegantly dressed like someone at a country club rather than on a deserted mountainside. Her husband had also changed clothes and his attire matched Roma's, as if they were taking part in some designer's fashion show. At almost the same time the two cousins arrived, and the musician couple and Carlos. Except for the last, who still had on his traveling clothes, everyone exhibited new outfits—which, in fact, appeared to be worn that day for the first time.

Afterward, on the porch, I reminded myself to make a note about the clothes Spallanzani was wearing the day he met Bufo. I took the pad from my pocket and wrote, *A pair of dark velvet pants and a white silk shirt with bouffant sleeves, loose on his body.*

"A writer's always on the job, isn't he?" said Orion, the conductor, sitting down beside me. During the trip in the wagon

Orion had asked me, after introducing himself, what my profession was. I tried to make one up, but nothing came to mind at the time, and I ended up saying I was a writer.

"Seeing the world about you, sticking your nose in things (no offense intended), appropriating people's souls like a metaphysical bird of prey (no offense intended), writing books that no one reads—" As he spoke, he made hand motions in the air like a batonless conductor and tried to disguise with a smile the unpleasant things he said.

"Words are, of course, the most powerful drug used by mankind," I said.

"Who said that?" the conductor asked.

At that moment Roma and Vaslav and the two cousins, Eurídice and Suzy, came onto the porch. They made themselves comfortable on the lounge chairs, dragging them from their position to form a semicircle.

"Kipling," I said.

"So the writer is a kind of drug dealer.".

"Who's a drug dealer?" Suzy asked.

"The writer. That's what our writer here said. In essence, of course," Orion said.

"I'd like to be a writer more than anything in the world," Eurídice said.

"It's not all that hard," Orion said.

"It's a trade like any other," I said.

Meanwhile, Juliana (who had been delayed by a second helping of the compote) and Carlos arrived on the porch.

"Making music is more difficult than making literature," the conductor said. "Domestic servants write books, retired military men write books, everybody writes books—beggars, politicians, athletes, disturbed adolescents, salesmen."

"Thieves and customs workers," I said, thinking of Genet and Kafka.

"Exactly. Biggs," the conductor said, "published a book."

I remembered Maugham's phrase: "It requires intelligence to write a good novel, but not of a very high order." Truly, there were more than a few of my professional colleagues whose intellectual level was quite low, but I wasn't going to give ammunition to the conductor. There must also be some idiot conductors.

"*Gone with the Wind* was written by a middle-aged housewife who never wrote anything else," Orion said, not disguising his aggressiveness. What could have caused such hostility, my size? It happens a lot; short men resent that I'm large and that women find me attractive.

"Orion said at lunch that you're writing a story that takes place here at the retreat, in which we're the characters," Juliana said amiably, perhaps attempting to change the tone the conversation had taken.

"I saw him looking at us and taking notes," Orion said.

"I guarantee it's not about you," I said. If Roma weren't there, staring at me with an enigmatic look that inflamed my heart, I'd have left for my bungalow long before.

"Will you show it to us?" Eurídice asked.

"I don't like to show a book before it's finished."

"Then he'll show it three days from now," Orion said.

"You write a book in three days?" Suzy asked.

"No, not in three days."

"How many days does it take you to write a book?" asked Carlos, who had been silent till that point.

"It depends. Flaubert took five years to write *Madame Bovary*. Working long hours, every day, without missing a day."

"That little book?" asked the conductor.

I thought about counterattacking by speaking ill of Mozart, but that would have been too ridiculous.

"On the other hand, Dostoyevski wrote *The Gambler* in thirty days," I said.

"Back in the days of soirees they used to provide a theme

and the poet would compose a poem, rhymed and metered, on the spot. Just ask yourself if music can be composed that way, cooked to order like french fries," Orion said.

"If I give you a theme will you write a poem?" I asked.

"I wouldn't say a poem. I personally don't care for poetry all that much. But prose. . . . Not only I but anyone can write it without difficulty."

"I agree with the maestro," Roma said in a playful tone. "Dancing is also more difficult than writing. Give me the theme and I'll write the text." She looked at me as if to say, I'd like to see you do an *entrechat* or even a simple *tour en l'air*. Then she looked at Vaslav, and they both laughed in amusement.

"Who else wants to play?" I asked.

"I can't spell," Eurídice said.

"Nobody can, can they? Proofreaders correct writers' spelling errors," Orion said.

"Let's agree that errors in Portuguese will not be taken into consideration," I said.

"I'm not going to enter," Eurídice said.

"I'll enter," Suzy said.

"Juliana?" I asked.

"My thing is singing."

"Which is also more difficult than writing," I said, before somebody else said it.

"Vaslav?"

"I never compete with my wife."

"Carlos?"

"No, thank you. Unlike the others, I find writing very difficult."

"Very well," I said. "I want your solemn promise not to reveal to anyone the theme you receive."

Despite the conductor's sourness, a happy air had come over us. "I swear," Roma said, "that not even Vaslav will know what my theme is."

"Vaslav can know," I said, "but no one else."

I cut a sheet of paper into three strips and wrote the themes. I folded the pieces of paper and shuffled them in my cupped hands. I gave a strip of folded paper to each player. They all read the papers immediately. Orion and Roma appeared extremely disturbed as they read the theme I had given them, especially Roma, who turned pale and began to tremble. Only much later would I discover the reason for this. She seemed to regain control and looked at Vaslav, in doubt as to whether to show him what she held in her trembling hand. She finally gave him the paper, observing Vaslav anxiously. Her husband's serene reaction seemed to calm her.

"Can I trade mine?" Suzy asked.

"No. Papers can't be traded or themes exchanged. That's how it was at the soirees, wasn't it, maestro?"

"Yes," Orion said.

Roma said something in her husband's ear, took him by the arm, and they withdrew, speaking in low voices.

I don't know what the other guests did in the afternoon. I put on my silk pajamas and stretched out on the bed, which would have been even more comfortable if it had been a bit longer. How good it was to sleep! Sleeping, eating, and loving—the delights of life.

I was stretching when someone knocked at the door. There are some people who can't hear a phone ring without feeling obliged to answer it immediately, even if it's not theirs. Others run to open the door as soon as the bell rings. I was immune to that type of urgency. I knew that other people's urgency was never mine.

Whoever was at the door wasn't very insistent. He waited for a time, until I again heard a light knock on wood. I went to the bathroom and examined my face in the mirror. I always woke up healthy and revitalized after a nap, and this was reflected in

my face. I combed my hair. I saw by my wristwatch that it was
5:00 P.M. I had slept three hours, more or less.

The person hadn't knocked again, but I knew he was still
there.

I opened the door.

"Did I wake you?" Carlos asked.

"No, I was combing my hair. Come in."

Carlos still had on the same clothes in which he'd arrived at
the retreat. He sat in the only armchair in the small living room.
I made myself comfortable on the sofa.

"I've read all your books," Carlos said. "Or nearly all."

I never know how to respond to a statement like that. Thank
you very much?

"The poems, the short stories, the novels. I've seen the plays."

Thank you very much?

"I also greatly enjoyed *The Snare,* a dizzying detective story.
Why haven't you written other detective works?"

"I don't know."

"*The Lovers* is completely different. A love story between a
blind woman and a deaf-mute."

"Love based on sensory inputs other than the visual and the
auditory," I said. (*See Hall.*)

"To me it's the story of two people who overcome their limitations and find happiness," Carlos said. His voice was strange.
There was something disquietingly feminine about him.

"Love is always the result of the perceptions we have of others.
Art in general has always exalted sight (form and movement)
and hearing (sound, music) as cognitive elements of love. Love
among my characters, on the contrary, arises from kinesthetic,
olfactory, and thermic perceptions. Perception comes from the
senses—Kant, et cetera; no need to go into that. What I mean
is that love is a form of perception and, in the case of *The Lovers,*
also a form of transcendence."

Carlos nodded his head. He seemed sadder upon hearing

this. He rose from the chair. "When you go to dinner, don't forget to take your flashlight," he said.

"I hadn't thought of that."

"The flashlight is in the drawer of the night table, in the bedroom."

"Thanks for reminding me."

"Do you know the road?"

"Yes. It's not hard."

He seemed to want to tell me something, undecided. Finally he said goodbye, extending and then withdrawing his hand. I saw him to the door of the bungalow. The air was cool and clean; birds sang in the trees as they do when night approaches. Carlos stood listening to the birds and said something I didn't catch. He always spoke very softly, a bit voiceless, like someone pitching his voice poorly.

I went back to the bedroom and tried to write Bufo & Spallanzani. My publisher wanted me to write another detective story like *The Snare*. "Don't get original, please," my publisher said. "You have loyal readers; give them what they want." The hardest thing for a publisher is to give the reader what he wants, for the simple reason that the reader doesn't know what he wants; like everybody, he knows what he doesn't want. And what he doesn't want, in fact, is anything new, different from what he's used to consuming. It could be said that if the reader knows he *doesn't* want what's new, he knows, *contrario sensu,* that he does want what's old, known, which allows him to enjoy the text with less anxiety.

OVERTURE TO BUFO & SPALLANZANI

The sage Spallanzani contemplated, from his window, the Romanesque bell tower known by the poetical name of La Ghirlandina, as it pealed twice. Then the scientist turned his attention to the couple with him in the large room, illuminated by a high skylight of dingy glass. Both of them, Bufo and Marina, appeared calm; Spallanzani, however, could not control his nervousness and paced back and forth in the room, his hands behind his back and his head thrust forward as was his wont.

The sage's life had always been a restless one. At fifteen he had entered the Jesuit school at Modena, taking his priestly vows very early. Instead of dedicating his life to the cloth, Spallanzani had enrolled at the University of Bologna to study law. At the university he met Laura Bassi, like him born in Scandiano. It is believed that it was Laura, who taught physics at the university, who led Spallanzani to abandon law for the study of biology. Spallanzani continued as a priest, however, since at the time this story took place no one left the Church, especially for as irrelevant a reason as lack of religious calling.

On that day, Spallanzani did not have on the black academic gown he habitually wore. He was wearing a pair of black velvet pants and a loose white silk shirt, for the sage preferred freedom of movement. On a broad square table of polished wood lay reams of paper, books, inkwells, and quills. Many of the sheets were covered with the scientist's tiny writing and meticulous drawings.

There was a knock at the door. It was a woman; when she was younger she must have been extraordinarily beautiful. With time she had acquired a majestic and dominating air. Bufo and Marina, with their lovely and dense golden eyes, followed the woman's movements as she entered the room. Spallanzani helped her remove the long cape she wore. Laura quickly sat down, and the four fell silent.

"I've found a name for the book," Spallanzani said. *"Prodromo di un'opera da imprimersi sopra la reproduzioni animali."*

The woman praised the title. Then she asked, "Are these . . ."

"Bufo and Marina."

"Marina, from *marinus*." The woman laughed, a full and vibrant sound rising from the depths of her chest. "They were on earth before us."

"They spoke before we did," Spallanzani replied.

"And they sang before we did; they invented music. And they're very old."

"We're mere upstarts," the sage said. "Let's begin."

Laura rose and went to the window.

"Don't you want to see it?" Spallanzani asked.

"What if Bufo doesn't want anything to do with her? My presence might inhibit him," Laura said, still at the window.

"That won't happen; I know him well."

Spallanzani took three candles from a drawer and lighted them.

"Look how well-developed Bufo's head is. Beautiful oval paratoids. Full of venom." The word "venom" was spoken with some hostility, as if the sage meant to indicate some defect in the individual before him.

"Marina's body would be extremely pretty, if it weren't for the papulous glands dispersed over her skin, those horny points that look like pustules," Laura said.

Bufo clasped Marina's dorsum tightly. After they had been thus embraced for some time, a long and sinuous gelatinous string of translucid ovules began to emerge from Marina's cloaca.

"He's so obsessed by his blind instinct of preservation of the species that he will feel nothing," Spallanzani said, using one of the candles to burn one of Bufo's feet.

"He has five toes. I had forgotten that," Laura said.

"The protohand," the sage said.

The burned muscle tissue and bony matter gave off a harsh odor that spread through the air.

"He has no teeth; did you know that?" Spallanzani said, still burning Bufo's foot. "And the poisonous secretions of his glands are expelled only if they're squeezed. Bufo has no control over them. In any case, his obsession overrides all else; it's the secret of his fantastic survival."

Bufo's foot was completely charred, but he maintained Marina, grasped between his arms. The scientist went on to burn Bufo's leg and thigh until they were fully incinerated.

"Does this member regenerate?"

"Not in toads. In tritons and salamanders, yes. There's a correlation between the potential for regeneration and the level of complexity of organisms. Lower organisms have a high regenerative ability. That capacity diminishes as complexity increases."

Spallanzani said this with undisguised pride, for he had made the discovery in that year of 1768 and hoped it might bring great benefits to humanity. He carefully moved on to burning Bufo's other foot. "Yesterday I cut off the leg of a *Bufo marinus* and he lasted thirteen hours clutching the female, finally dying in his nuptial embrace."

"Which is why he's been around for three hundred million years," Laura said.

Finally both of Bufo's legs were totally charred. Then, from his pristine bard's throat, from the first composer and singer on earth, came a strong, sweet sound full of harmony and beauty.

The song lasted only a short time.

"Is he dead?" Laura asked.

"Yes."

Spallanzani stood in thought. The glow no longer came through the skylight and the room was beginning to darken. The sage did not notice the pealing of the bell of Ghirlandina or the delicate weight of Laura's hand on his shoulder. Soon night fell coldly upon the deserted square. "Hell," Spallanzani whispered.

I stopped writing. I missed the TRS-80. I was hungry. I pinched my cheeks as I looked at my face in the bathroom mirror. How good to be awake, I thought.

A purple shadow covered the mountain. I walked in the direction of the Big House without turning on my flashlight, mentally telling myself that nature was beautiful.

Everyone was on the porch of the Big House watching it grow dark.

"Our chronicler has arrived," Orion said.

Roma and Vaslav had changed clothes again. They were dressed in the finest leather. To exhibit leather clothing is like exhibiting a hunting trophy, both a perversity and a perversion. My feelings toward Roma were still confused.

I had put the page with the opening of Bufo & Spallanzani in my pocket. I thought it would be interesting, given our game involving the theme, if I read them what I had written.

"Before I read it, I want to remind you—Orion, Suzy, and Roma—about the promise you made not to reveal the themes you received."

The three reaffirmed their promises.

"Then here goes: 'The sage Spallanzani contemplated. . . .' "

As I was reading I looked at my listeners. Suzy looked back at me and at the other two contestants as if she wanted to say something; I made a gesture of silence at her by bringing my finger to my lips. Orion frowned.

"You're a devil," Roma said when I finished.

I made the same gesture at her that I had with Suzy.

"I didn't understand very well what you mean with that story," Juliana said.

"It's just a story of toads & men. Nothing to do with the symbology of *Of Mice and Men*. On the jacket flap the publisher will say something to enlighten and motivate the reader. In France—for the book will be published in other countries, as has happened with my works—they'll say the book is a metaphor for the violence of knowledge. In Germany, that it's a denunciation of the abuses perpetrated by *Homo sapiens* against nature, not forgetting to mention that it is in Brazil, among all countries of the world, where such abuses are committed in greatest and most stupid measure (*see Amazon Rain Forest, Swamplands, etc.*). In the United States they'll define the book as a cruel reflection on the utopia of progress. The word 'hubris' will be used anathematically. We'll seduce the prospective buyer by creating quite a flap."

"So the thing is to sell?" Orion said.

"The writer is the victim of many curses," I said, "but the worst of all is the need to be read. Worse yet, to be bought. To have to reconcile his independence with the process of his consummation. Kafka is good because he didn't write to be read. But on the other hand, Shakespeare is good because he wrote with one eye on the shilling that he collected from each spectator. (*See Panofsky.*) Just as the theater will *not* save itself solely through the courage to write plays that no one wants to see, literature will not save itself solely through the courage to write more *Finnegans Wake*s."

"Those guilty of the present decadence of literature—you do agree that literature is decadent, don't you?—are the writers themselves," Orion said.

"Yes. They don't make writers like they used to," I said ironically.

"I read in an interview with Borges that he prided himself on never having written a difficult word that would send the reader to the dictionary. It seems to me that a spate of long words is only good for those French philosophers who go in and out of style periodically"—like the suit of Guedes the cop, I thought—"and who, having nothing to say, opt for cryptic logorrhea; just as doctors make their writing unintelligible on prescriptions to anoint themselves with greater authority."

"I also can be read without aid of dictionary," I told Orion. "Protohand. Hubris."

"The toad's was the first five-fingered hand to exist in the animal kingdom. Yes, protohand. Hubris is a beautiful hellenic cliché. Readers love it."

Maybe Orion was right and any idiot could be a writer, as long as he was a shameless exhibitionist with a large ego. There I was, reading a page of my novel, merely to show off to Roma, a page on which I had taken great care to give the impression that I was intelligent and cultured in addition to having mastered the difficult art of writing. A writer's being well informed isn't worth shit. To write *Death and Sport: Agony as Essence* I filled my computer with thousands of pieces of information—everything I had read in other people's books, who in turn had read it in other people's books, et cetera, ad nauseam. The computer stored that raw mass of data in the innumerable orders that interested me, and when it was time to write all I had to do was hit one or two keys and, within a second, the information I wanted appeared on the screen, at the right moment. *Death and Sport* is nothing but an immense quilt made of thousands of small old scraps that, assembled and stitched together, seem to be something original.

"I liked the trick of having us delay recognizing that Bufo and Marina were toads," Carlos said, in his muffled voice.

"Were you two given that theme?" Vaslav asked.

"Careful there!" I said, making the gesture of silence I had given Roma and Suzy.

Someone asked if Spallanzani had existed. Of course he had.

Initially I had thought of writing a book in which the main characters were a salamander and St. Catherine of Siena, both of whom were incombustible, according to legend. For reasons I didn't wish to reveal to the other guests, I changed the protagonists of the story and thus the story itself. I had always been interested in Spallanzani since high school. The first artificial insemination was done by him, on a bitch. He was the first to discover the acute sense of the bat, an animal that also interested me greatly. (*See my book* Dance of the Bat.) Spallanzani antedated Pasteur with his experiments in spontaneous generation. He studied the circulation of the blood, gastric digestion, and respiration, as well as, obviously, regeneration of amphibian appendages. Then, for a reason I didn't wish to reveal to my companions at the retreat, Bufo replaced the salamander and Spallanzani took the place of St. Catherine of Siena. The salamander, by the way, already had its own mad scientist, named Gesner, who also inflicted terrible suffering on individuals of the species that he studied in an unsuccessful attempt to prove his fanciful theories. But I'm not speaking just of madness when I use Spallanzani as a symbol of the scientist's authoritarian arrogance. (*See my book* Joseph Mengele, the Angel of Death.)

"It's going to be a hard book to read," Juliana said.

"Is that Catherine *the* Catherine, Catherine the Great?"

What can you say to a question like that? In reality the only great Catherine was Catherine of Siena, Caterina Benincasa, the only great illiterate writer in the history of world literature, with her texts dictated in the fourteenth century. She's the patron saint of Italy, but the aspect to be explored in my book would be the myth of incombustibility. I'd had my fill of hagiography.

I merely replied, "No."

At that instant Dona Rizoleta appeared to say that dinner was being served.

Dinner was even more delicious than lunch, a feat of Dona Rizoleta's that I would have considered impossible of achievement: carp cooked in butter without any aftertaste of earth (another accomplishment) and stewed rabbit with potatoes and string beans. There was also fresh asparagus—indescribable, even for a competent writer like me. Roma had sat down at a table near mine and there was a moment when, as I chewed the tender rabbit, I imagined—without lubricity—that I was chewing on her lush cheeks. Her cheekbones were prominent and noble, with the earthy and pure exuberance of the fruits of nature. An edible woman in every aspect.

The temperature had fallen by the time we finished eating. The fireplace was lit, and we all sat in comfortable easy chairs in the main hall.

"I greatly enjoyed your Manon," I told Juliana. "I was moved at hearing the *Adieu, notre petite table* aria sung by you." In reality, she was a little past the age the role called for, but it was still impressive that a woman of such bearing could play a beautiful and delicate heroine so well. "You have, more than anyone, the sensuality demanded by the role," I said in a soft voice so that Orion, who was talking to Vaslav, wouldn't hear. I think that in my abstinence I was beginning to get desperate.

"Excuse my saying so, but I don't like opera," said Eurídice, joining the conversation.

"You were also excellent in the aria of the seduction of Des Grieux, the priest," I said, ignoring Eurídice.

"Manon is one of the characters I like best," she said, in that same tone of complicity which I had imparted to the conversation. "But Puccini's, not Massenet's."

"I've never seen an opera," said Eurídice. Was she too ignorant to see she wasn't wanted? And she'd spoken the phrase so loudly that she caught the attention of Orion, who quickly butted into the conversation, as categorical as ever.

"The best thing about *Manon*, Massenet's version, is Guillot de Morfontaine's phrase, *La femme est un méchant animal*," Orion said. He must have been paying attention to my conversation with the woman the entire time. Gradually everyone began participating in the discussion.

"I prefer Turandot," Roma said.

"Because she cut off the heads of her suitors?" Orion asked.

"That, and because she was incomprehensible to men."

There I was, surrounded by women, women full of strength and mystery, those irresistible attributes of theirs, and not able to do anything, repressed and oppressed.

"You have to see the sky," Trindade said, coming in from the porch. He was holding a flashlight.

We all went to the center of the lawn in front of the Big House. Trindade turned off the light. In the dark night one couldn't see the face of those next to him. Fireflies in flight flashed on and off.

"The sky changes every hour," Trindade said. "It's nine o'clock and you can see Sirius to the west. We're between twenty and thirty degrees of latitude. Over there to the north is Arcturus. Antares to the east."

"Where's the Southern Cross?"

"To the south," Trindade said, laughing in pleasure, "next to Rigel."

No one found Rigel, but everyone found the Southern Cross, amid exclamations of joy.

"What about Aldebaran?"

"You can't see it this month. It comes out at five in the morning, or thereabouts, in July."

"And Betelgeuse?"

"Same thing. Both over to the east. Betelgeuse is near the constellation that bears our maestro's name."

"So you have a constellation with your name," Eurídice said.

"That's prestige for you, my dear," Orion said.

"It seems hard to believe that just a few days ago I was in São Paulo, which doesn't have a sky," Eurídice said.

"There's no sky like this anywhere in the world," Trindade said.

"I don't know," the conductor said. "This hurray-for-Brazil stuff bores me."

"Look at the fireflies," Eurídice said.

"How lovely," Juliana said.

"The fireflies?"

"The fireflies, the stars, the people, life. It makes me feel like singing," Juliana said, touching my hand lightly. Could it have been involuntarily?

"Control your rapture, my dear," Orion said.

"Sing something for us," Eurídice said. Led by Suzy, we repeated in chorus, "Sing something for us."

"Some other day she'll sing," Orion said.

"I'll sing now," Juliana said.

"This cold isn't good for you," Orion said.

"I'm going to sing," Juliana said, as if she were already onstage.

Suzy sat on the grass and Eurídice lay down with her head in her lap. Roma and Vaslav did the same, Roma with her head on her husband's chest. Good thing it was dark and I could barely see them, or it would have had the same effect on me as watching a pornographic film.

Juliana began to sing. I had already heard that aria of Bellini's several times, but I confess I found the setting magnificent: the starry sky and a feminine voice adding even more to the beauty and harmony of the universe. When Juliana finished—"*Quella pace, che regnar, regnar tu fai, tu fai nel ciel, tu fai nel ciel*"— none of us spoke.

"After that, the moon should come out, that ungrateful Casta Diva," Roma said.

The aesthetic pleasure had aggravated my satyriasis. I couldn't stay there even a second longer or I was at risk of committing an act of insanity. I left hurriedly, disappearing into the darkness. I noticed someone had come after me.

"Who is it? Is anyone there?" My heart beat hopefully.

"It's me." The muffled voice of Carlos. I remembered that his bungalow was in the same direction as mine.

I picked up the pace so he wouldn't get close to me. If there's anything that irritates me it's talking to a man. When I arrived at the path leading to my bungalow I shouted "Good night" into the darkness.

"Good night," Carlos answered. He was almost on top of me, and I hadn't sensed his nearness.

O wretched life, I thought sadly as I took off my clothes and put on my silk pajamas. Women will be the death of me yet; Guillot de Morfontaine is right. But a little later I murmured, as I stretched out, "How good it is to sleep." And I slept.

I awoke early, took a shower, and ran to the Big House. I should have spent the morning writing, but I didn't even glance at my notes on B & S. I wished Minolta were there to give me strength.

The tables in the dining room had just been set for breakfast. On a large, long table were breakfast delicacies—several kinds of cheese, including goat and sheep cheese, bananas large and small, oranges, mangoes, plums, papayas, jabuticabas, honey, corn fritters, cheese bread, toast, yogurt. I filled two plates with cheese, fritters, bread, and fruit, a container of butter, a bottle of yogurt, and honey, and went to one of the tables, my mouth filled with saliva. A maid served coffee with cream and asked me if I'd like some eggs. I said no, but Trindade, who was drinking coffee at a nearby table, said, "If I were you I'd try our eggs. Our hens roam at will; they spend their entire day in freedom, eating worms, insects, ants, working their legs the whole time without stopping. They don't have an ounce of fat on them; they're not like those bloated city hens. You'll see for yourself when you have the chicken in black sauce we serve at lunch. The eggs—look, I'm not going to say another word. Lucimar, bring two fried eggs for the gentleman."

Hearing about chicken in black sauce made me even happier. There's nothing better than thinking about food while you're eating. Trindade asked permission to sit at my table. He wanted to see me savor the eggs.

"Everything you eat here is produced on the farm, except the salt and olive oil," Trindade said with pride. The fried eggs arrived. The yolks were as red as rubies, surrounded by a scanty white that was merely a small snowy circumference, without that slimy look of fried eggs I was familiar with. The yolk was hard to cut, its consistency compact and dense and its taste lascivious and restful. I ordered two more eggs.

"Didn't I tell you?" Trindade smiled with satisfaction. "The yellow yolks of poultry farms don't have any taste or nutritional value compared to ours. Besides which, they're full of hormones. I'm under the impression"—he lowered his voice—"that the increase in homosexuality and other forms of sexual perversion comes from that, and from the crap they feed cattle. Don't you think so?"

As happy as I was to delight in these delicacies, ignorance always exasperates me. "Homosexuality isn't a perversion," I said. "Homosexuals are normal people just like you."

"Not like me!"

"Well, like me then."

Trindade stopped talking, not knowing what to say. With a piece of bread I scraped up the last of the yolk still on the plate, which shone clean and bright.

"I was thinking of taking you to see the garden," he said, as if he'd changed his mind.

"I insist on seeing your garden," I said.

I'd never seen a garden in my life. How pretty are collards, lettuces, cabbages, cauliflowers, chard, mustard greens, the broccoli sprouting from the ground like a colored carpet in a fairy tale. A purple cabbage is prettier than a rose, more luxuriant and luxurious (lush, libidinous). To see a garden is better than sitting down and writing. In fact, writing was becoming a tripalium (*see a Latin dictionary*), a suffering (suddenly I imagined myself suffering from Virginia Woolf syndrome and shuddered in fear); the devilish thing is that for a writer like me, who needs money to support his habit of living with women, every damned word, every *oh* in a hundred thousand terms, was worth a few pennies. Writing means cutting words, a writer once said, one who must not have had lovers. Writing means counting words, the more the better, said another writer, who, like me, needed to write a Bufo & Spallanzani every other year. Nevertheless, instead of working I was gazing raptly at a cabbage.

"Do you know how to cook?" Trindade asked, rather cunningly.

I thought before answering. I can cook, embroider, do crochet, sew, act as a wet nurse, dance ballet—but why waste time on other people's prejudices?

"I only know how to eat." This answer seemed to calm Trindade. He asked if I'd like to see the orchard. The greenness of the collards and chard made me want to see Roma; maybe she had already gone to the dining room for breakfast. I made an excuse and returned to the Big House.

Roma was in the dining room having breakfast, without Vaslav. She was wearing different clothes, an outfit of rustling linen, full of ruffles and pleats, that enveloped her as if she were a woman from another world. I worked it out: The *lex Oppiana* had been promulgated against her. Cato was thinking of a woman like her when he criticized feminine extravagance in the Roman senate. Surely in her delicate leather suitcase she kept purple apparel, colored with dyes from Tyre.

"May I join you?" I asked.

"Yes." She bit into a piece of toast, baring her teeth and looking at me. I got goose bumps.

"Did you sleep well?" I asked, imagining her in bed, lying on her side, face down, on her back.

"No, to tell the truth, I slept very badly."

"It must be the oxygen," I stammered.

"Maybe. The problem is that sleeping poorly makes me very irritated. I need at least eight hours a night." Every woman I ever met needed to sleep eight hours a night.

"And your life would make a novel," I said.

"Are you asking or telling?"

"Telling."

"A more electrifying one than you think," she said. "Did your priest say mass?"

"My priest?"

"Spallanzani."

"Yes. He continued to say mass, in Latin with an Umbrian accent, and to hear confessions. The world was full of sinners seeking absolution; the Council of Trent had established that complete confession of sins was by divine law necessary for all who had fallen since baptism. His faith didn't conflict with his science because he had no faith; God's designs weren't always clear to him. Why had God made Bufo? Evidently not to eat ants, which in turn were God's children. A stage in the evolution of man? Well, in those days the sun still revolved around the earth and Darwin hadn't been born. That's why he said 'hell' after having submitted the batrachian to that torture."

"I'm going to tell you something, which I don't want the maestro to hear: writing a book is a complicated thing," Roma said.

"*Quelle lourde machine à construire qu'un livre, et compliquée surtout,*" I said.

"That's true: *et compliquée surtout.*"

"Writing is a matter of patience and resistance, something like competing in a marathon, where one must run but mustn't be in a hurry." (I disliked the simile as soon as I said it. I hate sports.) "And speaking of which, how's your story coming?"

"You're horrible," Roma said, "giving me the theme of—"

I gestured for silence because at that moment Carlos was approaching our table. For the first time Carlos had taken off the loose velvet jacket and now wore a very loose and long sport shirt that gave him a singular look. At that same instant Vaslav arrived.

"Did you hear a violin last night?" Vaslav asked.

"It was the maestro," Roma said. "Our bungalow is near his."

"Roma woke me up to hear the violin," Vaslav said.

"Not so. I was awake, and since I can't stand being awake with someone sleeping beside me, I took advantage of the pretext and woke you up."

"Tell them what you saw," Vaslav said.

"I got up and went to the bungalow porch to hear better. Then I saw someone walking through the woods carrying a flashlight."

"It may have been Trindade. Or one of the workers," I said.

"Maybe. But the person was walking stealthily. I may have been influenced by that violin playing in the middle of the night. You know it's lovely, but at the same time there's something sinister about a violin playing in the darkness. I got scared, you know?"

From the musicians' table Juliana made an allegro gesture in my direction; Orion also, *ma non troppo*.

Trindade, in boots and a cowboy hat, came into the dining room and informed us that the horses were ready for anyone who wanted to take a ride around the retreat.

We all went to the place where the horses were, except Suzy and Eurídice. Both were tense, as if they had been fighting all night. Roma said she was going to change into her riding clothes.

"Where's the chestnut?" Carlos asked.

"Belzebum? He's a very mean horse. Ride this one here; it has an easy gait." Trindade pointed to a sorrel with a blaze on its muzzle.

Carlos looked at the sorrel and said, "I want Belzebum."

"Mr. Carlos, only one person rides Belzebum, and that's the Hermit, a man who lives up there on the peak with the wildcats and raises chickens for the falcons to eat. Once a week he comes down and rides Belzebum, so the animal doesn't totally revert to the wild state. Mr. Carlos, if you try to ride that horse you'll be thrown for sure and maybe get hurt."

"That's my problem," Carlos said dryly.

They went to get Belzebum. The horse appeared, shaking its head, its eyes wide. It took three men to put the bridle and saddle on Belzebum. Carlos went up to him and caressed the animal's muzzle. "This curb bit is too tight," he said, adjusting the metal chain of the bridle. Then he examined the cinch to see if the saddle was secure and checked the length of the stirrup straps. "Let him go," he said.

"I warned him," Trindade said, looking at us.

Holding the reins in his left hand, which rested on the pommel of the English saddle, Carlos placed his left foot in the stirrup and mounted slowly, effortlessly, throwing his right leg over Belzebum's haunches (the image of Delfina Delamare naked in bed, turning her back toward me, flashed through my mind!) and settled into the saddle without the slightest creak of leather. Belzebum remained immobile, as if made of iron. Carlos leaned forward and patted the horse's withers. Without our noting any command from the horseman, Carlos and Belzebum took off in a soft gallop through the grass of the meadow.

"Wow!" Trindade said. "Rizoleta should see this."

I looked at the horse that had fallen to me and decided not to risk it. We fat people don't make very good riders. "I've got a back pain," I lied. Roma too looked elegant as she rode, but not as elegant as Carlos. She had on black leather boots with brown trim, riding breeches that hugged her body, a polo shirt, and a riding hat on her head. There is nothing prettier than a pretty woman. She and Vaslav, while they waited for the others, who finally ended up not going, controlled their horses with much grace. Trindade explained that the horses were of Campolina stock, except for Belzebum, who was a quarter horse.

"No one else coming?" Trindade asked. The other horses were still being held by the workers. Like me, Juliana and Orion had no desire to look ridiculous after seeing the elegance and agility of Roma and Vaslav. Orion said he didn't have the right clothes; Juliana admitted candidly that she didn't know how to ride.

"I don't understand how anybody doesn't know how to ride," Roma said. "To me it's like not knowing how to read."

And they rode off, leaving us infantrymen standing in the dirt, feeling like failures. Watching Roma pull away, I thought, I don't want to mount a horse, I want to mount you; that's what I know how to do, mount mares like you. The idea so took control and excited me that I barely heard what Orion was saying.

". . . extraordinary. I wasn't sleepy; to tell the truth, because of our little game I began to write my story"—ah, so he was beginning to see just how easy it was to write. "I'm doubtful whether—anyway, I decided to get some fresh air. From my bungalow I can see a hill, located over there in that direction, that has a lot of trees with silvery leaves, and I was looking at the sky when I saw a flash of fire, intermittent, like a volcano spewing out flames at irregular intervals. I'm sure it was fire, but there wasn't any smoke, and when the brilliance ended I heard a sound so extraordinary that I think I must have been mistaken. The night was silent; there was no sound of crickets or toads. There are trees that moan, like the Australian pine. But this!"

"Just what was the sound anyway?" I asked.

"Laughter. It seemed like laughter. It *was* laughter."

"Laughter?"

"I don't know whether it was really loud or whether it seemed loud because of the silence."

"Is your bungalow near Roma and Vaslav's?"

"It's in the same area."

"Roma says she had insomnia and saw somebody walking through the woods with a flashlight. Did you see the fire before or after playing the violin?"

"Did you hear my violin?"

"Roma heard it."

"It was afterward. I stopped playing—it was one of Paganini's *capricci*—and spent a long time looking at the stars and thinking about what I wanted to write. That was when the fire started on the hillside."

"I was scared to death when Orion told me that this morning," Juliana said.

Suzy and Eurídice were leaning back in the canvas lounge chairs on the Big House porch. We sat down beside them, and soon Juliana was speaking of the laughter Orion had heard in the middle of the night.

"That doesn't surprise me," Suzy said. "I saw it in the cards."

"The cards?"

We learned that Suzy was a specialist in the occult. Her boutique was only a business; "I don't go there for days at a time." She knew astrology, the cabala, talismanic arts, numerology, palmistry, card reading, esoterica. She had laid out the cards and seen things she preferred not to talk about. But it wasn't only cards. She had looked into beryl and seen the same things. Beryl, she explained, was the stone used in crystal gazing. Despite having come to the retreat solely for rest, she had brought, besides two Tarot decks and the crystal, a book of the I Ching, a set of shells, a talismanic ring of mercury and cast lead, a jar of Paracelsus's lilium, and a bit of Frascator's diascordium, in purest form, with all the elements: storax, bloodroot, galbanium, fennel, bistort, and even the exceedingly rare Cretan dittany. (*See Sepharial.*)

"Besides, of course, my owl. I'm never without my owl."

"A real owl?"

"No, it's bronze. One of these days I'll show it to you!"

"I think that owl's horrible," Eurídice said.

"Clairvoyance—clear vision, precognition—should be used very cautiously," Suzy said. "Is Carlos horseback riding?"

At the time I didn't understand Suzy's interest in Carlos. But no one can decode the thousands of pieces of encrypted information that he receives each second.

"Then you're not going to tell us what you saw in the cards?" Juliana asked.

"I can't say anything," Suzy said, getting up quickly. "Let's go, Eurídice."

The chicken in black sauce at lunch was appetizing, delightful, luscious. Its color ran toward the dark auburn, which meant the chicken's blood had been used in a different way. Not even the presence of Orion and his annoying questions (he and Juliana had sat at my table) kept me from savoring the chicken with its bloody rice. Orion wanted to know why I didn't write a historical novel with the Duke of Caxias as a character. I attempted to explain to him that I didn't like heroes, powerful men and women (the men much less than the women) who made history. I didn't even like great history, with a capital *H*. I read the story of famous men with the greatest indifference, if not with disdain. But I could become rapt at the photograph of an "anonymous individual" in the middle of the street or perched on the platform of an old streetcar, imagining what sort of person he might have been. I was never interested in meeting famous men or women. But I would have really liked to meet, for example, that telephone operator with the large eyes and long dress who appeared in the photo of the inauguration of the first telephone exchange in Rio de Janeiro, in the nineteenth century. Orion replied that my idiosyncrasy must have a Freudian explanation. Luckily, Roma passed by and I asked her, "How was the ride?"

"Marvelous," she said, sitting down at our table. She told how Trindade had taken them to see lovely spots, crystalline streams, forest, et cetera. Carlos had accompanied them until a certain point. "Then we located the mysterious old man who raises falcons, and he and Carlos talked about the horse Carlos was riding, and they went off together toward the mountaintop. They looked like a couple of young goats."

"The old man doesn't raise falcons; he raises chicks for the falcons to eat," I said. "Good for him. Between falcons and chicks I prefer falcons."

I didn't wait for the desserts, which were always some kind of sweet in syrup and compotes made at the retreat. I don't have a sweet tooth, fortunately, or I'd weigh even more. And I also had no desire to stay at the same table as Orion. I've already said I don't like men.

I went to the porch and sat down in a lounge chair with my eyes closed. I wasn't feeling well. I couldn't forget that damned cop Guedes, the poor devil. I couldn't forget Delfina; she was my black hole, an irresistible gravitational force. I had proved thousands of times that "things separate" (*see Heraclitus*), and sooner or later I would separate from her. I, however, feared verifying that in the long run phlegm was stronger than passion, but in the long run we're all etc. There I was, suffering memories that could theoretically serve a therapeutic function if put down on paper, but writing is no cure; just the opposite—it twists our psyche (*see Braine*). When writing is good for one, it's bad for literature. Writing is a painful experience, exhausting, which is why there are so many alcoholics, drug users, suicides, misanthropes, fugitives, crazies, unhappy youths, and senile old men among us writers.

To cheer myself up I thought about the suckling pigs that must already be marinating for tomorrow's lunch, not overlooking the codfish to be served at dinner that evening. I opened my eyes and noticed Carlos and another rider coming across the meadow toward the Big House, side by side, their steeds in lockstep as if at a horse show. When they came nearer I noted that Carlos's companion was a man with long hair and a white beard, wearing a cowboy hat. It was probably the old man known as the Hermit, who lived on top of the mountain. They passed in front of the porch and the old man turned his wrinkled, sunburned face toward me, but I couldn't see his eyes, which were covered by his hat. They went to the stables, to take care of the animals.

In my bungalow I tried to continue writing Bufo, but without success. The only thing that kept my unhappiness from being complete was the prospect of dinner.

I was the first guest to arrive at the dining room, as usual. I smelled the aroma of the cod with potatoes, peppers, and olives that Dona Rizoleta had prepared. In the history of mankind millions of people have died, and still die, of starvation. Some, however, have died, and still die, from overeating. (I may yet become one of them.) For all of them, both the destitute and the surfeited, eating is the most important activity there is. Eating, eating! How good it is to eat! I'm not one to eat baked cod in thick slices, a gastronomic crudity second only to steak tartare. The slice of baked cod retains the harshness acquired at the moment of salting, even if placed in marinade twenty-hours before and sprinkled copiously with delicate olive oil when served, then washed down with swigs of tart Portuguese red wine. But with sliced potatoes arranged in alternating layers with slivers of cod, the roughness of the salt becomes sublimated to both, cod and potatoes, transforming them into something else at once strong-flavored yet delicate and jubilant. Of course one must know how to do this, as does Dona Rizoleta, for example. As soon as the steaming platter was placed before me, I saw that here was a masterpiece, an extraordinary demonstration of human wisdom. My heart swelled with peace and delight.

(This delicacy can be enjoyed equally well in the afternoon, as is most common, at night, or even in the morning. I have eaten cod in the morning upon waking up, then returned to bed, where a woman awaited me, asleep. I remember that day well. Her name was Regina and she pretended to be asleep when I returned to bed after eating the cod; she liked to pretend she was asleep, and while she pretended to be asleep I would pretend to believe she was asleep and possess her that way. Come to think of it, I always possessed her "asleep," with her moving her body to make things easier, moaning as if she were dreaming; and afterward she never mentioned the subject or allowed me to talk about it. She always found a way to go to bed before me and when I got there she was already asleep, etc.)

I had already finished eating and was at the table waiting for coffee when I noticed an interesting scene. When Carlos came into the dining room Eurídice, who was with Suzy at a table near mine, stared at the man with a rapt and expectant expression, like someone awaiting the chance to initiate an exchange of amorous glances. I had previously noted a certain interest in the young man on Eurídice's part and had also become aware that Suzy was irritated by this. When she saw Eurídice looking at Carlos, Suzy spoke sharply with her cousin. I heard her say "fool," "idiot," and an entire sentence: "Don't come begging for forgiveness later." In addition, Suzy pinched Eurídice forcefully.

Carlos was unaware that he was causing all this melodrama. Normally lost in his own thoughts, he seemed at that moment more abstracted than ever, eating without appetite. Only somebody who was really out of it could chew indifferently on such divine cod.

Juliana and Orion, who hadn't seen the fight between cousins, came up to Suzy's table and spoke about the promise Suzy had made to read the shells that night. Suzy tried to get out of it, but Roma and Vaslav sided with the musicians to make her honor her commitment. Finally Suzy agreed and said she'd go to her bungalow for the shells. I wound up getting involved in the affair.

"To tell the truth, I don't believe in voodoo of any type," Orion said.

"Reading shells isn't voodoo," Juliana said.

No one could explain just what reading seashells was all about. Someone suggested "a method of unveiling the mysteries of the future," but the term "method" was considered inadequate in the context. "How about divinatory hocus-pocus?" someone proposed.

Suzy returned from the bungalow carrying a black wooden box, accompanied by Eurídice. They appeared to have weathered the argument of a few minutes earlier and were holding hands and smiling.

We gathered around one of the tables in the game room. Several groups sprang up: Juliana and Eurídice, believers; Roma and Vaslav, neutral; Carlos, indifferent, detached; me, skeptical; Orion, I don't know.

Suzy took the shells from the box, shook them in her hands, then threw them on the tablecloth. "Ask your questions," she said in an intimidating tone.

No one dared ask: the believers out of fear of the answer; the skeptic, me, in order not to be viewed as a believer by the others; the indifferent ones because they didn't want to take an active role in the goings-on.

Suzy again cast the shells, which spread out over the table. I noticed that her face seemed to contract, her expression change, as if she'd seen a rat on the table, among the shells: a look of fear and repugnance. Here comes the flimflam, I thought.

"I see violent death," Suzy said.

"Death in an airplane?" Juliana asked. When her vacation was over, Juliana was going on a long tour, with planes as her principal means of transportation.

"No," Suzy said, "I don't see an airplane."

"Is the dead person a man or a woman?" Orion asked.

"A woman," Suzy said.

Silence.

"But it's a death that already took place. . . . I don't know . . . I can't see her face. . . . I see the person beside her. . . . I see clearly the person beside her . . . at that terrible moment . . . beside her . . . this person. . . ."

In the silence that prevailed, a small laugh from Orion, not very convincing, could be heard; it found no followers. Suzy gathered the shells and shook them in her hands. What kind of smile was that on her face?

"Enough!" Suzy said.

"Enough? Just when it was getting interesting?" Orion said. "Please go on."

"What was someone doing beside a dead woman? Where were they? *Who* were they?" Juliana asked.

"Enough," Suzy repeated. "Let's go, Eurídice."

The black box of seashells under her arm, Suzy left with Eurídice (who looked anxiously at Carlos as she passed him). Their walk as they left the game room revealed their tension.

"A real artist," I said. "She should do that act in the circus."

"Circus my foot, I'm scared to death," Juliana said.

"Don't overreact," Orion said.

Without Suzy's presence there was no reason to stay there, unless it was my lust for Roma. Everyone left for their bungalows. I remained by myself for a time, then walked through the woods. I was feeling a kind of frisson, an expectation of danger but only a little, enough to get me excited. I followed a path I'd never taken before, thinking about the poet Bocage: "I want to surfeit my heart with horrors." It must have been good, back in the days when hobgoblins and werewolves inhabited places like this. I lit the flashlight only when I feared falling into a precipice. Sometime during the walk I found a large log, where I sat down, turned off the light, and listened to sounds that seemed like moans, the beating of wings, footsteps, the murmurs of sorceresses.

I stayed there, frightened as an old monkey and enjoying the fear, until suddenly a diffuse yellow light spread through the sky, as if the woods had abruptly burst into flames. But the glow lasted only a short time and quickly went out, leaving the night around me even darker than before. That must have been what the conductor saw, for the sky immediately began to flash intermittently at irregular intervals. There was no doubt that those sudden flashes of light were caused by fire. But fire of that magnitude doesn't go on and off like a gigantic spotlight.

Wanting to find out what the phenomenon was, I set off through the woods toward the reflections. It wasn't an easy trek. I fell several times, tore my clothes, hurt my hands. Hurting my hands sent me into panic—I have been terrified of lockjaw ever since a friend of mine died of tetanus when I was a teenager. I started licking the wounds on my hands, like a dog, to cleanse them of the infectious bacilli. I was still licking myself when I arrived at the foot of the hill and saw a dragon, a dragon with a monkey's body, breathing flames that howled like the winds of hell as they tumbled over the ground. I was seeing things; it must be the effect of tetanus. A chill ran through my body as the muscles of my neck and jaw started to tighten. I knew no infection can attack the body so quickly, but then there was no such thing as a monkey dragon either.

"Die, damn you, die!" the monkey yelled.

Fortunately my dull-witted state was short-lived. I neither had lockjaw (yet) nor was the fearsome animal a dragon or a mere talking monkey. It was a man, holding a flamethrower, like those you see in the movies. The man, I saw to my relief, was Trindade.

"Mr. Trindade!" I shouted.

"I'm killing ants," he said in the darkness. "But I'm through, I'm through. You shouldn't wander around here at night."

"Why not?" I asked.

"You could fall into one of those crevices. Even animals, and they're animals, fall in, much less a person."

He was lying. A liar's voice gives him away in the dark.

"I'll take you to your bungalow."

"No need."

Despite myself, I ended up following him to my bungalow. I went in. I took off my torn clothing. I looked at my hand and saw that I had suffered only minor scratches. I went to the porch and stood listening to the noises coming from the darkness: toads, crickets, the hoot of an owl. I was in search of human sounds. Now I no longer wanted to feel fear. I turned on the flashlight and went into the woods. The distance to be covered seemed greater, but I finally arrived at the place where I had seen Trindade with the flamethrower. I examined the terrain with the flashlight. Scattered on the ground were charred animals that looked like pieces of melted wire, giving off a nauseating smell. With a stick I poked at one of the animals not totally destroyed by the fire. It was a gigantic spider the size of a pumpkin. That's why Trindade had been using the flamethrower; that animal couldn't be killed with clubs or even a hoe. And what if some still survived? What if the spiders grabbed me by the leg and threw me to the ground? I imagined them devouring me. They would begin with the nose and then the lips; lips are tender flesh. Then a smaller, more cunning spider would crawl into my pants, going up my leg until it reached my groin and devour, in order, my balls (balls are tender flesh, at least to spiders), and then my penis. . . . Enough! I thought; you don't play around with penis and balls. I ran back to my bungalow. How beautiful nature is? My body was starting to itch. I was covered with ticks.

I woke up completely swollen. I had pulled off the ticks but they had left behind their barbs. My body was full of red welts. Buboes had appeared in my groin and armpits. Now I really wouldn't be able to write. Without the TRS-80, and swollen all over! I had promised my new book for the first of the year, I'd already received the advance, my publisher was on my back— I think I already spoke of that. My publisher wanted a thick book, the bookseller wanted a thick book, the reader wanted a thick book (a good excuse for buying it and not reading it), because big things are impressive. The Eiffel tower is a horror but it's big; the pyramids are nothing but a heap of stones that pharaonic stupidity managed to pile on top of one another, but they're big. If someone succeeded in building a structure of shit, preferably human, the height of the World Trade Center, that fecal edifice would be considered the greatest artistic monument of all time, or perhaps a great religious icon. It might even be looked upon as God himself. The ticks' poison was starting to get to me.

When I got to the Big House I met Trindade, who didn't mention what had happened the night before. He did ask where I'd been to get bitten by so many ticks. He didn't want it known that there were giant poisonous spiders (and who knows what else) in his paradise.

In the breakfast room, a surprise. Eurídice and Carlos were having breakfast at the same table. I hadn't thought that Eurídice would have the courage to court the young man so spitefully after Suzy's fit of jealousy. Eurídice looked at Carlos like a woman in love, despite his not reciprocating; as always, he seemed distracted, introverted, and a bit melancholy. I feared a melodramatic scene with tears and shouting if Suzy showed up, but Suzy had asked for breakfast in her room. Despite feeling poorly, I ate all the breakfast tidbits—the jellies, cheeses, small cakes, toast, eggs, fried bacon. The waitress, as she poured my coffee, surreptitiously left on the table a piece of folded paper, which, also surreptitiously, I palmed and put in my pocket. My heart was beating wildly, for I had no doubt it was a note from Roma, who wasn't in the dining room.

As soon as I left the room, still on the porch, I read the note: *The maid who brought breakfast is taking you this note. Eurídice is going horseback riding, and I'll be at the bungalow all morning. Stop by. I need to talk to you. Suzy.* In the note was a sketch showing how to get to Suzy's bungalow.

Suzy! What the devil did she want? Her sexual preferences seemed pretty well defined, but still . . . I had been to bed with a few lesbians and couldn't distinguish any fundamental difference between hetero and homo. What rotten luck that I was all swollen from the tick bites. Anyway, it would take more than some lousy ticks to keep me from enjoying the choice morsels that were a woman's body.

I followed the directions in the drawing and soon found Suzy's bungalow. I knocked only once and she immediately opened the door.

"Well, here I am."

On the table in the sitting room I saw the owl she had mentioned, a sculpture about a foot high.

"What happened to you?" She laughed. "Sorry, you're probably suffering, but you look so funny with those red marks on your face and neck. Is the rest of your body like that too?"

"More or less," I replied, feeling a certain ill humor take control of me. "But I didn't come here to talk about ticks."

"You're right."

Suzy told me she had always been a compulsive reader of newspapers and magazines, especially those dedicated to gossip. She liked scandal, like everybody for that matter, and confessed that she was attracted by crime, swindles, embezzlement, confidence games, and dirty tricks. As the owner of a boutique and a student of the occult, she had a very great opportunity to satisfy her curiosity for gossip. "You bend over somebody's palm and in a few seconds, with a bit of encouragement, he'll tell you his lifelong darkest secrets."

After this *introitus*, she paused and looked at me, a cigarette between her fingers. Till then I'd never seen her smoke.

She continued. "Do you know there's a murderer among us?"

"Really?" I said.

"You're not surprised?"

"Nothing surprises a writer."

"Come off it."

"OK, I'm quite surprised."

"Your blasé air isn't very convincing," Suzy said. "Can I tell you the story I was going to write, for our game with the theme?"

"If you do, you'll be eliminated from the game."

"It doesn't matter. You'll like it. It's a love story."

"I really like love stories," I said, drawing closer to Suzy. "This is very lovely." Very lightly, I brushed my hand over Suzy's bust, which was covered by a silk blouse. She wasn't wearing a bra and I could feel the hard nipple of her breast. My mouth filled with water.

"Thank you," said Suzy, with calculated indifference, removing her body, bringing home to me the coarseness of my gesture. "The man in our story is twenty-four and the girl is twenty-one. They're rich, good-looking, tall, and in love. But they love in a possessive way, with the dark passion of the mad."

"All passion is mad," I said, thinking of Delfina Delamare. "But a man and a woman insanely in love is nothing new."

"I know. The difference is that these two made a love pact: whoever betrayed their partner would be killed by the other."

"Passion as terrible partnership, dark collusion, unbounded complicity. It's Greek tragedy, Latin melodrama," I said. "The onus of abundance is boredom. Beauty fades, pleasure dissipates, intelligence wearies. The death pact becomes a source of life. I like these pact makers." My heart ached as I said this.

"If you keep interrupting all the time I'll never finish the story," Suzy said.

"Oral stories are based on intrigue. So far it's only been social psychology."

"Oh? And what about your fortune-cookie philosophizing?"

"Let's not fight," I said. "What are the characters' names? Names are very important. *On ne peut plus changer un personage de nom que de peau.*" I knew I was talking too much.

"Maria and José. Maria spent the mornings at the equestrian academy riding her horses, which she did with exceptional skill."

I was very nervous, as if realizing what would come of that conversation. When I'm nervous I talk a lot. "Riding with open legs on horseback was for centuries forbidden to women as something obscene and abominable. Nowadays they compensate for that, that—"

"I gave you an important clue." Suzy cut me off. "Make a note of it."

"Noted," I said.

"José, for his part, carried out the masculine rituals. The rich are ritualistic, you know."

"I don't know. Preoccupation with the rich is typical of the marginal upper bourgeoisie, such as coiffeurs, restaurateurs, whores, jewelers, card readers, et cetera." (I recalled Minolta's words the day before my trip to the retreat, when I commented on my difficulty in writing Bufo & Spallanzani. "Your trouble," Minolta had said, "your trouble was not wanting to be black and poor, so you stopped really being a great writer; you made the wrong choice. You preferred being white and rich, and from the moment you made that choice you killed the best that was in you." Minolta said that, my Minolta! It could only have been a throwback to hippiedom. "What about Machado de Assis? He had the right to be white, didn't he?" I said. "But he was poor," Minolta replied.)

"It doesn't do any good to try and provoke me," Suzy said. "I'm not going to play your game."

"Go on then."

"The most beautiful body loses its seductiveness with exposure. As a writer you know that better than anyone. Love consumes like a flame. Can I read you something?" She took a piece of paper from her pocket and read it. " 'I was on that avenue when she passed me going in the opposite direction. It lasted only a few seconds. She was wearing a thin black dress, very flowing, as if of satiny silk. Her body was athletic, tall and slim. Her straight black hair was cut *à la garçonne*. The dress and the body were inseparable, a single object impelled by a stride of unsettling elegance. The dress, cut very low, was sleeveless, and the woman wore high heels and no jewelry. Her beauty was unforgettable. I felt her passing had left me burned.' "

Suzy lit another cigarette. "I carry that with me as if it were a prayer. Do you know who wrote it?"

"Baudelaire has a beautiful poem about a woman passing by," I said.

"No man could write like that; only a woman would be capable of writing like that about another woman," Suzy said. (Later I discovered that it was from an interview with M. Duras.) "And I read it to you because that's exactly what I felt when I saw . . . Maria for the first time. At the time I didn't understand what I was feeling, but it was like that, as if I had set fire to myself."

Suzy closed her eyes and appeared to recall her passion.

"As always—getting back to my story—it was the man who was unfaithful. Oh, yes, perhaps he loved her, I don't doubt that; men manage to love and betray at the same time. The woman didn't want to kill him, but the pact must be honored. She stood before him, a revolver in her hand, the vision of the man she loved, kneeling before her, her eyes misty with tears, and said, 'I don't want to kill you; I love you.' But even so she pulled the trigger. Do you know what made her pull the trigger? Pity. If she betrayed him, she wouldn't be able to go on living; she believed that he was as worthy as she and wanted to die to expiate the horror he had committed."

"What happened to her?" (My voice was quivering. Oh, how my voice was quivering!)

"She ran away. This part is interesting. Once I read her hand—it was when I fell in love—and foresaw, in general terms, what was going to happen. I didn't see her for some time, and we couldn't stay away from each other. It's destiny. Know where I met her again? You know where?"

"No."

"Prepare yourself for a surprise," she said.

"Nothing surprises a writer," I repeated, but less emphatically than the first time.

"You don't know. Tomorrow, or maybe tonight, I'll tell you, and everyone here, who she is. For today all I'll say is this: Her husband didn't die; in fact, he wasn't even wounded."

"Then she's not our murderer?"

"No, she's not our murderer."

"You're out of our game, did you know that? You didn't follow the theme," I said.

"My theme was the toad. Can anybody—yourself excluded, of course—write a story about toads?"

"I'm going to tell you a secret, but don't tell anyone, not even Eurídice. I gave all the others the toad theme too," I said.

"Clever, aren't you? Be careful, though; I've read the Tarot cards. I know what happened and also everything that's going to happen. The cards never lie."

When I publish a collection of stories they say they're inferior to my poems; my poems, in turn, are considered inferior to my novels; my detective novels are inferior to my love novels. Not to mention the misconceptions written about my plays. The world of art is the world of envy and jibes. When they can't say one of my books is bad, they say I'm a mulatto. I'm not interested in what others say or think of me, nor even in what women think of me, as long as they still go to bed with me. They call me a sexual maniac, but what would they have me do with my cock, which is constantly hard? A stiff prick was made to stick in a woman's cunt. Even the Indians know that. I went through long years of abstinence; I'm six-foot-two and weigh over two-twenty, as I think I already mentioned. Anyway, what's this I was saying? I was talking in circles; I felt feverish. How about a joke: I don't exercise and never have; I'm extremely lazy, and the only exercise I get is serving as pallbearer for my friends who exercise. (*See Churchill*.)

As soon as I got to my bungalow I threw myself onto the bed. She'd been playing a game of cat and mouse with me, and I was the mouse. I felt my body burning with fever; the itching had gotten worse.

In the bathroom mirror I saw my face and neck, red and swollen, and not only where I'd been bitten. My body was even worse. I must be allergic to tick bites. I went to the Big House and looked for Trindade, but he'd gone horseback riding with the guests and wouldn't be back till the afternoon. I asked Dona Rizoleta if there was some treatment they could give me. She said there was an injection but only Trindade knew how to give it. I wasn't about to wait for Trindade; I could be dead before he got back from the ride. I told her to bring me the medicine— an ampule of Phenergan—and a needle and syringe, disposable. I gave myself the injection in my left arm.

I felt a bit dizzy as I returned to the bungalow. I am very sensitive to pain-killing drugs. If I took a Valium I'd sleep for three straight days. The injection of Phenergan brought on such drowsiness that I forgot Suzy, forgot everything, even forgot lunch. I plopped onto the bed and immediately fell asleep.

I was awakened at night by Trindade. He says I took a long time to wake up. I know I was still pretty woozy when I opened the door and he burst into the bungalow exclaiming, "Dona Suzy's been killed!" At first I didn't quite understand what he was saying. Trindade had to repeat the story several times.

Trindade, Carlos, Eurídice, Juliana, Orion, Vaslav, and Roma had left right after breakfast for a picnic on the mountain. They arrived back at the retreat around four in the afternoon and Eurídice didn't find Suzy in the bungalow. She attached little importance to the fact and, tired from the outing, lay down for a nap until dinner. Shortly before nightfall an employee had found Suzy, dead, in a thicket not far from her bungalow. Trindade had radioed the police in Pereiras, but the policeman wouldn't arrive till the next day; it was impossible to reach the retreat at night.

"The police?" I asked. "Where do the police come into this?"

"Dona Suzy was murdered," Trindade said. He added that the other guests were meeting at that moment in the Big House and had requested my presence.

In the dining room of the Big House the tables had been pulled together and the guests were seated around them. When I came in with Trindade they stopped talking. I sat in one of the empty chairs. Orion cleared his throat. So he was going to be the spokesman! He waited a little longer before he spoke.

"We think that Suzy was killed this afternoon, when we were on the picnic." He gestured toward the other guests. Eurídice had her head between her hands; Carlos was even paler than usual; Juliana avoided looking at me; Roma and Vaslav were grave and pensive.

"Did you by any chance see her today? The last time the employees saw her was at lunchtime. But you didn't come to lunch, isn't that right?"

Somebody is always playing the policeman; it wouldn't do any good to kill all the Guedeses.

"I was bitten by ticks. I was all swollen and took an injection that knocked me out," I said.

I looked at my hands and shut up. I raised my sleeve and looked at my arms. My hands and arms were back to normal. I got up, followed by everyone's eyes, went to a mirror on the dining room wall, and looked at my face. There wasn't the slightest sign of tick bites. I returned, sat down, and said, "That injection works wonders."

Another silence. A furtive look from Juliana. Eurídice still had her head stuck between her hands. Eurídice must be the woman who tried to kill her husband.

I tried to remember in detail the talk I'd had with Suzy that morning. Only Eurídice could be the Maria in Suzy's story; it couldn't be Roma, nor could it be Juliana. Suzy, irritated at Eurídice because of her flirtation with Carlos, had decided to denounce her lover. There was, however, something wrong with my reasoning. Could it all be something Suzy made up? Orion cleared his throat again, cutting off my reasoning process.

"A chambermaid says she gave you a note from Suzy this morning." The conductor's voice was solemn, like a judge's.

"What is this? Do you think I killed Suzy? Are you all crazy?" I got up, knocking over the chair.

"Take it easy, Mr. Gustavo, take it easy," Trindade said. Only then did I see he had a revolver in his belt, the butt of which he grasped and then released.

"No one's saying that. We're just concerned," Roma said. "You know something? I wrote my story based on the theme you gave me."

"That Hermit fellow was seen wandering around the retreat," Vaslav said.

"This is all absurd," Carlos said with such vehemence that his voice sounded like a woman's. "Neither the Hermit nor Gustavo had anything to do with Suzy's death."

"*Somebody* killed her," Orion said.

BUFO & SPALLANZANI / 159

"And here we are, on top of a mountain, unable to leave, surrounded by virgin forest, in the company of a murderer," said Roma.

"Tomorrow the inspector from Pereiras will be here," Trindade said.

"Where's her body?" I asked.

"In the bungalow. Eurídice will spend the night here in the Big House. We fixed up a room for her near ours. Rizoleta is taking care of her," Trindade said.

"I'm going to sleep. Good night," I said. "What about you, Eurídice? Anything to say?"

She continued to clutch her head in her hands.

I left the others sitting around the table.

That day, in a single day, I had skipped lunch and dinner for the first time since Minolta made a new man of me.

And I also couldn't sleep, which was unusual. I tossed and turned the entire night. I remembered Delfina Delamare, I remembered the cornmeal mush with cinnamon that my mother made when I was a child, I even remembered the poor gravedigger at St. John the Baptist Cemetery.

The inspector from Pereiras arrived at eleven. From the porch of the Big House I could see the tractor and wagon slowly approaching. The inspector must be the man with the thick mustache who was sitting in the front seat with two other men. In the rear seat was a woman that I recognized with enormous surprise and delight. It was Minolta, my beloved Minolta.

But I had an even greater surprise. In the last seat, hidden from view by the others, was a man wearing a grubby jacket, and when I saw him my heart raced in fright. It was Guedes. Guedes, the cop I thought I'd never see again in my life.

IV

THE
PROSTITUTE
OF
THE
PROOF

1

The church that Guedes the cop attended considered confession
one of the fundamental elements of the sacrament of penitence:
repentance of sin, without which there can be no salvation. The
law—the penal code to which he subjected himself—considered
spontaneous confession of a crime committed by person or persons unknown or attributed to another party as a factor mitigating
severity of sentence. As an old cop and an old Catholic, Guedes
knew, however, that confession by the criminal or the sinner
only had value if corroborated by other elements of conviction.

He had stopped going to confession while still a boy; he found
it humiliating and to some extent absurd to kneel before another
man to relate his sins, affirm his repentance, and seek re-
demption from his faults (*see Tenth Council of Trent, Session
14, chapters 1–9*).

Confession also repelled him in the police, for it was obtained
through violence, physical or psychological—which amounted
to the same thing; for many, fear was the worst form of torture.

To have an aversion to all forms of confession and be a member
of two institutions that believed in the essential role of the
confiteor perhaps explained the tortuous reasoning of the cop
that I'm calmly trying to make clear.

When Agenor Silva confessed at the precinct that he had

killed Delfina Delamare, Guedes's first worry was to ascertain if the confession had been obtained through torture.

Since the homicide, more serious than the attempted robbery, had been committed in his precinct's jurisdiction, Guedes was able to get the prisoner transferred. He went himself, accompanied by a detective from the 14th, to pick up Agenor. When Guedes arrived with the transfer order for Agenor, the duty officer, Wilfredo, said, "We did your work for you. The guy told us everything."

Guedes knew Wilfredo. He knew he wasn't violent. He asked, "Was it you who interrogated the man?"

"No. Take a look at his sheet."

Guedes took the arrest record that Wilfredo removed from a drawer.

"OK to take this with me?"

"Sure."

"Who did interrogate Agenor?"

It had been one Ribas, fresh out of the police academy. Guedes asked if he could talk to Ribas.

The precinct was in an old two-story building on Mareshal Floriano. Downstairs, by the entrance, was the duty officer's room. In back were a room for the jailers and the lockup. Upstairs were the offices of the various services that made up the precinct.

Guedes climbed a rickety wooden staircase, whose handrail had been chewed away by termites, to the second floor. He found Ribas in a small room with broken windows. He was a tall, thin man with a beard; he had on his leather coat, still wet from the rain falling in the street, and a red-and-black wool cap on his head.

"I'm from the 14th," Guedes said. "I'm here to pick up Agenor Silva."

"The lockup's downstairs," Ribas said.

"I know. I wanted to talk to you. Got a minute?"

"What's up?"

"Did you squeeze Agenor to get him to confess he killed that woman?"

"I never laid a hand on him. I don't go in for that sort of thing."

Ribas told how the arrest had occurred. He and his partner were patrolling in a paddy wagon in the Benfica district when a woman stopped the vehicle and said that a man was holding up a bakery on Prefeito Olímpio de Mello. "It was seven P.M. We were slow to arrive, thanks to our driver's stupidity, but luckily the man was still there, pointing his revolver at the Portuguese guy behind the register. When he saw us he threw down the revolver and raised his hands. When we took him to the wagon he said there was no need to beat him, he'd confess everything. But at the time we didn't want to hear it and stuck him in the wagon. When we got here he said he wanted to talk to me about a private matter. I said I wouldn't discuss any private matters with him and told him he could talk in front of everybody. When he said he'd killed that society lady I brought him here to do the job right. I didn't even make a face at him. He talked and I listened."

According to Agenor's confession, Delfina was stopped at a traffic light on a street in Leblon at the wheel of her Mercedes, at night, when he decided to rob her. It wasn't the first time he'd pulled this type of holdup. He entered the vehicle quickly by the right door and pointed the revolver at Delfina.

Some people must have seen the attack, but no one did anything, perhaps because the light changed and Agenor ordered Delfina to get the car out of there. They drove around the city. He was looking for a place to rape the woman, but the places he selected weren't right: there was a patrol car in one; in another, he noticed some people in a car watching them and was afraid they'd call the police. Finally he decided to go to Tijuca Forest, but neither he nor the woman knew the way and they wound up on a dead-end street (Diamantina, where the body had been found). When they got to that street Agenor became nervous and told the woman to turn around and get them out of there at once. But she was frightened and the car stalled. He struck her, not very hard, and she started screaming. Fearful that someone would come, Agenor shot the woman. Then he opened her purse, took a gold cigarette holder, and got out of the car as fast as he could.

"Why didn't he take the gold wristwatch she was wearing?"

"Why? I can't say. I didn't ask. I didn't know she was wearing a gold wristwatch. Look, Guedes, the guy wasn't leaned on. He was dying to confess everything. There's people like that; you know that better than I do, since I'm new on the job. The guy's conscience hurts and he has to do something about it. I didn't twist his arm. Why should I lie to you? You're not from Internal Affairs."

Ribas wasn't lying, Guedes thought. They went down to the lockup.

In a cell with room for fifteen (if they lay down side by side) were thirty prisoners. The weaker had to sleep standing up. Some among the weakest were periodically killed to relieve the pressure and, through public repercussions, force the authorities to improve living conditions for the incarcerated. It was something like what rats do, except for the protest aspect.

Agenor was lying in half a yard of cell space, and another prisoner was fanning him with sheets of newspaper, like a caliph. It wasn't summer, but it was very hot in that overcrowded cell.

The jailer banged his key ring on the bars and shouted, "Agenor Silva, Agenor Silva!"

Agenor got up hurriedly upon hearing his name and said, "That's me, that's me." He opened a path—or, rather, the prisoners squeezed together to make way for him.

"Come on," the jailer said, opening the door of iron bars.

Agenor accompanied the jailer to Ribas's office.

"You're being transferred to the lockup at the 14th," Ribas said. "Inspector Guedes will take you there."

"The 14th? Why?" He looked worried.

"You killed the woman in our jurisdiction," Guedes said.

Ribas took Agenor by the arm to take him to Detective Wilfredo's office.

"Is he big man in the cell?" Guedes asked.

"Him? No, the guy's a chickenshit, a nobody," Ribas replied, not giving the slightest importance to the prisoner, who was listening to the dialogue between the two cops.

In Wilfredo's office, Guedes took a better look at the prisoner: fidgety, biting his nails. "Can I make a phone call, sir?"

"Go ahead," Guedes said, making a sign toward Wilfredo.

"How's the gang at the 14th?" Wilfredo asked. "I heard Ferreira got transferred to Bangu. That mustn't have made him very happy."

"So far there's been nothing in the *Bulletin*," Guedes said.

Guedes was talking to Wilfredo but was interested in what Agenor was saying on the telephone. "Tell him I'm goin' to the 14th in Leblon. You know who. Dumb broad."

"There are worse places than Bangu," Wilfredo said.

"That's true," Guedes said.

"Don't forget. The 14th," Agenor said, hanging up the phone. "Thank you, sir."

Guedes pretended not to hear Agenor's thanks. He spoke a while longer with Wilfredo, thinking about Agenor's phone conversation. Whom had he told the woman ("dumb broad") to advise that he'd been transferred to the 14th? A lawyer? If he already had a lawyer, why hadn't he called him direct? If he wasn't the cell boss, why was somebody fanning him? He didn't have the money to buy that much comfort and security, or the physical strength and courage to win space in that cubicle.

"Let's go," Guedes said.

They got into a van from the 14th that was waiting for them.

Guedes placed Agenor between himself and the driver. "I have to make a stop," Guedes said. "Let us off near Candelária."

Guedes and Agenor got out at Candelária, at the corner of Quitanda Street. "This way," Guedes said.

Quitanda was closed to vehicular traffic. The cop and his prisoner walked down the middle of the street. Anyone seeing them wouldn't have known they were together. Guedes walked a bit ahead, looking at the numbers on the buildings as if searching for an address. Agenor followed, tense and frightened. Twice he stopped in the street, perplexed, looking about hurriedly, first at the cop's back as he walked away, then at the other end of the street. But on both occasions he soon increased his pace and caught up with Guedes.

From Quitanda Street they went to the Menezes Cortes parking garage, on São José, where Guedes asked if he'd like some coffee. They drank their coffee standing up, in one of the building's galleries. People crowded through the garage's passageways like insects in a giant termites' nest. From there they went to Erasmo Braga Street, and at one point Agenor almost became separated from Guedes among that vibrant throng of people.

They caught an air-conditioned bus, the Castelo–Leblon. When they reached the Flamengo highway, Guedes said, "I forgot my St. George's medal. I don't like to go anywhere without it." An untrue statement with which Guedes was attempting to start a conversation with Agenor. By the cop's calculations, Agenor must be a follower of St. George, a member of the Mangueira samba school (based on his place of residence, which he had seen in his records at the precinct), and a Flamengo soccer fan. He planned to talk with the prisoner about these subjects during the trip. Two of his hunches were right. But Agenor was no Flamengo fan, rooting instead for Vasco da Gama.

"I'm a Vasco supporter myself," Guedes said.

They talked about soccer and Carnival on the trip.

"Don't guess I'll see my Mangueira paradin' again anytime

soon," Agenor said, his eyes moist with tears. "Or Vasco at the stadium."

"You should've thought of that before doing something stupid," Guedes said.

"But I——" Agenor stopped talking, and wiped his eyes.

They arrived at the 14th, where Guedes signed the prisoner in and told the jailer to take him to the lockup. The 14th's lockup was even more crowded than at the other precinct. The records clerk showed up to verify that Guedes had brought Agenor, for he planned to take his statement that day.

"Not today," Guedes requested. "Leave it till tomorrow. I want to talk to him first."

"Ferreira wants to expedite the investigation," the clerk said.

"You can take his statement tomorrow," Guedes said. "Feed Ferreira some BS. He doesn't even know the guy's here." The clerk, who got along well with the cop, had no choice but to comply.

Guedes had other things to do, things having no connection to me or this story, which I won't relate here.

At night, when he got to his apartment, Guedes took a sheet of paper and jotted down:

1. Arrested for robbery (which he did not complete), confessed to homicide of which he wasn't even a suspect. Criminal record shows no previous robbery. Or homicide.
2. Boss of his cell, even though a coward.
3. Says he drove around with woman looking for place to commit rape. No previous record of rape.
4. He's a thief but fails to steal gold watch, claiming lack of time. (Had time to open deceased's purse.)
5. Has various chances to run away and doesn't.

On another sheet of paper:

1. Investigate phone call from precinct. (Who was Agenor talking to? Who did he order advised about his transfer to the 14th?)
2. Find out where the .22 came from. Where was it bought?
3. Thief, confidence man, fence, pimp, procurer, forger. No violent crimes. Just a con artist.

Next Guedes examined Agenor's rap sheet. He had committed crimes against property (Articles 155, 168, 171, 180), morals offenses (Articles 227 and 230), a family-related crime (Article 238), and a crime against validity of documents (Article 297). His criminal activity did not include a single "crime against the person," as stipulated in the penal code.*

He put the papers on his night table. My book *The Lovers* was there, but he didn't pick it up to continue the reading he had begun days earlier. I believe he'd come to the conclusion that the relation between an author's life and what he writes is such a superficial and untruthful one it wouldn't be worth his time to read four hundred pages and find out nothing. He lay down, but his was not the easy sleep of minor public employees who have done their duty. He awoke several times during the night and reread his notes, besides going to the bathroom to urinate.

*To whom it may concern: The crimes referred to are, in order: theft, unlawful appropriation, swindling, receiving stolen property; acting as intermediary for carnal acts of another, hooliganism; impersonation of a member of the clergy to perform a marriage; and forgery of a public document.

2

The next day Guedes arrived at the 14th even earlier than usual. He went to the lockup. The lockup was a large cell, packed with prisoners. Agenor was there, lying on a mat, with a light gray blanket covering his body. He was still sleeping.

"Take Agenor to my office," Guedes told the jailer.

Agenor was yawning as he came into Guedes's office.

"Did you sleep well?" Guedes asked.

"Yeah. I was real tired," Agenor said.

"Were you able to sleep all right? Wasn't the cell pretty full?"

"Yeah, but the guys there are great. We get along, nobody fights. You know how it is when everybody cooperates; life is good."

"Nice people. I can see that; they even found a mat for you. Want to go out for some coffee?"

The other policemen saw Guedes leaving with the prisoner, but the grubby cop was too respected for anyone to try to stop him or even criticize him for it.

They had coffee on Ataulfo de Paiva.

"Why did you kill the woman? That's not your style; you're a con man."

"It was crazy," Agenor replied.

"Tell me about it."

"I don't like talkin' about it, Mr. Guedes."

"You're going to have to talk to me about it." Softly, but irrefutably.

"I already told you what happened."

"Tell me again."

Agenor told his story again.

"How did you shoot her?"

"How did I shoot her?"

"Yeah. Take your time to think."

Agenor scratched his cheek. He had the habit of doing that when he was nervous.

"How do you shoot somebody? You point the revolver at her and shoot."

"Were you inside the car or outside?"

"Inside. I was sittin' beside her."

"Did you rest the gun against her body when you shot?"

"No. I don't remember. I was nervous, she was yellin' a lot."

"Had you ever shot anyone before?"

"No."

"Where did you get the .22?"

"I bought it from a guy that lives near me."

"Who?"

"I'm not gonna finger a buddy."

"You can tell me his name. I'm not going to do anything to him."

"Gibi."

"There's lots of Gibis in Mangueira. Tell me what he looks like."

"Light-skinned mulatto. Plays tambourine for the samba school. A good guy."

"OK. So you shot the woman. Then what?"

"Then I beat it."

"What about the cigarette case?"

"Oh, yeah, the cigarette case. I opened her purse and took the cigarette case."

"What about the watch?"

"What watch?"

"She was wearing a gold watch."

"I didn't see it."

"You were with the woman for a long time and she was driving the car, and you didn't see a solid gold watch on her wrist?"

"I didn't see it."

"And just why was it you decided to stop on that street?"

"I wanted to go to Tijuca Forest, and I thought that street went there."

"You wanted to go to Tijuca Forest to rape the woman?"

"Yeah."

"Did you ever rape anyone before? Your rap sheet doesn't show any rapes."

"It was gonna be the first. She was a real knockout, wasn't she?"

"Let's go back to the moment when you shot the woman. Tell me again what happened."

"We got to that street and I saw there wasn't any way out. I told the woman to back up. The car stalled and I got nervous and hit her. She started yellin' and I lost my head and shot her."

"Continue."

"After I shot, all I could think of was gettin' out of there. The car was stalled and I don't know how to drive. I took off."

"What about the cigarette case? You always forget the cigarette case."

"I opened her purse and took the cigarette case."

"You didn't see the watch."

"I didn't see the watch."

"Let's go back to the moment when you shot her. Want another cup of coffee?"

"Yeah. Thanks."

Guedes ordered two more coffees. They were standing up at

the counter of a bar. They were the only ones there. It was still quite early and the place had just opened. The cop and the prisoner looked like two friends chatting in a low voice about some private matter.

"You shot the woman. How was she yelling?"

"Just yellin'."

"Was she trying to get out of the car? Did she try to defend herself by attacking you? Every person yells in a different way; some tear their hair, others sort of shrink into themselves—everybody acts in their own way. What was she like? She must have been one of those who tear their hair, for you to get that nervous."

"And how."

"And how? And how what?"

"And how she tore her hair."

"The revolver. What did you do with the .22?"

"I dropped it somewhere."

"You dropped it somewhere."

"Uh, no. I mean, I put it in the woman's hand so it'd look like suicide."

"And you didn't see the gold watch."

"I put the revolver in her right hand. The watch must've been on her left."

"Do you know why I brought you here to this bar to talk about this matter?"

"No."

"To give you a chance to tell the truth. I'm giving you a break."

"Yes, you are, Mr. Guedes. Thank you very much."

"Meanwhile you lie through your teeth to me."

"No, sir."

"You say you don't know how to drive but I saw in your file that you used to be a cabby."

"But I—"

"Let me speak. You forced the police to arrest you for holding up the bakery so you'd have a chance to confess to killing the woman. A second-class chickenshit con man lying on a mat in lockup and being fanned. You think I'm some kind of idiot? You know I'm no fool, Agenor. You didn't kill that woman. Tearing her hair! Not a hair was out of place, you dummy; she looked as if she were on her way to a dance. And whoever shot her opened her silk blouse and shot her and then buttoned her blouse. You're a real son of a bitch. More coffee?"

"No." Agenor braced himself against the counter as if about to fall.

"Let's go to the precinct," Guedes said, and, as they walked, "If you want to run away, you can. But you don't want to run away, do you? You depend on others for orders and don't know if they want you to run away or not, so in case of doubt you do nothing."

Agenor didn't answer.

"They paid you to confess to killing the woman, they offered you protection, they had their bosses in the cell guarantee you a soft life in the lockup. But they're just waiting for you to make a statement at the hearing and for the clerk to get it all down on paper and have you sign the confession in front of two witnesses so everything'll be nice and official. That's what they're waiting for. You know why?"

Agenor didn't answer. His hands were shaking, and he grabbed Guedes by the arm.

"I don't know what you thought of this," Guedes continued. "By now they've already picked the chump who'll confess to killing you—'He tried to cornhole me, sir'—one of those boys in the lockup with you. And they'll use a noose made of old shirts or a sheet; knifing you would dirty the cell and there's little enough space as it is. I don't know how an old con man like you could fall for such a story."

Agenor sighed.

"The records clerk wanted to take your statement yesterday. I didn't let him. I don't know if he's involved in this. If you had given a statement yesterday, you'd already be dead. But you'll have to today, regardless. I can't stop it."

"I'll deny everything. I'll say I didn't kill the woman."

"You're dead just the same. How'd you get yourself into this mess?"

They were at the door of the precinct, but Guedes continued walking toward the Rowing Stadium. The stadium's door was open, and they went in and sat down in the bleachers. They sat there watching the racing boats practicing in the lake.

"My life was shit, and things are rough for people in my line of work," Agenor said.

"I know; only the really big con men make it."

"A man I know, a big shot in the Jacaré, said he was lookin' for a guy who knew how to talk, to confess to killing a society lady. Fifty thousand up front and fifty more later, plus a guarantee I'd go to Ilha Grande and they'd bust me out. The Jacaré people have a pipeline set up. Gettin' somebody out of Ilha's a piece of cake."

"I know. The only problem is that you weren't going to Ilha. You were going to Caju. Did you already get the dough?"

"Yeah. It's stashed."

"You're not going to get to spend it."

"You mean I'm fucked?"

"Yeah, you're fucked. Was it the Jacaré guy who gave you the dough?"

"Uh-huh. But it was a lawyer who told me what to say."

"Tell me about it."

"The Jacaré man told me to meet him at the Plataforma barbecue joint. When I got there he was at a table with a guy he

said was a lawyer. We ate lunch, and the lawyer told me everything I was supposed to do. He even drove me to the street
where the woman got killed."

"You know his name?"

"Mr. Jorge."

"What's his last name?"

"The rest of his name I don't know."

"Who'd you call from the precinct?"

"My wife. She was supposed to tell the lawyer I was bein'
transferred. We agreed ahead of time to warn him if anything
happened."

"What's his phone number?"

"Two four six six two one four."

"I'll tell you one thing: You guys really screwed up."

"Good thing too, or I'd already be history. Isn't there any way
to get me out of this?"

"I should tell you to make a statement telling the truth, the
whole story. I should promise you protection, but I know that
sooner or later they'll get you. I don't want your death on my
shoulders."

"But it will be. You know I'm gonna die and don't do anything."

The boats had left and the lake was deserted. The sun glis-
tened on the surface of the water.

"Do you have someplace to hide? Somewhere outside Rio?"

"Yeah, a long way from here. Are you gonna give me a
chance? Promise?"

"A con man talking about promises. Life is funny."

"I believe you. I won't be stupid enough to offer you money.
Swindlers hang out with other swindlers; even the mark is tryin'
a swindle. But we know when a guy is honest."

"You can go," Guedes said. "Don't pull any more foolish
stunts."

"The good guys *and* the bad guys after me, and you think I'm gonna slip up? God bless you."

"Leave God out of this."

"God bless you anyway."

"Get out of here before I change my mind."

A small sailboat pulled out from Piraquê and navigated toward Cantagalo Point. The sun was stronger now and Guedes began to feel the heat.

Agenor's flight didn't cause any great problems for the cop. Detective Ferreira called Guedes in and told him the Minister of Security was furious and that he'd probably be suspended. But days passed, and no suspension was published in the *Bulletin* and no inquiry into the escape was held.

Guedes continued his bird-dogging activities.

It wasn't difficult to find out the full name of Mr. Jorge, the lawyer who had set up the imposture in which Agenor had been the main player. His name was Jorge Delfim. He was part of a large firm that handled civil cases, mostly commercial and financial law. None of the members of the firm was a criminal lawyer. Which explains the screwup they pulled, Guedes thought.

He didn't call Mr. Jorge. He picked up the phone and dialed the home of Eugênio Delamare. It was the afternoon of the day he had let Agenor Silva escape.

"Is Mr. Eugênio Delamare there?"

Guedes was counting on luck. Besides the Principle of Perfection, he believed in another, Hohenstaufens's Principle of Risk Reward: The reward is always proportional to the risk— or, in plain English: Nothing ventured, nothing gained.

"Who's calling?"

"His lawyer, Jorge Delfim."

Eugênio Delamare was not long in coming.

"Mr. Delfim?" (So Jorge and Eugênio weren't close. Maybe he wouldn't notice the voice was different.)

"The man escaped," Guedes said.

"I know. The minister phoned me. We should have foreseen that. Our police are shit. I rang your office but they told me you were in São Paulo."

Guedes had the impression that Delamare was drunk. The idle rich always begin drinking at lunch.

"I just got back," Guedes said.

"What now?"

"We'll see if we can get a default judgment against him as your wife's murderer. Isn't that what you wanted—to establish the blame?"

"And the case closed," replied Delamare. "I don't want him showing up tomorrow saying he didn't kill her, understand?"

"Nothing to worry about."

"Those friends of yours will take care of everything?"

"Nothing to worry about."

"If you need more money let me know. Goodbye."

Guedes's investigations led him to another important discovery. Every night of late he had been covering the two possible paths taken by Delfina's killer as he fled Diamantina Street: first by Faro, down to Jardim Botânico; then a more complicated route, Itaipava to Benjamim Batista, and then alternating among the three streets perpendicular to Jardim Botânico: Abade Ramos, Nina Rodrigues, and Nascimento Bittencourt. And also the stairs that led to Pio XI Square.

It was a stroke of luck to run into the witness he had sought for so long (more sweat than luck). She was an elderly lady walking a dog. Her name was Bernarda.

When Denise Albuquerque arrived home from France, she wasn't expecting to find an invitation to go to the 14th Precinct.

Of course she didn't go. She sent a lawyer instead. But the cop wanted to see the woman and did not easily back down. I don't know if what happened was the result of an agreement with the lawyer or with Denise herself. The fact is that Denise made an appointment with the cop in her house.

She had just separated from her husband, and it was a matter of notoriety that she had won the largest financial settlement in Brazilian history. According to rumor, her husband had committed peccadilloes (like virtually all great financiers), and Denise had threatened to tell all at the divorce trial.

Denise liked the cop; she felt a certain tenderness toward poor, badly dressed people. Guedes liked her too, perhaps because of the frank way she answered his questions.

"I read the letter you wrote Dona Delfina."

"Isn't that a crime, opening someone else's mail? Or are the police allowed to do that?"

"They're not. But it was important for me to know Dona Delfina had a lover."

"I never thought that when Delfina had an affair it would be with a guy like that, a stuck-up mulatto. I always thought if she had an affair it'd be with somebody like Tony Borges. Tony was crazy about Delfina."

"Do you think that individual could have killed Delfina?"

"Who, the writer? No. Do you suspect him?"

"I suspect no one and everyone. Even her husband."

"I'm going to tell you something. Eugênio Delamare is from an old and very rich family; in both tradition and money they can only be compared to the Guinles. Both the men and the women always married money, the one exception being Eugênio's marriage to Delfina, but Delfina as a human being was a million times better than her husband. Eugênio is a bastard. When a guy from a good family is rotten he can be a bigger son of a bitch than anyone. It wouldn't surprise me if he ordered her killed. I'm going to tell you what happened to me when I spent a week at the Delamares' ranch in Mato Grosso. I never told this to anyone; you're the first person to hear the story. I was still married to Albuquerque, and he went too. I don't know what we women were doing there in the marshlands. The men spent the time hunting and fishing. As a matter of fact, I went along with them once and was horrified seeing them with their telescopic rifles killing defenseless animals. One day Delfina went for a boat ride with Albuquerque—I stayed behind because I get sick in boats—and Delamare offered to keep me company because they'd be gone nearly all day. When we were alone, at the first opportunity, Eugênio came on to me. I pretended not to understand what he wanted; after all, he was a friend of my husband. It was a very sticky situation. Know what he did? He grabbed me by force, in my room, and had me. He raped me, the bastard. I didn't have the courage to say anything to Albuquerque or Delfina. I told Albuquerque I was feeling very bad—and I really was—and that I wanted to go back to Rio. The next day we boarded our Lear jet, which was on the ranch's airstrip, and returned to Rio. That s.o.b. Eugênio went on pursuing us, inviting us to dinners, as if nothing had happened."

"Do you think he could have had Dona Delfina killed?"

"I don't know if he'd go that far, but it wouldn't surprise me. He knew that Delfina was having an affair with that writer, and he wasn't the kind of man to take it gracefully."

The meeting with Dona Bernarda:

"Aren't you afraid of being in the street this late at night?" Guedes asked when he ran into her. It was one in the morning, and Abade Ramos Street was deserted.

Dona Bernarda looked at him through her thick-framed glasses.

"I'm too old to be afraid. Besides, my Adolfo is sick and has to be walked at this hour and there's no one else to take him."

Guedes bent over and patted the dog's head. "What's wrong with him?"

"I don't know. At this time of night he starts to howl, and if I don't take him out he gets convulsions and drools all over himself and even worse, the poor dear. The veterinarian doesn't know what's wrong either. What about you—aren't you afraid to be in the street this late?"

"I'm a policeman," Guedes said. "I'm working."

Dona Bernarda was very observant. Yes, she had seen a man like the one the cop described; he had tripped over Adolfo, two houses up. Yes, of course she could recognize him. The date was quite easy to remember: it was Adolfo's birthday and she'd given him some candy—Adolfo was crazy about candy. She knew Adolfo couldn't eat candy, but once a year couldn't hurt that much. But it did. She wasn't likely to forget a day like that.

3

Meanwhile, in Iguaba, Minolta woke in the middle of the night and saw a shape standing beside the bed. Since it was very dark, all she could make out was the outline of the figure's white clothing, which shined phosphorescently.

"Who are you?" she asked, terrified.

"A friend," the shape said in a hoarse voice.

"What do you want?"

"Time is passing," the ghost said. And disappeared.

Minolta got up, threw some clothes in a small tote bag, and sat in a chair to await daybreak. That morning she caught a bus to Rio de Janeiro.

Arriving at Rio, she went to the travel agency where I had made my reservations for Falconcrest Retreat. She was told there wouldn't be any transportation to the retreat for three days. "To get to the retreat you have to take a special vehicle that leaves Pereiras once a week."

A young man who was listening to Minolta's conversation with the travel agent broke in to say that he had spoken that morning with their contact in Pereiras, the store owner, who had told him that the next day a special transport would be leaving to take a police detective to the retreat. It was known that a homicide had been committed at the retreat.

"That's what the shape was trying to tell me," Minolta said. "How do you get to Pereiras?"

"Do you have a car?"

"No."

"Ouch." The man scratched his head. "Look, like this. . . . Better write it down or you'll get lost."

Seeing there was no time to lose, as soon as she finished writing down the instructions the man had given her, Minolta left the agency in a run. On her way out she bumped into a man who was going in and had to grab him to keep from falling.

"Sorry," Minolta said.

"My fault," the yellow-eyed man in a grubby jacket said.

At the Novo Rio bus station Minolta caught a bus to Resende; from there, a bus to Queluz. In Queluz she took a bus to Areias, always following the directions of the young man at the agency. From Areias, a bus to Pereiras. Despite being immersed in deep thought, Minolta noticed that the man in the grubby jacket was on the same bus.

She got to Pereiras at nine o'clock at night, got off, and didn't see where the man went. She'd been traveling or waiting in bus stations since dawn, but she wasn't tired. It wasn't hard to find the little square described to her by the man at the agency; it was the only one in the small village.

She spent the night sitting on a bench in the square. At daybreak, as the birds began to sing in the trees, the man in the grubby jacket appeared. The sun was shining when a jeep arrived and three men got out.

"Have you been here very long?" one of them asked her.

"Are you going to the retreat?" asked another.

They were behind schedule, and Minolta's answer calmed

them. The bus to the retreat still hadn't arrived. The late-comers were the detective, the clerk, and the forensic expert from the Pereiras police. The detective was always late when he had to be somewhere very early. That day his wife, assisted by the clerk, had had to throw cold water in his face to wake him up.

V

THE
CURSE

1

Every novel suffers from a curse, one especially, among others: that of ending weakly. If this were a novel it would be no exception to the rule and would also have a second-rate ending. (Every novel ends feebly—*see Forster*—"because the plot requires to be wound up. Why is there not a convention which allows a novelist to stop as soon as he feels muddled or bored? Alas, he has to round things off, and usually the characters go dead while he is at work, and our final impression of them is through deadness.") It has been said (*see James*) that the novel's only obligation is to be interesting. But this, I repeat, is not a novel. Therefore (*see Nava*), "Fuck you, you asshole. Now listen."

Memoirs, like these I'm writing, also suffer from a curse of their own. Writers of memoirs are condemned to bitterness and lies. I began by saying I am a satyr and a glutton in order to rid myself of the anathema—no lies; I established this from the outset. I should mention parenthetically that beginning a book is no more difficult than ending it, as some claim, alleging that it's preferable to disappoint the reader at the end than have him stop reading at the beginning.

I took from my bookshelf, at random, twelve books by world-famous writers and read the opening sentences of each:

There is, as every schoolboy knows in this scientific age, a very close chemical relation between coal and diamonds.

Our prison stood at the edge of the fortress grounds, close to the fortress wall.

There was no possibility of taking a walk that day.

A small, rather smart, well-sprung four-wheeled carriage with a folding top drove through the gates of an inn of the provincial town of N.

Sitting beside the road, watching the wagon mount the hill toward her, Lena thinks.

Mother died today. Or, maybe, yesterday; I can't be sure.

Nunc et in hora mortis nostrae. Amen.

Here we are, alone again. It's all so slow, so heavy, so sad.

I am the doctor who is sometimes spoken of in rather unflattering terms in this novel.

Eh bien, mon prince, so Genoa and Lucca are now no more than private estates of the Bonaparte family.

For a long time I used to go to bed early.

It was the afternoon of my eighty-first birthday, and I was in bed with my catamite when Ali announced that the archbishop had come to see me.*

---

*Books and authors, by paragraph order: *Victory*, Conrad; *The House of the Dead*, Dostoyevski; *Jane Eyre*, Brontë; *Dead Souls*, Gogol; *Light in August*, Faulkner; *The Stranger*, Camus; *The Leopard*, Lampedusa; *Death on the Installment Plan*, Céline; *Confessions of Zeno*, Svevo; *War and Peace*, Tolstoy; *Swann's Way*, Proust; *Earthly Powers*, Burgess. All are foreigners and dead (with the exception of Burgess). Some are not my favorite authors. Authors who wrote in the Portuguese language are deliberately excluded, although Portuguese-language literature is in no way inferior to that of the aforementioned authors—i.e., English, Russian, French, and Italian. I repeat that, once this preliminary exclusion was made, the selection was random, books grabbed off the shelf by chance. To me there's no such thing as the ten, or one hundred, or one thousand masterpieces of world literature.

By coincidence, the sentences even seem to make some kind of sense, which proves the theory (if it doesn't already exist, I'm inventing it as of this moment) that words brought together, in any manner whatever, always exhibit a certain nexus. (*See Burroughs*.)

A novel, therefore, can start any way the author wishes. Can a book that begins "For a long time I used to go to bed early" interest the reader ab initio? Can anyone really want to know what a narrator who goes to bed early thinks? Or take this one: "The story of Hans Castorp, which we would set forth, not on his own account, for in him the reader will make acquaintance with a simple-minded though pleasing young man, but for the sake of the story itself, which seems to us highly worth telling—" This is how Mann begins *The Magic Mountain*. Could there be a sillier beginning for a book than this, in which the author admits that Hans, the main character, is a bore and that the author himself wants to tell the story out of love for his own compulsive talkativeness? The truth is that no book was ever not read for lack of an intriguing opening.

"Of everything that is written, I appreciate only that which someone writes with his own blood," said Nietzsche, for whom blood and spirit were the same thing. My first books were written with blood. Hidden in a house for ten years, it was inevitable that in my spirit would finally emerge the same revolt that impelled the Marquis de Sade.

In the years of imprisonment after I fled the asylum (you might say that I myself built the dungeon around me, which isn't far from the truth, but I had no alternative other than hiding like a wounded and pursued animal), I came to feel disdain for humanity in general and for powerful people in particular.

I asked Minolta to bring me books about the end of the world by nuclear war. I liked to imagine the catastrophe, the burn victims immediately decimated, the wounded lying writhing in agony without medical attention, those exposed to radiation who would slowly perish, and those who would die from hunger and thirst and cold and insanity even before the radiation took effect. I read what the Russians had written (Bayev, Bochkov, Moiseyev, Sagdeyev, Aleksandrov) and the Americans (Holdren, Sagan, Ehrlich, Roberts, Malone). The horrible end of the world was near, but neither the scientists nor the poets nor the saints could do a thing to prevent it. The species was living on borrowed time.

I was beginning to go mad when Minolta saved me. The human species may still be living on borrowed time, but at least madness is no longer knocking at my door. I don't want to think about hecatombs in a morbid fashion. Until the end comes, and to avoid its coming, man must love. That's what Minolta taught me. And that hope was conveyed to me in bed, fucking, and at the table, eating. The only way man can truly survive is by finding ever greater enjoyment in living. This is such an obvious view of salvation that it takes on the trappings of absolute stupidity.

I know I talk a lot, and that's why I've been called a conceited mulatto. Conceit, as everyone knows, is related to concept: that is, thought, notion. Yes, I'm conceited, in the sense of brazen, affected, cocksure, and also thoughtful, for I'm always thinking. The better the writer, the more conceited—that is, thoughtful— he is.

2

I was on the porch when the tractor arrived with Minolta, Guedes, and the policemen from Pereiras. Guedes's presence in a way undermined the joy I felt at seeing Minolta. He came up to me and said hello.

"I'm on vacation and didn't know where to go. Then I recalled you'd mentioned this place."

Of course I didn't believe him, even less after seeing him closet himself with Trindade in the administrator's office.

The policemen from Pereiras went by jeep to the bungalow where Suzy's body had been found. Sometime later the expert returned with Suzy's body wrapped in a black plastic bag. With Trindade's help he placed the body in the tractor.

The expert got in the jeep and went back to the bungalow. We stood watching that black bundle in the tractor wagon, both obscene and attractive in its fragile solidity. It gave off a pestilent odor—or was that my imagination? With the exception of Eurídice, who at Roma's advice had disappeared as soon as the tractor arrived with the policemen, we were all there, our number now increased by Guedes, who acted in the face of events with that distracted air cops and cats like to affect when extremely interested in something: First he watched a hummingbird suck sugar water from a colored plastic feeder hanging on the porch;

then he looked at a distant tree as if he saw a chimpanzee or a jaguar on one of its branches; he even yawned.

We heard the sound of the jeep. The three policemen were now in it. They got out beside the tractor and spoke in low voices. The forensic expert, carrying a pillowcase with an object inside, got into the wagon and sat down beside the black bundle, and the tractor slowly pulled away.

Trindade's office became the cops' work area. The detective from Pereiras had decided to take statements right there at the retreat, since there were no hotels in Pereiras where people could stay while the clerk did his work. I was the first.

Summarizing questions and answers, my statement went more or less like this (after the customary identification, etc.):

"Did you know the victim?"

"I met her here."

"You'd never seen her before?"

"Never."

"Were you with her the day before yesterday, the day she died?"

"I was with her the day before yesterday, yes."

"Where?"

"In her bungalow. I received a note asking me to go there to talk to her." I took the note from my pocket and gave it to the detective. Till that moment I was undecided whether or not to show the note. It was a sudden decision.

The detective read aloud: " 'The maid who brought breakfast is taking you this note. Eurídice is going horseback riding and I'll be at the bungalow all morning. Stop by. I need to talk to you. Suzy.' " He immediately handed the note to the clerk. "We'll keep this," he said, adding, "for your own good."

For my own good? What did he mean by that?

"What was it she wanted to discuss with you?"

I wasn't going to tell the detective anything about the story of Maria, the would-be murderer, whose real name must be

Eurídice. I had to make up some plausible story, which wouldn't be difficult for someone like me, a specialist in creating praiseworthy and believable cock-and-bull stories.

"She felt I had the gift—undeveloped, of course—of clairvoyance."

"What's that?"

"She also referred to it as clear vision. Let's call it the ability to see the future."

"And you have that ability?" A quick glance at the clerk.

"No. I can't even see the past straight, much less the future. But Suzy believed in such things. She also told me that Trindade had undeveloped mediumistic talents. Anyway, we talked a bit and she became discouraged by my skepticism, which I didn't display in words but which was evident nevertheless. The basic requisite to developing our gifts, she said in recrimination, is to believe in them. I wasn't in the bungalow very long."

"And you didn't see her after that?"

"No."

"When you were in the bungalow did you see a bronze statuette?"

"The owl? It was on the table in the living room."

"Whoever killed her used the owl as a blunt instrument," the detective said. "Several blows to the head, the first one most likely to the base of the skull. The expert thinks she died when that blow hit her."

The detective dictated some of my statements to the clerk. Others he must have considered irrelevant because he didn't record them.

"Do you suspect anyone?" he asked at one point.

"No," I replied.

Minolta was waiting on the porch for me to finish my statement. She was talking excitedly with Orion and Juliana. In another corner Roma, Vaslav, and Carlos were sitting in silence. Guedes was nowhere in sight. Carlos was called in to give his statement. He was worried; I could feel the tension in his body. His hands were shaking.

The entire morning was taken up by the statements, and nobody budged from the porch, not even Minolta, who had just arrived from her journey. One of the cops entered and left the interrogation room several times on mysterious and hurried errands.

The cops had lunch in the dining room, at a table removed from the other guests. Eurídice ate in her room. Trindade explained that she wasn't feeling well. For lunch there was a delicious armadillo stew, caught right there on the retreat, but the only one (besides the cops) who ate with gusto was me. The cops seemed unconcerned and laughed a lot, like people on vacation after completing a difficult task.

After lunch the cops locked themselves in the room that served as an improvised headquarters. They studied the statements. In additon to the guests, some of the staff had also given statements.

For obvious reasons, I invited Minolta to go with me to rest in my bungalow. She responded that she wanted to stay on the porch with the others, to see what was going to happen. There was a climate of mutual suspicion in the air, exchanges of oblique glances. The only person who appeared calm was Guedes the cop, who sat in a corner of the porch, pretending to doze.

Finally one of the cops came out of the room to summon Trindade. The cops spoke with Trindade with the door open. Then the detective and Trindade came over to the group of guests.

"The detective has a statement to make," Trindade said.

"Ladies and gentlemen. My colleagues and I have good reason to believe that we know who killed Dona Suzy."

This said, he fell silent, like a detective in a suspense film.

"Who was it?" asked Juliana, just as Roma opened her mouth, probably to ask the same question.

"The individual known as the Hermit," the detective said. He explained that the Hermit had been seen on the porch of Suzy's bungalow by a woman who worked in the laundry. He had his ear pressed against the door in a suspicious manner. And it wasn't one of the days that he came down to ride Belzebum. There was no reason for him to be at the retreat.

"I can't believe the man's a murderer," Carlos said.

"Horse tracks were found at the site where the body was discovered, tracks identical to those found in front of the bungalow. We're certain the tracks were made by the Hermit's horse."

"How do you know they don't belong to some horse here at the ranch?" Carlos asked.

"No horse at the ranch passed that way, and the marks have a distinguishing feature: One of the hooves is missing a shoe. And Alcides, our expert, examined every horse here and none of them is missing a shoe."

A moment of general reflection.

"What could the motive have been, rape?" I asked.

"No, robbery," the detective said. "According to what Dona Eurídice told us, the victim's jewels have disappeared. We still don't have a complete list of the stolen objects because Dona Eurídice is in no condition to make a statement, but missing so far are a gold chain with a beryl stone, a solid gold necklace shaped like a snake and encrusted with precious stones, two rings, also gold, one with a large diamond, and a bracelet."

"All that's left is to catch the man," the clerk added.

"To do so I'm going to ask for outside troops. It won't be easy. Mr. Trindade told me he knows these hills better than anyone.

But they'll get him. They've got people who were born and raised right here in the mountains."

Soon afterward the tractor carrying Suzy's body arrived. The cops got into the wagon and left, in that arrogant way cops have of simplifying things. First the detective calmed Juliana by saying that he didn't think the killer would have the courage to return to the retreat.

"What could that man want with the jewelry?" Carlos asked.

"To sell it," Juliana said.

"He has no need of money up there where he lives, in the middle of the woods," Carlos said.

"He may have stolen it for his own use. He must look good in earrings," someone said. The climate was becoming more relaxed. The guilty party, a stranger, had been discovered and would surely soon be punished. The world was back on track. A maid arrived with a tray of coffee.

"I ended up not carrying out my part in our little game," Orion said in a good humor.

"But I did mine. I wrote my story," Roma said.

"Then you were the only one. I don't think . . . did she write something?" Orion looked at me questioningly.

"Not that I know of." The story of Maria, the would-be murderer, told by Suzy, had nothing to do with our game.

"Then you won," Orion told Roma. "I'll confess one thing. My story is in my head, all in place, but when I sit down to write it I can't. I admit I was wrong; writing is harder than I thought. I mean, it requires a very great physical effort. I think the muscular effort is more than the mental. Isn't that so? Tell the truth." Before I could answer, the maestro continued, "If a person could think and have it go down on paper automatically, I guarantee my story would be marvelous."

"What's your story about?"

"Well, it's a love triangle. A famous conductor, the concertmaster of the orchestra, and his wife. Do you all know what the function of the concertmaster is in an orchestra?"

Everyone knew.

"Well, the conductor was the lover of the concertmaster's wife—"

"Why not the other way around?" Vaslav asked.

"He's upholding the conductor class. Adulterer yes, cuckold never," Roma said.

"Are you going to let me tell the story or not?"

"Please, let's allow him to talk," I said.

"One day the concertmaster discovered what was going on. It was a rehearsal day. The concertmaster accused the conductor, the two started to argue, and a fight broke out. In the fight the conductor destroyed the concertmaster's violin. I still don't know how the violin gets destroyed. I thought it might be at the rehearsal, with the conductor trying to kick the concertmaster but missing and hitting the violin."

"That would look rather funny. Why should the conductor kick the deceived husband?"

"Right. Which is why I abandoned the idea of kicking the violin. Anyway, somehow or other the concertmaster's violin is destroyed. The violin was a Janzen, but you don't know what that means. Everybody's heard of the Stradivarius, considered the greatest violin in the world and which no one has ever been able to imitate. Of course many violin makers attempted to copy the Cremona pattern, which passed through the Amatis and the Guarneris and was established by Antonio Stradivari. There were other famous names like Vuillaume, Fendt, Gilkes, Lupot, and Pique, who manufactured good instruments without ever attaining the superb quality of the Stradivarius. Am I boring you?"

"Not at all; I'm fascinated," said Minolta, who liked to learn things.

"This is where the Janzen comes into the story. Gustav Janzen was born in Russia but came to Brazil as a boy, where he lived in Santa Catarina. At thirteen he built his first violin, probably a crude thing; we have no way of knowing. He worked as a cabinetmaker and began his study of acoustics quite young. He had learned of the history of the Stradivarius and, in an audacious act of youthful folly, decided to construct a violin as good as that of the great master from Cremona. For fifty years Janzen researched the construction of that violin. At one period in his life he lived in Canada, but he didn't take to the cold climate and returned to Brazil, settling in Mato Grosso. It's said he went to Mato Grosso because it was good for his lungs, but there's another version that maintains that Janzen had discovered that the sun of Mato Grosso is the best in the world for drying the violin's varnish, even better than in Cremona. The thing is that it was in Mato Grosso that he finally achieved the feat that famous violin makers through the centuries had attempted in vain: to build a violin equal to the Stradivarius."

"How wonderful," Roma said. "I have the greatest admiration for obsessive people like that."

"The Stradivarius's structure isn't impossible to copy, nor is it difficult to master the principles of its acoustics. The materials needed are rare but obtainable. The problem for Stradivarius imitators, as for imitators of any of the great Cremona masters, is in the varnish. No one has ever managed to make an identical varnish. In recent decades Nobel laureates in chemistry, craftsmen, voodoo practitioners, artists, mathematicians and their computers, NASA scientists, whatever—all have been brought together to try to make an identical varnish, without success. Well then, they say that Janzen discovered the secret formula for the varnish from del Gesu himself. Janzen won't talk about it. What's definite is that he manufactured a violin that many consider better than the Stradivarius. The first time a Janzen of that quality was used was in a concert at Cecília Meireles Hall, in 1983. The honor went to the violinist Jerzy Milewski. Milewski used to perform his concerts on a Camilo Camini, a violin built in 1710, worth a fortune, but someone took a Janzen to him and Milewski gave up the Camini to play the Janzen. He was so enthusiastic about the quality of the new violin that he bought one to give to Isaac Stern. Currently Menuhin, Ricci, the greatest violinists in the world are using Janzens. Now do you see the importance of the instrument that the protagonist in my story broke with a kick?"

"It can't be with a kick. It makes no sense," Roma said.

"How about a punch? Is that all right?" Minolta asked.

"Could a punch break a violin? What wood are violins made of?" Vaslav asked.

"Certain hardwoods such as ebony, for example, or brazilwood, used in the bows. Speaking of that, Janzen also discovered other woods, like the faveiro, a tree common in the central part of Brazil, to make the bows. Could a punch break it? I think so but I'm not sure; no one would ever have the courage to hit a violin."

"Except your seducer-conductor. What about your violin? What kind is it?"

"Mine's a Guadagnini from 1780, a precious thing. If I lost my violin I think I'd die of grief," Orion said. "But getting back to Janzen, he wrote a book, *Luftsäulenraum, Akustik und Geigenbau*—"

"Hold on, didn't you say he was Russian?"

"He was born in a city settled by Germans, his mother tongue was German, and he spoke German at home when he was small, here in Brazil. But in this book Janzen, besides stating that he discovered the acoustical laws of Stradivarius—he says nothing about the varnish—declares that the violin goes through several crisis points, true evolutionary variations, before achieving its maturity. The first, after six hours of use. The second, more furious, after being played for sixty hours. Then the violin goes into a depression from which it emerges only after eight to ten hours of exercise. A violin, one might say, only attains its highest potential after sixty years of life, and therefore we can't know yet if Janzen really is the new Stradivarius. But for some reason, the great violinists who've had the opportunity to use it once couldn't put it down. Sixty years from now—I heard this from the mouth of Milewski, and I think Lehninger said the same thing—its perfection and excellence will be shown to be without equal."

"You were going to put all that in your story?"

"Of course not. Professional distortion is a very unpleasant thing. My enthusiasm carried me away. I was going to concentrate more on the love triangle. It must be a distressing sensation to discover that your wife is with another man."

"I don't know if distressing is the right word," I said.

"Some go around shooting," Roma said.

"I think it varies from person to person," Juliana said.

At that instant Carlos, who had remained silent, got up from his chair and, after looking at me as if he wanted to say something, left the porch. In the corner of the porch Guedes buttoned his grubby jacket because, as always at twilight, it was starting to get cold.

"An affair with the concertmaster's wife wouldn't have caused the conductor pangs of conscience, but breaking the Janzen—with a kick, punch, whatever—left the conductor in a state of collapse. He knew how much the concertmaster loved his violin; he had witnessed the concertmaster's artistic development since he began using the Janzen. The concertmaster, who was a good musician (that's why he was number one in the orchestra), had coaxed a fantastic sound from the violin. The entire orchestra had benefited from that; each piece of music was executed with greater brilliance and purity. And the conductor knew this had come about because of the concertmaster's Janzen. The conductor began to suffer unbearable guilt; he began to waste away, so great was his contrition. Every genius has an in-genuous side."

"They say Mozart was an idiot," Roma said.

"All geniuses are idiots."

"Newton wasn't."

"Does that mean an idiot can be an artistic genius but not a scientific genius?"

"Einstein was an idiot."

"Wagner was an idiot. Beethoven was a deaf idiot."

"Flaubert was an idiot."

"Who isn't an idiot?"

"Dona Rizoleta," I said. "No idiot could make an armadillo stew like the one she made today."

"Let's allow Orion to finish his story," Minolta said.

"I'm lost. Where was I?"

"The conductor was starting to waste away from contrition over breaking the Janzen of the husband he was cuckolding."

"Oh, yes. He goes into a depression and his friends want to send him away for sleep therapy; they want him to undergo analysis; they want him to take a trip."

"What about the deceived husband?"

"I confess that I didn't know what to do with him, so I dropped him. He disappears from the story as soon as the violin is broken."

"Too bad," I said. "Deceived husbands have an interesting pathetic side: lost illusion and confidence, the betrayal they suffer—they deserve more attention, but even amateurs like you leave them by the wayside."

"Right. The conductor gets worse and worse and arrives at the point where he loses interest in music. He becomes irres-olute, spends his days in bed, doesn't bathe, doesn't shave."

"Was he married or single?"

"I didn't work that out. Maybe it would be better if he were single. Single men, for unexplained reasons, go crazy more than married men."

"So he got really bad, went crazy, went insane, and that's how the story ends?"

"He didn't really go insane and the story can't end here because I still haven't used the theme I was given, the theme selected by Gustavo."

"What's your theme?" Roma asked.

"We'll see. Our conductor, then, had sunk into the depths of depression when he decided to take a friend's suggestion and remove himself to the bucolic tranquillity of a ranch like this one here. I planned to describe everything I've seen—the landscape, the people, animals—in short, relate life here at the retreat, to flesh out my story. That's what a good writer does, isn't it? He uses people, incidents, settings from real life in his books, doesn't he?"

"He uses them, but he doesn't abuse them. A writer can be considered good only when he can, first, write without inspiration and, second, write using only his imagination."

"A rule I'm not obliged to follow," Orion said. "So here's our conductor, in the throes of a soul-searching depression, at lunchtime, looking at the armadillo stew they've served him, feeling a certain nausea at the food, unhappy and wanting to die."

"I think that's overdoing it," Roma said.

"At twilight—twilight in the story is like here, a pinkish light spreads over the mountain, giving a dreamlike touch to the landscape, but for him it was a nightmare—the conductor's despair increases. That's when he's convinced he's going to die—"

Roma interrupted. "I still think it's too dramatic. After all, all the guy did was break a violin."

"A Janzen, don't forget. Pains of the soul are very subjective—as Counselor Acácio said," Orion said quickly, seeing that Roma was about to interrupt him again. "The conductor remained on the porch of his bungalow, without the strength to go to dinner, without the will to live. Night had fallen, so dark he couldn't see the very hand that rested on his forehead to support his head. Then he heard a sound coming from the darkness, an odd sound like a tuning fork, followed by isolated voices, rising and falling sounds that stopped suddenly. The silence lasted only a short time; a harmonious chorus of voices filled the night and seemed to rise toward the firmament. The conductor rose from his chair and walked through the darkness, orienting himself by the voices as if seeing the ground he trod, until he came to the edge of a lake. There the indescribable beauty of the chorus could be heard in all its unsurpassable grandeur. He had already heard the greatest and most harmonious choruses in the world, some of which he himself had directed, but none had left him so moved. At this moment of ecstasy, the moon appeared in the heavens and enveloped the lake in shimmering silver light. Now the conductor could see the singers. They were about fifty toads, grouped around a toad sitting on a rock. They all looked toward this toad, who appeared larger than the others and who with movements of his grotesque head, like a God, directed this fantastic batrachian chorus."

"Bravo!" I exclaimed.

"So your theme was the toad? Just like mine?" Roma said.

"Just like everyone's. The theme for everybody was the toad," I said.

"And then? What happened?" Minolta asked.

"Well, the conductor, seeing that these toads were capable of creating such beauty and harmony in the middle of the forest, learned a lesson: The greatest joy a man can have—"

"Or a toad." It was Roma again.

"—is to create that which is beautiful. And so he went back to his orchestra, made his peace with the concertmaster, and they lived happily ever after—in a ménage à trois, if you prefer, Roma. It's a fairy tale of sorts, or would be if I had written it."

"I think you did reasonably well. You didn't write it, but you told it. Oral literature counts, doesn't it, Gustavo?"

"No. The bet was about writing. Any gossip can tell a story."

"How about Caterina Benincasa?" Orion asked.

It was a good question, one I didn't get to answer. Trindade came onto the porch breathlessly to say that Carlos had ordered Belzebum, the wild quarter horse, saddled up and had galloped off, no one knew for where. This had happened over an hour earlier and Trindade was worried. It would soon be nightfall and he was afraid Carlos would get lost on the mountain. There had already been one tragedy like that; a rider got lost and wasn't found till a week later, dead. He and the horse had fallen into a ravine. These mountains were treacherous, etc.

While this was going on, Guedes the grubby cop maintained a discreet silence. Just what was it he wanted? Why was he really here?

Roma ran back to her bungalow and brought her story.

"Don't show it to anyone," she said.

Night was falling. I took Minolta by the arm and told her it was time to do she knew what.

Someone wrote that the old novels were the good ones. Their heroes weren't forever engaged in feverish and grotesque—I believe the word was different, something to do with the circus—screwing. But how could they do any type of screwing at all when they were like cartoon animals, dolls with eyes, a nose, ears, hands, fingers, everything but genitalia, capable only of expressing platonic or metaphorized passions? My heroes, and I myself, have sex and engage in libidinous and pleasurable activities whenever possible. I am a delicate man who is horrified by coarseness, a man who has great consideration for people, and my desire for women is a form of consideration, of attention, of respect, of generosity. Even the feminists know that.

As soon as we got into the bungalow Minolta and I took off our clothes. I grabbed her and hooked her around my hips; her long muscular legs were perfect for it. She crossed her feet over my kidneys and the warm, wet lips of her pussy opened pulsatingly, desiring my prodigious member that would penetrate and pierce her to her depths. Oh, oh! My mouth was filled with saliva! We walked around the room in what might be called peripatetic fornication. "Yes, sink into me like those damned ticks, oh, so good! that's right, my love. . . . Do you want to go outside, fuck under the refulgent mantle of the stars? Oh, oh! Let's go there, naked as kangaroos, hold back your orgasm, wait for the stars a second longer; there! Here they are, many have already died a thousand years ago and all that remains of them is their light traveling through space! Do you want us to come together? Sing, toads! Now! Goddam! Omigod! I'm coming, heavenly dome, I'm coming!"

After some time Minolta said, "I'm getting cramps in my legs."

"Must be from the cold. We've been out in the open a long time."

"Aren't you tired of carrying me?"

"Sweetheart, I never get tired when I'm making love. But maybe we'd better go in so I can read the story that Roma wrote."

"Did she turn you on?"

"Yes. She still does. You know all pretty women turn me on."

"Did you screw her?"

"No."

"Did you try?"

"No. So much has happened. I was bitten by ticks; you can't tell now, but I was all swollen. Then that woman was killed. . . . Would you believe they suspected me? I'd been at her place, where I heard a strange story. Suzy's manner made me nervous. Maybe she knew about my case."

"What case?"

"The gravedigger, the asylum, all that stuff."

"That happened a long time ago, love. Twenty years."

"Did you see the disappointment on Guedes's face? I think he believed I killed Suzy. He's dying to prove I killed somebody, whoever it is."

Our naked bodies were cold. With Minolta still wrapped around my hips, we went into the bungalow. I put Minolta on the bed and we fucked again. Then I got the sheets of paper Roma had given me. Minolta picked up the first and only pages I had succeeded in writing of Bufo & Spallanzani.

"This is all you've written in all this time?"

"Yes. I told you things have been complicated."

I began reading Roma's text.

"You know something?" Minolta said.

"What?" I put down Roma's papers and looked at Minolta. She looked at me with the loving expression she always used when she discovered one of my shortcomings.

"This is pretty bad, love," she said. "What happened to you?"

"It's bad?"

I took the two sheets of paper from her hand. I read: "The sage Spallanzani contemplated, from his window, the cathedral of St. Geminiano—" etc.

"It *is* bad," I said when I finished.

"What's with you? Do you miss your computer?"

"Maybe. But it's not just that. I think the end is coming. The time to do memoirs, an old man's writing."

"You're barely past forty," Minolta said. "Don't talk foolishness. We ought to lock the door. The killer might show up."

I closed the door. But I didn't think the Hermit would return, not after what he'd done. I went back to reading the story Roma had written.

"What about that Carlos fellow? Where do you think he went?" Minolta asked.

"I have a hunch."

Minolta didn't want to know what it was. I continued reading Roma's story. It was in tiny handwriting. I detest reading anything handwritten. When I finished reading this story about toads, Nietzsche's phrase came to mind (the next pseudonym I adopt, if I ever have to go into hiding again, will be Frederick William—but that's a subject for some other time). As I was saying, his phrase came into my head: "It is in that which your nature has that is savage that you reestablish the best of your perversity, by which I mean your spirituality."

3

Roma's story, like the one Orion had told, was autobiographical. I think I already said that. What a strange coincidence had made me give them that theme! I was writing a story of toads and men, but I didn't necessarily have to give them that theme for our game.

"What do you think?" Minolta asked when she saw I'd finished reading.

"If it weren't so long it could perhaps be considered an interesting confession," I said. "Want to read it?"

"What horrible handwriting," Minolta said, without taking the paper. "Does she talk about the toad?"

"Yes. And it explains why she got so nervous when she saw the theme I'd chosen for her."

"Give me a summary," Minolta said, resting her head on my chest.

"Well, there are these two ballet dancers. They meet, still quite young, at the ballet school of the Municipal Theater of Rio de Janeiro. She is rich and he is poor. His mother makes his dancing shoes. Vaslav—his real name is Sílvio— possesses great physical vigor and even greater technical virtuosity and can do the *entrechat dix* or the *entrechat royal*, which consists of leaping and crossing the legs ten times before landing, something few dancers in the history of ballet have achieved. Maybe only Nijinsky. Then a guy enters the story— I don't know if he's the villain—an Argentine named Ricardo Berlinsko, choreographer and artistic director of the Colón, in Buenos Aires, a former dancer, a homosexual who dyes his hair."

"Is he the villain because he's homosexual or because he dyes his hair?"

"He also has very thin legs and probably had plastic surgery on his face. But Roma recognizes that he's a charming, erudite, and intelligent man."

"Is Roma her real name?"

"No. But I want to go on calling her that. I like the name. Berlinsko, who attends a rehearsal of Sílvio's in Rio, invites him to go to Buenos Aires with him. They go. Under Berlinsko's guidance the young Sílvio develops his technique and talent even further. He begins frequenting Buenos Aires high society. I'll skip the part describing socialite parties. Rich people's parties are the same everywhere in the world. But there's one character who says something interesting: 'I'm like that Orson Welles character: If I throw away a million dollars a year, know how long before I'm poor? Sixty years.' I like prodigals."

"Who says that, Berlinsko?"

"No. Berlinsko is an artist. It's said by one of those superrich types who never worked a day in their lives, like our Eugênio Delamare."

"Your voice sounds funny inside there, in your lungs," Minolta said, turning her head and placing her ear against my chest.

"There's a huge section about the decadent habits of the rich. But rich people snorting cocaine is too much of a commonplace, so I'll skip that section. There's also a part where

Sílvio dresses as a woman, in clothes copied from a Gains-borough painting."

"High-class people," Minolta said.

"Under Berlinsko's direction Sílvio succeeds in doing the *entrechat onze*, which we should perhaps call the *entrechat Sílvio*, and other complicated steps. He's considered a genius; people come to watch him rehearse. Berlinsko prepares a sensational debut for him. Now I'll read you what Roma wrote: 'Ricardo wanted Sílvio to dance the same program, on his debut on May seventeenth, that Nijinsky had danced in his debut in Paris on May 17, 1909—exactly the same repertoire, which consisted of *Le pavillon d'Armide* by Tcherepnin, a divertissement entitled *Festin*, and Borodin's *Prince Igor*. The choreography was the same that Fokine had done for the Russian's debut.' "

"What's a divertissement?"

"Well, that *Festin* one, according to what's written here, is a kind of arrangement based on music of several Russian composers, Rimsky-Korsakov, Tchaikovsky, Glazunov, and on a *pas classique hongrois*."

"I like it," Minolta said, laughing. "A la mode."

"The original sets and costumes of Kerovine, Benois, and Bakst done for Nijinsky's debut in Paris were copied. Only a person as meticulous as Berlinsko, Roma says, could success-fully execute a project as crazy as that."

"Was Berlinsko going with Sílvio?"

"Well, Roma doesn't make that clear, but I think so. Sílvio's dancing shoes are now made of the finest plush, and he has dozens of them, French and Italian. There's always a dressing room reserved for his exclusive use. As the date of the debut approaches, rehearsals extend to fill the entire day. Dancers, choreographers, wardrobe people, set designers, and all that immense entourage of people involved in the production of the spectacle begin taking their meals in the theater. Of them all, the one who rehearses with the greatest dedication is Sílvio. Daily in his exercises he destroys several sets of shoes, maniacally repeating complicated steps like the *grand fouetté à la seconde*. Et cetera."

"You always told me you hated ballet, and now you tell this story drooling all over yourself. I can guarantee you're adding to what you're reading."

"Roma's text is interesting. You should read it. I'm not adding a thing." I placed the papers in my hand in front of Minolta's face.

"I don't want to. You read it to me. Or better yet, go on with the summary."

"Blah, blah, blah, Sílvio isn't sleeping well, he's very nervous. Roma and Berlinsko think it's the result of the natural tension that Sílvio must be experiencing on the eve of such an important debut. On May seventeenth, Berlinsko says, Sílvio will be known as the greatest dancer in the world, comparable only to Nijinsky."

"Is Nijinsky the one who went crazy and starting talking to God?"

"That's him. So, on May seventeenth everything was ready, with sets and costumes carefully copied from the original 1909 production. The Colón itself had undergone a modest remodeling, not that it needed it, but because of Berlinsko's superstition that anything done to the Châtelet in Paris at the time of Nijinsky's debut should be done to the Colón. Interesting guy, that Berlinsko."

"You think all that's true?"

"I haven't the slightest doubt, sweetie. Do you think Roma has the imagination to make up something like this? Sílvio arrives at the theater early, three hours before the show. On stage, behind closed curtains, he does exercises for an hour and a half, just as Nijinsky had done in 1909. In Roma's words, 'There on that dark and empty stage he was not just a man; he was sublime. There was a moment when he hovered in the air after a *grand jeté* like a bird, like an angel.' After the exercises Sílvio locks himself in his dressing room with his makeup man, a Hungarian who had worked with Zeffirelli, and the hairdresser, both of whom came directly from Alexandre's Parisian salon. When the makeup is done, the costume designer comes in with her assistants, and they dress Sílvio in his outfit for the first ballet, which is—let me check— yes, *Le pavillon d'Armide*. All these preparations end five minutes before the curtains go up. The theater is packed; people have come from all over the world, from the most distant places, to see this new phenomenon of dance. At nine o'clock everything is ready for the show to begin. The maestro, the famous Levine, come especially from New York for the occasion, ascends the podium to delirious applause, an indication of the climate of enthusiasm in the theater. The lights go down and the first strains of *Le pavillon d'Armide* are heard. The orchestra, possessed by the excitement that has taken hold of everyone that night, creates a sound of such bravura and brilliance for that mediocre overture that when it's over the sophisticated and proper public of Buenos Aires applauds with fervor.''

"Bravo!" Minolta said.

"Again I read Roma's words: 'Fokine's choreography demands that the dancer, as soon as he comes on stage or very shortly thereafter, execute a *grand jeté en tournant*.' ''

"What's that?"

"I think he jumps with his legs straight out in front while making a complete turn in the air, or a series of turns. Let's see. Blah, blah, she doesn't explain; she talks about *tours en l'air, pliés*, and other things, but I'm not going to read that. I'll limit myself to the drama. So, Sílvio has to make that great whirling leap, and do you know what happened? He's stuck to the ground as if made of lead, immobile, before the dumb-founded gaze of all spectators, dancers, musicians. After a few moments of astonishment the crowd, first in the second balcony, then in the entire theater, begins to boo. It was a horror, Roma says. Levine doesn't know what to do; some of the dancers flee the stage. Then the curtains are rung down and someone from the Colón management comes to the proscenium and says that due to sudden illness suffered by the leading dancer the show will not be presented."

"How embarrassing," Minolta said.

"Roma takes Sílvio home and calls a doctor. The doctor says Sílvio has manifested latent schizophrenia and suggests elec-troshock therapy. Another doctor says that Sílvio had an attack of manic-depressive psychosis and suggests massive doses of drugs. Sílvio, the whole time, seems to be dreaming with his eyes open."

"Maybe he was so fond of Nijinsky that he decided to flip out like his idol," Minolta said.

"No one comes to see him; he's like a leper with AIDS. Not even Berlinsko will have anything to do with him. Finally Roma brings Sílvio back to Brazil. I forgot to mention that Roma, as she herself clarifies here, is a very rich woman."

"She looks like a rich woman," Minolta said.

"What does a rich woman look like?" I asked.

"A mixture of arrogance and boredom."

"That's a wretched cliché."

"Just because it's a cliché, does that mean it isn't true?"

"Every morning Roma takes Sílvio to walk along the sidewalk of Ipanema beach. Madness seems to have made Sílvio even more handsome. Every woman that passes looks at him; even joggers turn their heads to see the beautiful man a bit longer. Since Brazilian doctors have confirmed that he's an incurable schizophrenic, all that's left to Roma is to seek help in the world of magic, voodoo, the supernatural—where there are even more charlatans than in medicine. She goes to voodoo sites recommended to her, from umbanda to quimbanda, consults fortune-tellers and mediums who 'embody' the most diverse and preposterous 'entities.' One day Roma takes Sílvio to a woman with great powers, named Santinha, in Caxias, on the outskirts of Rio de Janeiro. Now I'll read what Roma wrote: 'When I saw Santinha I was shocked. She was a little girl, ten years old or even younger. She had long hair that reached to her waist in little curls; she was very pale, her hands with very thin fingers'—I'm reading it exactly as Roma wrote it—'and wrists so delicate they gave the impression that they would break at the slightest effort she made. Her lips were grayish and her widely spaced teeth, all her widely spaced teeth, gave me the idea of a large white bat or a badly done angel. Sílvio and I sat down; she remained standing, and I noticed that she saw at once that it was he, Sílvio, who needed help. She did not look at me for an instant. She went up to Sílvio and cradled his head between her tiny rickety breasts. Her body began to tremble and her hair stood on end as if she were being lashed by a strong wind. But nothing happened to Sílvio; it was Santinha who became disturbed and exhausted. There was no time to feel disappointment at this initial failure. She immediately left the room and returned at once, carrying in her hand an enormous toad that—' "

"There's the toad. It took long enough to make an appearance," Minolta said.

" 'An enormous toad that she held by the neck'—I'm still reading Roma's text—'or whatever the place behind a toad's head is called. Held in this way, the toad stuck out its leg and looked enormous, immense. When it came into the room, carried by Santinha, the toad looked at me, at my face, then at Sílvio, as if it knew us, as if it knew who we were and what we were doing there—a look of intelligence, of conspiracy, a human look, terrifying. Santinha stood before Sílvio with the toad in her hand. Get up, she told Sílvio. Take it, she said, and gave Sílvio the toad to hold. Sílvio held the toad in both hands, placing the disgusting snout of the animal at the same level as his face. Sílvio and the animal stared into each other's eyes, and I noticed a fleeting smile pass over Sílvio's lips. Then he brought the toad's head to his face, each always staring into the other's eyes, closer and closer, and the lips of one and the lips of the other came nearer, and to my horror and revulsion the toad stuck its immense tongue in Sílvio's mouth, in a long and passionate kiss.' "

"Ugh! I'd rather stay a schizophrenic my whole life," Minolta said.

"Let me finish: 'Then a bright red light, as if we had stepped into a tube of neon gas, flooded the room with a brilliance so strong it blinded me, and for moments I could not see Sílvio, or the toad, or Santinha. Little by little my vision returned to normal and I saw Sílvio, still in scarlet half-light, reverently hand the toad to Santinha, who left the room carrying the animal, but not before it gave me a last, knowing look.' A lovely passage, I must admit."

"Is that all?"

I arranged the papers with Roma's minuscule handwriting and placed them on the night table.

"Well," I said, "after that Sílvio got well and went back to dancing. It's a story with a happy ending."

"Do you believe her?"

"Of course I do. Have you forgotten what we did with that toad twenty years ago? The *Bufo marinus*? Ceresso? Memory's a weak thing!"

"Did he stop being a homosexual?"

"Roma doesn't say. But what's that got to do with happiness?"

"Could he go crazy again?"

"All you need to go crazy is to be sane. The healthier you are, the more severe the attack of insanity." I put that reasoning together myself. "Confessions bore me, did you know?"

But sweet Minolta was snoring at my side. It wasn't exactly a snore; it was that little sound women make in deep sleep. How good it is to sleep! I thought. And I slept.

4

The next morning, when we got to the dining room of the Big
House for breakfast (I was late for obvious reasons; I now had
a woman sleeping with me), everyone was already there, even
Eurídice, at Sílvio and Roma's table (we'll go on calling her
that). At another, Orion and Juliana. Only Carlos was missing.

Minolta ate very little, and I had already finished her breakfast
when Trindade came into the room and said he'd seen Carlos
and the Hermit, on horses, coming down the mountainside. He
thought they were heading for the Big House. Everyone got up
and ran to the porch, with me carrying a plate of cheese bread
and corn muffins.

There they came, already in the meadow extending beyond
the Big House, in a trot that became a gentle gallop when they
saw us on the porch. The two horsemen passed in front of the
porch and disappeared in the direction of the stables.

"They went away," Juliana said, fifteen minutes later. But at
that moment both of them, Carlos and the Hermit, reappeared
from the stables. They were talking, or rather Carlos was talking
and the Hermit was listening.

They made a dramatic entrance on the porch, covered with
dust and mud.

"We went to take care of the horses," Carlos said. "We rode
all night, and they were exhausted."

No one answered. Carlos bit his lips. I noticed, for the first time, that he was completely hairless, like an Indian—that is, if there could be an Indian with such delicate white features. Despite his having ridden all night, there wasn't the slightest sign of a beard on his face. Finally Juliana broke the silence.

"Is it raining?" An incongruous question, for the sun was shining outside.

"On the hill it is," Carlos said.

"It rains a lot there," the Hermit said. He had a heavy, rough voice, a disconnected way of speaking, like someone not in the habit of talking.

Another silence.

"Tell them," Carlos said. His voice held a secret suffering.

The Hermit scratched his beard.

"Go on," Carlos said.

"No," the Hermit said. I had the impression that he meant he didn't know how to tell his story.

"Besides coming here to exercise Belzebum every week, there are occasions when he secretly meets Dona Belinha, who works in the kitchen," Carlos said. Undecided and unhappy, the pale youth fell silent.

"Oh, my God!" Eurídice said. A thin sob made its way from her throat.

Suddenly everything was clear to me. Whan an imbecile I'd been! I'd had all the pieces of the puzzle and hadn't put them together. Now I understood everything. I knew who Maria was, the woman referred to in the story Suzy had told me in the bungalow the day she was killed. I even knew who had killed her.

"Go on," said Guedes, who had appeared from somewhere or other. He was the only calm person on the porch.

"Dona Belinha didn't show up for our meeting. I took my horse to the creek for water," the Hermit said.

"Is your horse missing a shoe?" Guedes asked.

"Yes."

"Go on," Guedes said, softly but with authority.

"Then when I was on my way back, I heard shouts in one of the bungalows. I went to see what it was. It was two people arguing. I heard a scream. I went to the porch and I saw everything. Then I left. It was none of my business."

"What did you see?"

"One girl hit the other in the head with that doll. I didn't think she'd killed her. It was none of my business, so I left. My place is up there."

"It wasn't intentional, I swear it wasn't," Eurídice murmured, tears running down her face. "She started saying bad things about you, said she was going to tell everybody who you were."

"That didn't matter in the least," Carlos shouted.

"I didn't think you wanted anyone to know," Eurídice said, sobbing.

Maria-Carlos took Eurídice in her arms.

"What did it matter if they knew I'm a woman? I'm a woman, are all of you satisfied?" said Maria-Carlos, looking at us with hatred. I imagined her dressed as a woman, in high heels, displaying the physical splendor of her athletic body, which I now took notice of, disguised under the loose clothes she wore, inflaming the hearts of men and women who saw her pass with her "stride of unsettling elegance." I thought of Guimarães Rosa's Diadorim, another woman who masqueraded as a man, but I saw at once that, other than the disguise and their equestrian skills, there was no resemblance between the two.

We were all perplexed, excited, and confused—all but Guedes the cop. Everyone had understood the story, up to a certain point. Carlos was a woman disguised as a man, and there existed between him—I mean her—and Suzy and Eurídice a hitherto clandestine relationship of love and jealousy that had ended in death. We all stood there wide-eyed and hardly breathing. I alone knew that Maria-Carlos had tried to kill her husband,

and I intended to keep that secret, a decision reinforced by the pathetic sight of Eurídice crying on Maria's shoulder.

"Can I leave now?" the Hermit asked. The question was directed to Guedes.

"Let me speak to the detective in Pereiras first, to cancel the warrant on you."

While Guedes left for the room housing the radio that Trindade used to contact Pereiras, I said to him, "Tell Trindade to get the wagon ready. I want to leave here as soon as possible."

"So do we," said the other guests.

I went with Minolta to the bungalow. We packed our bags.

"Aren't you relieved?" Minolta asked.

"No. I'm worried about Guedes."

"Why worried? Are you hiding something from me?"

"What could I be hiding from you?"

"Don't pay any attention to that idiot of a cop," Minolta said.

"He's no idiot."

The wagon with the detective didn't arrive till after lunch, which was rather spartan that day, though tasty. Dona Belinha, who worked in the kitchen, had decided to give notice and go live in the woods with the Hermit. She spent the morning getting her things together. Rizoleta had been so upset when she learned that Eurídice, for whom she had developed a motherly affection in the short time the woman had been under her care, was a killer, that she had an attack of nerves and took to her bed. It was Trindade who made lunch, and fortunately he was a good cook, though obviously not as good as his wife. In any case, he managed to make some quite delectable pork chops, sausage, and manioc flour, as well as shredded kale and a bean dish, both delicious.

The clerk took the Hermit's statement at the retreat, in the Big House. The detective had wanted the Hermit to go to Pereiras. "Over my dead body, sir," he answered, and the detective saw the man was telling the truth and ordered the clerk to take his statement on the spot.

Finally, Suzy's jewels hadn't disappeared. They were all in a purse inside a suitcase. The detective made a list of them and asked me to sign as a witness. I declined. I wanted the least involvement possible with the police.

Before we all went down to Pereiras in the wagon, Guedes managed to get a moment alone with me. We were in the kitchen, where I had come for a cup of coffee.

"When I arrived, there was all that commotion and I wasn't able to tell you something," he said.

"So tell me."

He told me. I felt my legs tremble when Guedes finished talking.

"It's not true," I said. "It's absurd."

"Want me to tell you how I discovered it?" he asked.

"Ah, there you are," Minolta shouted from the other side of the dining room. "Everybody's waiting for you. The wagon's about to leave."

During the descent in the wagon, Guedes and I didn't talk. In fact, I didn't talk with anyone.

"What's with you?" Minolta asked.

I didn't answer. What *was* with me? . . . I was thinking, Until the hour of his death no one can guarantee that his is a happy life. . . . Sophoclean pain. . . . I remembered: I don't want death to find me and put an end to me in the dirty, painful, humiliating way it chose for me. . . . Death is always something dirty, the doctor told me when I went to see him; it may not be painful, it may not even be humiliating, but it's always dirty. . . . *Valentudinis adversae impatientia*.

We got to Pereiras in time to catch the bus to Cruzeiro, where connections could be made to Rio and São Paulo.

"What did you do with my story?" Roma asked me in Cruzeiro.

"Nothing. I just read it, as you wanted."

"I needed to get that off my chest," Roma said. "Things happened just the way I described it."

"Even the kiss on the toad's mouth?"

"Exactly like that, all of it. Incredible that you chose precisely that theme to give us. But that was good; it had to be told to somebody."

I removed the papers from the suitcase. Roma took the papers and stood there looking at them. Then, with a sudden gesture, she tore them into small pieces and threw them into a nearby trash basket. Perhaps that's the final destiny of all writing: letters, books, wills, diaries, contracts, deeds, written statements—into the trash.

I wrote down Roma and Sílvio's address; I wrote down Juliana and Orion's address. I knew I'd never see them again. Just as I'd never see Maria-Carlos and Eurídice. I regret not having paid more attention to Carlos—I mean Maria. She was an interesting person, and that triangle, the three women with interlocking loves, contained intriguing mysteries worth deciphering. I felt sorry for Maria and Eurídice, at that moment in the doubtlessly cold and ugly Pereiras police station, facing the cops' sordid bureaucracy unprotected. When I asked Maria (it was no use trying to talk to Eurídice, who was in an almost catatonic state) if she needed help she said no; from Cruzeiro she'd call a lawyer in São Paulo, a very competent one. A courageous woman.

I slept in the bus, resting on Minolta's shoulder. When we got to the Novo Rio bus station, after we got our bags, Guedes the cop told me, "I'll stop by your house tomorrow."

5

Guedes arrived at ten o'clock. I knew his habits. He had surely been prowling around outside my house, like a mangy, hungry dog, since daybreak.

"I'd like to be alone with him, please," I told Minolta.

Hurt, she left the living room. I heard the door slam.

"She's going to find out anyway," Guedes said.

"Find out what?"

"No crime ever occurs in isolation, in a pure state, if I may put it that way. Around it orbit other acts and criminal omissions, a constellation of turpitude and depravity. Evil is contagious," Guedes said.

"For some it's inspiring and provocative. Let's philosophize, inspector."

Guedes sniffed and cleaned his nose. "I came here to tell you I have witnesses who saw you near Diamantina Street on the night Delfina Delamare was found dead."

"You're crazy. If I were Victor Hugo, you'd be one of my characters."

"Bernarda saw you. Remember Bernarda? She was walking her dog. On Abade Ramos Street."

"I was never on Abade Ramos Street. What about the robber who confessed to killing Delfina?"

"We'll talk about that later. But I can tell you right now that Agenor's confession was false. He was paid by the husband to confess."

"And how is it that woman remembers the day she supposedly saw me?"

"It was Adolfo's birthday. Adolfo is the dog."

"The husband's the guilty one. You're the only one who can't see it. He knew we were lovers. Mr. Guedes, I've got a lot to do. I need to write my book Bufo & Spallanzani; I think I already spoke to you about that."

"Yes . . . yes. . . ." For a few seconds he appeared to have discontinued our conversation. That had happened once before when we were together, when the cop had also removed himself from the dialogue he was having with me and begun to look at me pensively. What conjectures were going through his head at that moment? I had agreed to receive Guedes only to find out if he'd discovered anything connected to my dark past, the crime involving the gravedigger.

"I didn't come here hoping to get you to sign a confession. I'm in no hurry. A short time ago you mentioned Agenor Silva, the confidence artist who confessed killing Delfina Delamare. He was murdered."

"And what does that have to do with me?"

"The people who killed him plan to murder another person. That's what I came here to tell you."

"I already told you I wasn't interested in that subject."

"The other person they plan to kill is you."

The cop left without telling me who the people were who planned to kill me. But I knew. Until then I'd thought I would never feel anything as horrible as the threat of being caught again. As soon as I fled the asylum, the few times I left my hiding place I saw an agent of the law in every passerby, an enemy, particularly if the guy wore a beard. I was especially afraid of bearded men. I thought they were psychiatrists with the power to order shock treatments, informers, detectives who would arrest me, law officers, public prosecutors ready to accuse me right there in the middle of the street. It was a hellish thing, a suffering I found the most unbearable of all. But the worst torment, I discovered that day as soon as Guedes left my house, is knowing there's someone who wants to kill you, be it from hatred or for money. At the time of the Estrucho case, at Panamerican, I had also felt threatened, but not as personally and tangibly as now.

What can a peaceful citizen like me do when he learns someone wants to kill him? The first thing that goes through anyone's head is to call the police. But I didn't trust the police, and I couldn't and wouldn't ask for their help. And I didn't believe Guedes was interested in protecting me. With his warped sense of ethics he probably considered it just for me to get killed, as long as he could catch the murderer and, most important, the man who ordered it. I return to the question I asked before: What should a peaceful citizen threatened with death do? First, identify his pursuer. I knew who he was, even without Guedes saying anything. It was Eugênio Delamare. His hatred for me must be beyond measure. He must surely have found the letters I wrote to Delfina. In those letters, besides speaking of our favorite poets like Baudelaire, Pessoa, Pound, Drummond, Auden, and Bocage, I had reminded her of what we had done in bed, abrasive libidinous acts, deliriously lubricious, candidly sordid, described in the rawest terms, accounts that would have left Bataille dead with envy at not having written them. I think Delamare still hadn't read the letters when he came to visit me, when he discovered I was Delfina's lover and threatened to castrate me and "let you bleed like a pig till you die." He must have found them after Delfina died. And if he wanted to do that to me before seeing the letters, I could imagine what his plans must be now.

OK, I thought that day when the grubby detective Guedes came to my house like a messenger bearing bad news, the first step has been taken—identifying my executioner.

Immediately I could do two things:

1. Run away from him—Delamare. Living is knowing how to escape. (*See Greene*.) That's all I'd been doing for the last twenty years.

2. Render inoperative the power that threatened me; that is, put an end to Eugênio Delamare before he put an end to me. This hypothesis was somewhat repugnant to me at first. But after considering the baseness of Delamare's character, and the fact that he didn't have children or other relatives who would suffer from his death (which gave rise to the happy prospect of his entire fortune going to the national treasury), I began to get used to, and then to like, the idea of killing him. Maybe "like" isn't the right word; it wasn't exactly that his death would give me pleasure. Relief, yes; that's what I craved with his death. Relief from fear.

But how could I kill Eugênio Delamare? I had killed—well, the gravedigger had been killed involuntarily, by accident, through ineptitude; in reality my experience as a murderer wasn't anything great. Should I kill Delamare with my own hands, by strangling him? Or beating him with a club? A knife? Kicking? Biting? (No, obviously not biting. First, I didn't bite men, not even in self-defense; second, to bite a man to death you have to be a tiger or a mad dog.) Bullets. That was the best way. I'd have no physical contact with Eugênio and would run no risk. After all, he was an athlete, a strong and muscular man capable of resisting and struggling.

I was no urban wanderer like Guedes the cop, but there

were many downtown streets that I especially liked, such as República do Líbano, Constituição, and Larga, among a few others. I liked to stop and look in the window of stores that sold musical instruments, electronic equipment, the secondhand stores that sold everything including used bedpans, but especially the sporting goods stores, with their rifles, carbines, revolvers, fishing reels, and underwater spear guns. And the stores that sold animals—fish, turtles, cavies, dogs, birds, cats, snakes, lizards, you name it. One day I was standing outside a sporting goods store looking at a rifle with a telescopic sight when a guy came up to me. He asked if I was interested in a firearm.

"I'll sell it for half price. Got a great selection," he said.

"I'm just looking."

"No need to register it with the police. Total confidentiality."

He probably thought I looked like a crook, maybe a bank robber.

"I've got an Ina machine gun, with ammo."

I left hurriedly and never again stopped in front of that or any other weapons shop.

But now here I was, to see if the same fellow, or somebody else, would show up with a similar offer. I wasted hours on end, for nothing, going from the door of one shop to the next. No one appeared.

Let's go back a little and see what happened shortly before Guedes went to meet me at Falconcrest Retreat. Agenor had been found dead in a dark street in Caxias (the city where Roma had discovered Santinha, who had cured her dancer husband's insanity), near the Luxembourg Motel, beside Brasil Avenue. He had been killed with three shots in the head, three in the chest, and three in the abdomen. About fifteen feet away lay a woman, who the police, when they arrived on the scene, thought was dead too. The woman had been shot twice in the back but, despite the caliber of the weapon used, was still alive. The police had concluded that two .45 pistols had been employed, the projectiles had hard metal jackets, and the shots heard by witnesses had been fired in rapid succession, indicative of an automatic. Agenor had been killed by shots from a single weapon, probably with a nine-bullet clip.

It took two days for Guedes to learn of Agenor's death. As soon as he found out he left in a flash for Caxias to talk with the detective in charge of the investigation.

"The woman was with Agenor; maybe she'd come from the Luxembourg, but the motel employees deny it. The killers, at least two in number, were interested in getting Agenor. The woman just happened to be in the wrong place at the wrong time. She came running out and caught two bullets in the back. They didn't waste time making sure she was dead. The guy who hit Agenor was careful. He put a bullet in each temple and another in the right ear; he wanted to avoid the possibility of a fluke, the bullets being diverted by the bones of the skull. That's happened, you know. Besides which he put three bullets in the gut. If he'd done it in the ICU, with doctors all over the place ready to operate, Agenor would still be fucked. The woman was lucky."

"Where is she?"

"In the hospital here in Caxias. They operated and she's doing OK."

"Have you talked to her?"

"I'm going there today. Want to come along?"

When they got to the hospital, Guedes and the policeman from Caxias, a Paraiban who looked like a marine sergeant and whose name was Bráulio, were taken by the doctor on duty to the bed where the woman lay. There were tubes inserted into her arm and nose.

"She's still in no condition to talk," the doctor said.

At that instant the woman opened her eyes and looked at the ceiling. Her eyes were gray and opaque. If there had been anything to be seen on the ceiling, she wouldn't have seen it. The woman still hadn't been identified. Her fingerprints weren't on file.

Bráulio believed the couple must have been going into the motel; it was no dumping ground for people killed elsewhere. And in any case the residents wouldn't have moved a dead man and a live woman. The couple must have been entering the motel, not coming out; to get into the motel you had to stop in the street, a favorable situation for the killers' purposes.

Guedes felt Bráulio's reasoning was sound. The woman in the hospital must not be Agenor's wife. "This business of taking your own wife to a motel is a middle-class thing," the cop said. If so, Agenor's wife, who must know something, was still alive and in hiding somewhere. Guedes thought it best not to tell Bráulio about his investigations involving Eugênio Delamare and Agenor Silva.

"What's she look like?" Bráulio asked.

"I don't know."

"In that case it's easy," Bráulio said jokingly.

The woman died the evening of the day the cops visited her, without being identified and without revealing anything. Her body was removed to the coroner's for autopsy. It would remain there for a time and later be buried in a pauper's grave.

Guedes had correctly deduced (I feel like using the adverb "intelligently," but my antipathy for the cop won't allow me) that the killers who had murdered Agenor and the woman were also after me. That was the real reason Guedes rushed off to the retreat. Not that he'd have been upset at my death, just that he found it inconvenient and, at that moment, detrimental to his investigation. I think I already said that.

6

Getting back to my wanderings in search of a revolver, on the second day a small, bilious-looking guy came up to me in the door of a gun shop and asked if I was interested in something.

"Yes."

"Follow me."

He started walking without looking back. We walked toward Camerino Street. As we crossed it I saw my old high school building. Suddenly I had a melancholy revelation: That had been the only happy time of my life. With great sadness I realized the extent of my unhappiness since becoming an adult. I had done nothing but deceive myself and escape, through sex and food.

I was imagining the story of a writer—hedonistic, epicurean, etc.—who decides to purify himself through asceticism, when the bilious little guy scrambled through the door of a two-story building where a sign read PHOTOGRAPHY—5 MINUTES.

When I got to the door of the building the guy was climbing a flight of wooden stairs, leaning on the handrail. I went up behind him. He waited for me on the landing.

"This way."

We went into the photographer's waiting room. The guy took a key from his pocket and opened a door. We entered a darkened room devoid of furniture, and he tapped a code with his fingers on a thick door that appeared to be reinforced with iron. A light went on in the empty room, a peephole opened in the heavy door, and a pair of eyes stared at me. Sometime later the door opened and we went into a large room with a table, several wooden cabinets, and steel filing cabinets.

"He wants a revolver," the bilious little guy said.

"A .22, .38, or .45?" the fellow who was in the room asked.

"It's to kill a man," I said.

"You really wanna waste him—blow away his nose, his teeth, the top of his head—besides killing him?" the man asked.

"How does it work?" I asked.

"With a .22 you just kill. With a .45 and dumdum bullets you make hamburger out of him."

"What's a dumdum bullet?"

The two men looked at each other disdainfully.

"Our friend here's a civilian. He don't know for shit. You remove the metal from the nose and expose the lead. Then you make an X in the lead. When it impacts, the lead spreads out. You can imagine the effect."

"A .45 with dumdums," I said.

The guy opened a cabinet and took out an enormous black pistol. "Seven shots in the clip and one in the chamber," he said. "It's butt-loaded, like this. When you slide it you introduce the cartridge into the chamber. Now you just pull the trigger." The guy also explained how the safety worked. "When you're not using it, push the safety catch, which locks the hammer and the sear. Automatics are real treacherous."

Before I left I asked, "Is this revolver really good? Can I trust it?"

"It's not a revolver, it's a pistol. A revolver has a drum, a cylinder. You see any cylinder on that weapon?" The man shook his head. When I left the room I heard him say under his breath, "Holy shit, confusing a pistol with a revolver!"

When I got home I put the revolver—I mean the pistol—on the table beside the TRS-80 and stood looking at the two machines. The pistol struck me as the prettier of the two; I don't know why, but it inspired me, made me feel like writing.

I turned on the TRS-80. First the printer, an Epson FX-80, connected to the computer. Then I put Superscripsit in Drive 0 and a floppy disk in Drive 1 for the file. The red light over the drives came on, then went out when TRSDOS was loaded. Month, day, year, ENTER; hour, minutes, seconds, ENTER; the red light going on and off over both drives: READY. I wrote SS and hit ENTER. The program's menu appeared on the screen. I typed the letter O.

Name of document to open?
I wrote Bufo.
ENTER.
On the screen, *Open Document Options:*

Document name: Bufo: 1
Author: Gustavo Flávio
Operator: GF
Comments: Novel
Printer type: LP8
Lines per page: 54
Pitch: P
Line spacing (to 3 +, "+" = ½): 1
1st page to include header: 1
1st page to include footer: 1

Again, ENTER.

The screen page appeared: the tab line, with the ghost cursor and the status line and the document's printing parameters. At the top of the page the cursor blinked. Everything was ready for writing.

The words appeared on the screen as I wrote:

File material. Spallanzani considers Bufo a stupid individual. Bufo's sexual and gastronomic appetite. Bufo and me. Parallel. So many writers, Conrad for instance, have been aided by being brought up in a metier utterly unrelated to literature. English is the Latin of modern times. Lévi-Strauss: I am not in fact very optimistic about the future of a humanity that reproduces so rapidly that it has become a threat to its own survival, even before it begins to run out of essential elements such as air, water, and space. I look at the revolver, I mean pistol, at my side. Enough idle talk.

I stopped writing.

Print command: I held down the CONTROL key and typed P. I listened to the rapid clattering of the Epson. I stacked the sheets of paper filled with the characters I had printed and threw them in the trash can ("the writer's best friend"—Singer). Why should I keep that in the computer's memory? I defined a block by pressing CONTROL and X. On the status line appeared:

Delete Copy Move Adjust Search Freeze Hyph Print Linespace?
I hit the D key, meaning Delete.

On the status line: *You have asked to remove this block. Are you sure? (Y or N)* Superscripsit is always very careful when you order it to erase anything longer than a paragraph. I typed Y for yes, and immediately that pile of letters vanished from the screen and was eliminated from memory. I held down CON-

TROL and hit Q, quitting the document, returning to the main menu. On the screen:

(O) Open a document
(D) Display disk directory
(S) System setup utility
(P) Proofread a document
(C) Compress a document
(A) ASCII text conversion utility
(E) Exit to TRSDOS

I hit E. *TRSDOS Ready.*

I wrote: KILL BUFO: 1. I hit ENTER.

TRSDOS looked for and found what there was in Drive 1 about Bufo & Spallanzani and erased it all, the overture I had put in the file containing the meeting between the scientist and the batrachian, the first appearance of Laura, the La Ghirlandina tower with its bell, the story of Spallanzani's boyhood, my notes, the general outline of the book—everything was extinct, destroyed in a fraction of a second. Bufo & Spallanzani no longer existed on the face of the earth; it was all thrown into the great trash can of oblivion. The KILL command is so preemptory that the computer obeys without question the order received.

KILL. Destroy. To kill Delamare it was also sufficient to apply pressure to the trigger of the gun beside me. My imagination wandered.

There was a knock at the door.

I saw through the opening that it was a guy carrying an enormous bouquet of roses decorated with colored ribbons.

"Gustavo Flávio?" he asked.

Then I understood everything and tried to shut the door, but it was too late. He put the gun against my chest and said, "Inside."

He entered behind me, closing the door with his foot. He threw the flowers to the floor indifferently.

"Put your hands behind you," he said. He deftly hand-cuffed my wrists. "Lay down," he said coldly, pointing to the floor. I lay down on my stomach. I heard him dialing the phone.

"I'm in. Piece of cake. The fucker had an old Colt." He hung up.

"Listen," I began.

"Shut up." He spoke not in anger but in a dry and intimidating tone.

With difficulty I turned my head to see where the guy was. He had sat down in one of the armchairs in the living room, his back straight, his hands resting on his legs. My pistol was gone. He looked at me impassively. If there was anything to be read in his inscrutable face it was an enormous lack of interest in me.

The doorbell rang, making my heart pound. I heard the man open the door. By the sounds, two people must have just arrived. When I tried to turn my head to see who it was, I was hit with a gun butt on the back of the neck.

"Keep quiet."

I felt my belt being loosened and my pants unzipped. My pants were pulled down.

"Hey!" I protested.

The gun butt again, followed by a fine pain in the buttock. They'd given me an injection. One of the men moved into my field of vision. He had a black beard.

Memories of the days in the asylum pierced my head. Psychiatrists. Detectives. Public prosecutors. Judges. Flowers on a grave. The tombstone opened as in a vampire film and a man all in black, with a white flower in his lapel, smiled at me and said, Pleased to meet you, I'm Maurício Estrucho.

"The worst form of authority," said Estrucho, "the slyest and

most arrogant, is that of the artist: He judges, implacably, anyone he thinks different from himself, always pretending to be
fair and impartial." Just as I was beginning to find Estrucho's
speech strange, his face started to age, a white beard appeared
on his face, and it was Tolstoy saying, "When are you going to
finish that piece of shit Bufo & Spallanzani?" I was about to
say that Bufo & Spallanzani had been KILLED by the computer
when the dream ended.

7

I could hear voices. I was in an uncomfortable airplane seat. Since I was large and fat, travel in narrow airplane seats was uncomfortable for me. The chair where I sat was tight, just like all the others. I opened my eyes and saw a pair of raised naked legs. The legs were mine! What kind of nightmare was this? I closed my eyes again.

Somebody hit me in the face. Lightly at first, then harder. I tried to understand what was happening. A guy I knew was there.

"I know who you are," I babbled.

"The fucker's still doped."

"You're Eugênio Delamare," I said.

"Can you count backward from a hundred?" Delamare asked.

"Sure," I said. "One hundred . . . ninety . . . ninety . . ."

"I want him to be wide awake to see and feel everything," Delamare told one of the men at my side. There were three men with him, wrapped in fog.

"This is a wine cellar," I said. I tried to point to the infinity of wine bottles resting in shelves along the walls, but my hands were tied.

"Did you close the door upstairs?" Delamare said.

"Yes," one of the men said. It was his chauffeur. Images were beginning to come into focus.

"Do you see this?" Delamare asked.

It was a knife. It shone, reflecting light onto the ceiling.

I felt a chill on my naked legs. I felt a chill in my heart. I noticed then that I was tied to an obstetrical table, like a woman about to give birth.

"I'm going to tear out your balls. Remember that I promised I would?" Delamare said.

The men around him laughed. One of them was the one who delivered the flowers.

I started thrashing about in panic, but my arms, my legs, and my chest were tightly held by wires that tore my skin. Blood began running down my body.

"I've done this a lot, with my cattle on the ranch. But it's more enjoyable with you," Delamare said.

I closed my eyes.

I'd always heard that when a pain is too intense you don't feel it. That's true.

"Make him open his eyes."

Someone slapped me violently.

"Know what this is?" Delamare brought his hand near my face. Between his thumb and index finger he held a small beige-colored sphere like a wedge of jackfruit, oval, smooth, dull, compact. "This is one of your balls, stud."

With his fingernails Delamare tore the egg apart, unrolling the long stringlike tubes as if the testicle were a ball of thick yarn.

"Did you ever see two pit dogs fight?" Delamare asked as he unraveled the strings of my testicle. "Whenever I go to England I always see a dogfight; they're the best in the world. The English know how to do such things, they've got class, they've got tradition. When it's still a pup the pit bull terrier, a cross between a bulldog and a terrier, begins being taught to desire the blood and flesh of other dogs for food."

Delamare took on the air of a lecturer. My testicle was now

a long, thin strand that dragged on the ground. His henchmen listened respectfully.

"When he reaches fighting age the dog is left without food for several days in the presence of a weaker animal, in whose body bloody wounds have been inflicted. I don't need to tell you what happens. The bull terrier rips the other dog to pieces. This is repeated several times during the training phase. Later they use an unwounded dog, who is also torn to bits and devoured. The bull terrier then comes to see any and every dog as an enemy to be shredded and eaten. I'm not going to do that to you; I'm not some ferocious dog. I'm just going to cut off your balls, one after the other, slowly, without haste—I promised you that, remember?—and afterward, to climax the party, I'm going to cut off your penis and throw everything in the garbage. I hope that doesn't have a negative effect on your creativity. I enjoy your books. Besides that, it's kind of late for you to begin a career in bel canto, and I don't think they hire castrati in the opera houses anymore."

Delamare carefully cut into the other side of my scrotum and delicately withdrew my second and last testicle. That was when I fainted from terror.

I awoke in the hospital. The first thing the doctor told me was that my life wasn't in danger. I'd lost some blood but they had decided against a transfusion, given the risk of AIDS, hepatitis, etc.

Delamare hadn't had time to cut off my penis. Guedes, the grubby cop, who had been trailing the millionaire, arrived with other policemen in time to prevent that from happening. Delamare and the criminals with him died in the gunfight in the wine cellar on Sara Vilela Street. Two policemen had died also.

I no longer had testicles. The doctor assured me that the only deficiency I would suffer from this would be sterility. My sexual potency would not be affected by the testicular ablation. For psychological reasons he advised me to have a prosthesis made, to implant plastic testicles "with the same shape and weight of the real ones."

"How are they going to know the shape and weight of the real ones?"

"We'll estimate; it's not difficult," he said.

I didn't believe a thing the doctor was saying. I was also disinclined to accept his suggestion to consult a psychologist, analyst, or whatever.

I was in the hospital for only a few days. As soon as I could I went home. Not to my house, to Minolta's in Iguaba.

"You're different, but I think it's a good idea to get away for a time."

The house had television, but I avoided watching the news. I didn't want to know about the "Delamare case." Minolta, however, told me some of what she'd seen on TV. In summary:

The millionaire Eugênio Delamare had hired the professional killer Agenor Silva of the criminal gang known as the Jacaré faction, which controlled the prisons in Rio de Janeiro, to kill his wife Delfina Delamare when he discovered she was the lover of the writer Gustavo Flávio. Agenor Silva had been arrested by the police following the crime but mysteriously managed to escape. Other gunmen from the Jacaré faction—Pedro de Alcântara, aka Chanfra, and Jorge Luis, aka Big Lead—killed Agenor in a typical rubout of witnesses, to prevent his identifying Eugênio Delamare as the one who arranged his wife's murder. The millionaire Delamare also wanted revenge against his wife's lover. At his orders, Chanfra and Big Lead kidnapped the writer Gustavo Flávio to kill him after subjecting him to abuse. Inspector Guedes and two assistants broke into the millionaire's residence just as the writer was being tortured. Killed in the shoot-out between police and criminals were Delamare, Big Lead, Chanfra, and the millionaire's chauffeur, one Matinho, who had also tortured the writer. The two policemen accompanying Guedes were wounded and died on the way to the hospital. Guedes's role is being investigated by the law. It was believed that Guedes had been with the millionaire before Agenor's flight and that Delamare had bribed the cop to facilitate the gunman's escape, thus allowing his death immediately thereafter. The slaughter led by Guedes in the millionaire's home was possibly the policeman's way of eliminating everyone who could incriminate him by denouncing his role in the complicated affair. He had been relieved of duties pending an investigation.

"Worse than any lie is half the truth," I said. (*See Blake*.*) "Did they describe the so-called abuse that I suffered?"

Minolta hesitated. "More or less. Know something? I think all this is going to help the sale of your books."

"What? Somebody buys the writer's book just because he was castrated?"

Minolta said nothing.

"The one who must be happy is Zilda."

"I hadn't thought about her," Minolta said. "But there's no danger. You're quite different."

"I feel sorry for Guedes."

"Sorry for the cop? The guy hounded you like that and you feel sorry for him?"

We were silent for a time.

"I wonder if my dick will ever get hard again."

Minolta sat down beside me and pulled my head to her shoulder. I pushed her away.

"Why go on living if your dick won't get hard?"

"There are other things that matter," Minolta said.

"See?" I said, disheartened. "You think I've become a eunuch too."

"Don't be silly."

---

*Blake didn't say exactly that. What he said was: "A truth that's told with bad intent/Beats all the lies you can invent."

"All we men have to give the world is a hard penis. But you women created everything—fire, the wheel, pottery, agriculture, the city, museums, astronomy, fashion, cooking, pleasure, art." (*See Mumford*.) "The only thing men have is a stiff prick. And I don't even have that anymore."

"Stop talking nonsense," Minolta said.

We went to bed and I pretended to sleep. But I didn't fool Minolta.

"Ivan? Are you awake?"

"Yes."

"Do you want to talk about women?"

"I can't."

"I feel you want to tell me something. I feel you're hiding something from me. I've been through a lot with you."

I didn't say anything. The night passed, and both of us remained awake without speaking to each other.

Day began to break.

"I'm going to talk, but you don't interrupt. OK?"

"OK," Minolta said.

"Don't say a word while I'm talking."

"Not a word."

8

"Normally I met Delfina in my apartment, as I already told you, at one in the afternoon. Eugênio hadn't yet returned from the trip they took together, that trip to Europe. She had come back early to take advantage of the freedom and said she wanted to attend the rehearsal of my play, which began at eleven at night. We never went out at night when her husband was in Brazil. We went. It's funny seeing actors knocking themselves out over the intentions they discover in my dialogues. That day the best thing was one of the actresses, a very young woman. When I arrived I didn't give her the least notice. But little by little I began to pay attention to her legs, to her body movements under the strong light of the reflectors. I remember I created an idiotic reflection on movement for Delfina, something like: Rivers are more beautiful than mountains because they move, and horses more beautiful than rivers because they move wherever they wish, and men—that is, women—are more beautiful than horses because they invent movements. Something like that, inspired by the young woman. I thought it would be good for me to fall in love with her. I think Delfina sensed that. From the rehearsal we went to my apartment. Lying in bed with her, I realized I wasn't as enthused by Delfina as usual. To excite me, she asked which of her friends I'd like to take to bed. Denise, I replied, and she asked if I'd do with Denise what I did with her.

"Unexpectedly, Delfina mentioned that her grandmother, the one who raised her as a girl, used to say that on Good Friday in the past all radio stations—there wasn't any television yet—played only classical music, preferably funeral marches. Then she added that she hadn't been feeling well and was going to see the doctor, Dr. Baran, the next day to find out the results of some tests she'd had done before her trip.

"Dr. Baran told her she had an incurable cancer and had only a few months to live. You can imagine the horror of the situation, someone hearing the news that they're suffering from a terminal disease. Today I know there are worse things.

"She left Dr. Baran's office and went to my apartment. Feigning calm and even a certain sangfroid, she said she had leukemia. When I saw her so self-controlled, I was astonished. I never thought she was so brave.

" 'Death chose a dirty, painful, and humiliating way for me to say goodbye,' Delfina said with a sad smile. But she wanted to say farewell in her own way and not as Death had decided. Now she spoke of Death as if it were someone she knew. She must be thinking of killing herself with barbiturates, I thought. And Delfina had in fact contemplated ending her life that way and had spent the night with a bottle of pills beside her bed. 'Do you remember your book *The Snare*? The woman who commits suicide with a shot in the heart from a .22 revolver? You said her death was instantaneous, that she didn't suffer at all, and that she didn't even stain herself with blood,' Delfina said. I explained that it was a novel, and I didn't know if the person suffered or not, if she stained her clothing or not, etc. We talked about it for a long time, until I came to agree with her. If someone wanted to kill himself, a bullet in the heart would be the quickest and cleanest way. But if she didn't have the courage to kill herself by swallowing some pills, she wouldn't have the courage to pull the trigger.

"You're going to pull the trigger, as if you were me, Delfina said. 'Don't ask that of me,' I begged. 'For the love of God, don't ask something like that of me!' But she insisted, and the more desperate I became, the calmer and more rational Delfina became. We spent all day arguing about it. Several times I felt like running away and leaving her alone in my apartment, disappearing in the streets. There was even a moment, shortly before Delfina finally convinced me, that I myself longed for death, to escape the mental torture I was being subjected to. She placed a nickel-plated revolver in my hand; I don't know where she got it. I let it fall to the floor in repulsion and fear. But, truthfully, I was already convinced that killing her would be an act of kindness on my part, even one of repentance and generosity. The car was her idea. Delfina chose the car because it wouldn't incriminate anyone and because the body would be found quickly. The street was my suggestion; I knew it was a dead end and so there would be little traffic. I had gotten lost there once trying to find a house in Jardim Botânico.

"It was midnight when we got to Diamantina Street. We wanted the street to be deserted, as it was. Delfina asked if there was some way to keep from ruining her blouse; she didn't want to appear disheveled to whoever found her. I opened the buttons of her silk blouse and the pink flesh of her breasts rose, weakly illuminated by the streetlight. She ran her hand over my face and dried my tears. 'I love you, thank you very much,' she said. I tried to see her eyes, whether there still lived in them that heat and passion, the same unyielding flame that shone in Bufo's eyes. But Delfina, in a gesture of circumspection and farewell, closed her eyelids. I planned to have her hold the gun and close her finger on the trigger; any reader of detective stories knows there are powder marks on the hands of people who commit suicide by firearm. But when she told me, so generously trying to appease my soul, that she loved me, all I could think of was ending her suffering quickly. I shot into that unhappy heart at the exact moment that she smiled at me. As in my book, no blood came from the wound, and her blouse, which I carefully rebuttoned, was unstained. Her smile dissolved, but on her face, behind the closed eyes, I could see that Delfina hadn't suffered and was glad, I think even happy, in her final instant of lucidity, of life. That's what happened. It's the truth. Don't look at me like that; I can't bring her back to life, to die of cancer. Don't call me a sly demon. If you want, I can go right now and tell Guedes everything, hand myself over to the police. Life means nothing to me anymore. Do you want me to? Go on, tell me."